T0166635

THE REVIEW *of* CONTEMPORARY FICTION AUTOFICTIONS

FALL 2013 / VOL. XXXIII, NO.3

EDITOR
JOHN O'BRIEN

ASSOCIATE EDITOR
IRVING MALIN

MANAGING EDITOR
JEREMY M. DAVIES

PRODUCTION
TIM PETERS

INTERN
ALEKS SIERAKOWSKI

REVIEW OF CONTEMPORARY FICTION
Fall 2013
Vol. XXXIII, No. 3

The *Review of Contemporary Fiction* is published three times each year
(March, August, November). Subscription prices are as follows:

Single volume (three issues):
Individuals: $17.00 U.S.; $22.60 Canada; $32.60 all other countries
Institutions: $26.00 U.S.; $31.60 Canada; $41.60 all other countries

ISSN: 0276-0045
ISBN: 978-1-56478-933-4

Partially funded by a grant from the Illinois Arts Council, a state agency, and by
the University of Illinois at Urbana-Champaign

Indexed in *Humanities International Complete, International Bibliography of Periodical Literature, International Bibliography of Book Reviews, MLA Bibliography*, and *Book Review Index*.
Abstracted in *Abstracts of English Studies*.

The *Review of Contemporary Fiction* is also available on 16mm microfilm, 35mm microfilm, and
105mm microfiche from University Microfilms International, 300 North Zeeb Road, Ann Arbor,
MI 48106-1346.

Address all correspondence to:
Review of Contemporary Fiction
University of Illinois
1805 S. Wright Street, MC-011
Champaign, IL 61820

www.dalkeyarchive.com

THE REVIEW OF CONTEMPORARY FICTION

BACK ISSUES AVAILABLE

Back issues are still available for the following numbers of the
Review of Contemporary Fiction ($8 each unless otherwise noted):

William Eastlake / Aidan Higgins
William S. Burroughs ($15)
Camilo José Cela
Chandler Brossard
Samuel Beckett
Claude Ollier / Carlos Fuentes
Joseph McElroy
John Barth / David Markson
Donald Barthelme / Toby Olson
William H. Gass / Manuel Puig
Robert Walser
José Donoso / Jerome Charyn
William T. Vollmann / Susan Daitch /
   David Foster Wallace ($15)
Angela Carter / Tadeusz Konwicki
Stanley Elkin / Alasdair Gray
Brigid Brophy / Robert Creeley /
   Osman Lins
Edmund White / Samuel R. Delany
Mario Vargas Llosa / Josef Škvorecký
Wilson Harris / Alan Burns
Raymond Queneau / Carole Maso
Curtis White / Milorad Pavić
Richard Powers / Rikki Ducornet
Edward Sanders
Writers on Writing: The Best of The *Review of*
   Contemporary Fiction
Bradford Morrow
Jean Rhys / John Hawkes /
   Paul Bowles / Marguerite Young
Henry Green / James Kelman / Ariel Dorfman

David Antin
Janice Galloway / Thomas Bernhard /
   Robert Steiner / Elizabeth Bowen
Gilbert Sorrentino / William Gaddis /
   Mary Caponegro / Margery Latimer
Italo Calvino / Ursule Molinaro /
   B. S. Johnson
Louis Zukofsky / Nicholas Mosley /
   Coleman Dowell
Casebook Study of Gilbert
   Sorrentino's *Imaginative Qualities of*
   Actual Things
Rick Moody / Ann Quin /
   Silas Flannery
Diane Williams / Aidan Higgins /
   Patricia Eakins
Douglas Glover / Blaise Cendrars /
   Severo Sarduy
Robert Creeley / Louis-Ferdinand Céline /
   Janet Frame
William H. Gass
Gert Jonke / Kazuo Ishiguro /
   Emily Holmes Coleman
William H. Gass / Robert Lowry /
   Ross Feld
Flann O'Brien / Guy Davenport /
   Aldous Huxley
Steven Millhauser
William Eastlake / Julieta Campos /
   Jane Bowles

Novelist as Critic: Essays by Garrett, Barth, Sorrentino, Wallace, Ollier, Brooke-Rose, Creeley, Mathews, Kelly, Abbott, West, McCourt, McGonigle, and McCarthy

New Finnish Fiction: Fiction by Eskelinen, Jäntti, Kontio, Krohn, Paltto, Sairanen, Selo, Siekkinen, Sund, and Valkeapää

New Italian Fiction: Interviews and fiction by Malerba, Tabucchi, Zanotto, Ferrucci, Busi, Corti, Rasy, Cherchi, Balduino, Ceresa, Capriolo, Carrera, Valesio, and Gramigna

Grove Press Number: Contributions by Allen, Beckett, Corso, Ferlinghetti, Jordan, McClure, Rechy, Rosset, Selby, Sorrentino, and others

New Danish Fiction: Fiction by Brøgger, Høeg, Andersen, Grøndahl, Holst, Jensen, Thorup, Michael, Sibast, Ryum, Lynggaard, Grønfeldt, Willumsen, and Holm

New Latvian Fiction: Fiction by Ikstena, Bankovskis, Berelis, Kolmanis, Ziedonis, and others

The Future of Fiction: Essays by Birkerts, Caponegro, Franzen, Galloway, Maso, Morrow, Vollmann, White, and others ($15)

New Japanese Fiction: Interviews and fiction by Ohara, Shimada, Shono, Takahashi, Tsutsui, McCaffery, Gregory, Kotani, Tatsumi, Koshikawa, and others

New Cuban Fiction: Fiction by Ponte, Mejides, Aguilar, Bahr, Curbelo, Plasencia, Serova, and others

Special Fiction Issue: Juan Emar: Fiction and illustrations by Juan Emar, translated by Daniel Borzutzky

New Australian Fiction: Fiction by Murnane, Tsiolkas, Falconer, Wilding, Bird, Yu, and others

New Catalan Fiction: Fiction by Rodoreda, Espriu, Ibarz, Monsó, Serra, Moliner, Serés, and others

Writers on Writing: Essays by Gail Scott, William H. Gass, Gert Jonke, Nicholas Delbanco, and others

Georges Perec Issue: Essays by Perec, Harry Mathews, David Bellos, Marcel Bénabou, and others

Special Fiction Issue: *; or The Whale*: Radically abridged *Moby-Dick*, edited by Damion Searls

Individuals receive a 10% discount on orders of one issue and a
20% discount on orders of two or more issues. To place an order,
use the form on the last page of this issue.

CONTENTS

THE REVIEW *of* CONTEMPORARY FICTION

EDITOR'S NOTE

Beginning as another issue in the line of past favorites such as "The Novelist as Critic" and "New Writing on Writing," this number of the *Review of Contemporary Fiction* evolved over time to focus on writing without a clear allegiance to any one of the categories of fiction, memoir, or essay. Here you'll find a long and entertaining interview with Gerald Murnane, who refuses the designation of "novel" for his longer fiction, and who has led many an unwary reader into the error of confusing his writing with autobiography. This is followed by John Griswold's report of his trip to Hannibal, Missouri for the centenary of Mark Twain's death, asking, "Why do we go looking for writers beyond their work? They are, after all, *unpleasant* people."

After this comes Luis Chitarroni's brief, semi-fictional portraits of such authors as William Gerhardie and Gerard Manley Hopkins; and then S. D. Chrostowska's parables on the efficacy of parables and other "instructive" or ethical fictions. Jacques Jouet's "Suppositions" on Flaubert blend playful hypotheses with serious criticism, while Thalia Field takes to pieces the presumed rationality of the novel and by extension, reality (or vice versa). Lily Hoang and Bhanu Kapil provide a punning and harrowing guide to the uses of the colon, while Warren Motte gives us a preview of his upcoming book *Mirror Gazing* by outlining the story of his literary preoccupation with mirror scenes in fiction. Adrian West takes a personal journey into the underworld of the "autoportraits" and fictions of Edouard Levé, before, finally, Jacques Houis provides a long-overdue overview of a little known—even suppressed— branch of the French literary counterculture of the 1960s, itself focused on often bizarre and grotesque auto-fictionalization.

ANTONI JACH

An Interview with Gerald Murname

ANTONI JACH: Welcome to the Melbourne Writers' Festival. We respectfully acknowledge we're meeting on the traditional lands of the Wurundjeri people, belonging to the Kulin Nation and we pay respect to their elders, and all of the elders in Victoria. Now, it gives me very great pleasure to introduce a friend of mine, Gerald Murnane, to you. Some of you might know Gerald—some of you might have been taught by Gerald. Anyone taught by Gerald? Yes, thank you. I had Gerald speak to my students at RMIT in 1987 and, Gerald may or may not remember this, but he gave a wonderful lecture on his published books and he picked up one after another, and he went through the books, told us a bit about the plot and told us much more about the themes, and that was fabulous. Gerald's latest book is *Barley Patch,* Giramondo the [Australian] publisher—my publishers as well—the amazing Ivor Indyk is the publisher—*Invisible Yet Enduring Lilacs* was the previous one, wasn't it?

GERALD MURNANE: Yes, and there was also a first—a reissue of *Tamarisk Row,* which is not a new book, but Giramondo published that recently, about two years ago.

AJ: And Text has republished *The Plains,* right?

GM: *The Plains* is in print with Text, yes.[1] And while we're on that subject, there's a French edition. We've been trying to interest the French through agents and publishers working—I think every publisher in France by now, during the last twenty years, would have seen at some time, and rejected *The*

1. In the US, *The Plains* is available from New Issues Poetry & Prose at Western Michigan University.

Plains, but just recently thanks to the exertions of Michael Heywood and Penny Hueston at Text, a French *Plains* is coming out[2] and I only heard from Michael five minutes ago that it's coming out next February.

AJ: It's great work, Michael, wherever you are. Thank you very much, that's terrific. As a way of introducing—this might sound a little bit like bragging, but there is a reason. [Holds up book to show to Murname and the audience.] After the *Celebration: Australian Fiction 1989 to 2007*[3]—have you seen this, Gerald?

GM: No, I know about it, yeah. I keep away from books like that.

AJ: Well, I'm going to bring some of that up today, so we'll see what your reaction is. You'll get your chance to talk back. Um, [reading] "Gerald Murnane might be contrasted with another Australian Postmodern novelist, Antoni Jach"—that's myself, I'm Antoni Jach, hi—so there's a bit of serendipity in terms of the two of us being here together. And Gerald's fiction was certainly influential on my fiction, back in the '80s, and *The Plains* in particular was very important to me, because it showed me that there was an Australian writer who was actually writing in a modernist style. And, I was someone who loved Marcel Proust and still love Marcel Proust, and I could see something Proustian in Gerald's work that I really admired. Gerald, could you tell us a bit about Proust?

GM: Well, I'll tell you first that I don't like talking about—using in my speech or talks—words such as *postmodern* because—and you might laugh at this and think I'm striking a pose—but I do not quite understand what the expression "postmodern" means, and I don't see it as any of my business to understand it, and I welcome people using it about me and I feel that it must be something that I should be proud of, and so I am a little bit proud but without fully understanding it.

2. *Les Plaines*, in Brice Matthieussent's translation, was indeed published in February 2011 by Editions P.O.L, Paris.

3. By Ken Gelder and Paul Salzman, published by Melbourne University Press in 2009.

My way of writing is not to sit down and try to fulfil somebody's expectations—to say, "Now I've written a realistic novel, it's about time I tried a postmodern novel." My way of writing starts with just a small image or collection of images, and it expands in all directions from that. And of course I've been influenced—unconsciously perhaps—by Marcel Proust. And strange to say, one of the things that first got me going and into my stride with *Tamarisk Row* which took eight years to finish from the time I started it—was a book which I don't think that I'd be at all impressed by now if I read it again, called *The Tin Drum* by Günter Grass. It came out in 1962, when I was trying to be a poet and drafting a few scribbled versions of what became *Tamarisk Row* years later. And something about the crazy passages in the *The Tin Drum* liberated me from being just another Australian writer who wrote about characters and plots and all. It was a feeling that if they can do it in Europe, I can do it here. Anyone can do it. And that's—I've gone off the subject a bit but it won't be the last time I'll do that today.

And Proust, I don't just worship or respect him as a writer, but as a thinker. My kind of thinker. He thought in images. He didn't think in philosophical terms. And I can't think—I almost failed Philosophy 1 at Melbourne University. I only passed it by pretending I was a philosopher. When I was doing the exam, I thought—if I understood what philosophy was about, how would I answer this question? So I got through. So that's not my way of thinking. But the imagery in Proust says it all. I've managed to read Proust twice. I don't know if I've got time to read him a third time yet.

AJ: Yeah, and it's the intense interiority, the absence of action—I presume these are two of the qualities that—

GM: There's a passage in *Barley Patch*—I was looking at it on the train coming in this morning. A passage in which the narrator of *Barley Patch* directly refers to Marcel Proust's work—and to a passage in the first part of the work, in which place names are listed—place names along the coast of Normandy. And for each name, the narrator of *Remembrance of Things Past* describes visual imagery. And the visual imagery arises from the vowels in the names. The final *e* acute vowel in one particular name—I wish I could quote them from memory—to him had a colour, or a texture, or an architectural feature associated . . . So, Proust was of such a sensitive or alert frame of mind, that he could read a name on a map, and see a coloured landscape or a coloured building, or just pure colour. And I envy him that kind of skill. And I perhaps have it to a small extent.

AJ: Following up from that, what do names like Glass Land and New Arcadia do for you?

GM: Well, Glass Land takes me to the—it's in *Barley Patch* of course, but a better question would be, What was I thinking about?

AJ: Gerald, what were you thinking about?

GM: What was I thinking about when I used those words in *Barley Patch*? Ah, now this is something that you'd be interested to hear—most of you, anyway. Some of my books have grown out of other books. I didn't intend, for quite a while, to write. And I want to have a rest from writing this year and next year. But I've started working on a book which I think has actually grown out of my interest in stained glass or coloured glass. I don't work with stained glass—I just look at it and think about it. And the Glass Land in there wasn't just a reference to the Glass Land that the Brontës described in their . . . Not their published works but that strange—they had a secret sort of land or series of lands called Gondal. One of them was called Gondal. And they had all these little handwritten accounts of the goings on in this mysterious imaginary country. The girls did it and so did that poor—what was his name?—Branwell, the drunken brother. So the Brontës had this fantasy world, and one of the big cities in it was called Glass Land.

So my Glass Land—I've always been inspired by the Brontës and their shameless, shameless dedication to nonexistent things; to the reality of imaginary places. And *Barley Patch,* whether you've read it or not or understood it or not, *Barley Patch* is full of references to things existing on the other side of works of art. And imaginary places. And Gondal lies on the other side of *Wuthering Heights,* which is one of my favourite books. So, Glass Lands, there's all these multiple references. But it also—I love the sound of the word "glass" itself. And it's lead me—my love of that sound and what it connotes—has lead me to start the book that I'm writing now. What was the other reference?

AJ: New Arcadia, but just while we're on Glass Land, it connects to grassland which is one of your big themes, isn't it.

GM: You get that—it's just the fortuitousness of the English language that provides that, but if you're a writer like me you fasten onto connections like that.

AJ: So what does New Arcadia do for you?

GM: New Arcadia, ah, is, ah, you'll have to wait till twenty years after I'm dead to find out. I have, um, I was hoping I'd get the excuse to mention this: I have, in my little work room, I think . . . I counted them before I left too . . . it's thirty-two or forty . . . one or the other. I think there are forty filing cabinet drawers, but only thirty-two of them are full at present. So I've still got eight drawers left to fill. And what are they filled with? Well for those, probably most of you don't know, I started keeping all my letters, all my autobiographical writings and they are very—I've written far far more autobiographical writing—well, as much autobiographical writing as—it could fill three or four books. All unpublished, never to be published, and to go to some library. My executors of my estate will decide where after I'm dead. And twenty years later, after certain other people have died, hopefully the stuff in my filing cabinets will be available for reading and then the mystery of what New Arcadia is will be revealed. But if you read *Barley Patch* with alertness you'll probably get a very strong hint. And also if you go back to the book *Emerald Blue,* one of my—a book I always feel a bit sorry for, that it didn't get the, ah—came out at a time when I wasn't the flavour of the month, I hadn't written anything for five or six—I hadn't had anything published for five or six years—and there's a story in *Emerald Blue*, or a piece of fiction, called "The Interior of Gaaldine," and uh, if you read that and then read *Barley Patch* carefully you get an idea of what New Arcadia refers to.

AJ: Yeah, and *O, Dem Golden Slippers?*

GM: *O, Dem Golden Slippers* was the title of the big book that I didn't ever finish. In fact, in the filing cabinet drawers that—the archives, as I call them, are three. There's the personal archive—or the chronological archive—which fills about twenty filing cabinet drawers. Unfortunately I haven't got anything from my childhood. We moved—I lived at about thirteen different addresses in the first thirteen years, and we just couldn't keep stuff. Dad would say, "We're moving again," and we used to tell this old joke: the chooks, on hearing those words, used to lie on their backs and put their feet up so we could tie their legs together. And Dad would—we used old boxes called tea chests. They apparently were used for—tea merchants used to buy the tea from China and Ceylon, in these big tea chests with zinc lining, and Dad had a collection of them. They were our packing cases, and always one was for our toys. And we had a few toys and treasures as we called them and—I wrote little plays and stories at the age of eight or nine, but none of them survived. But back to the archives. My first writings in the archives date from 1956, just as I was leaving school. I wanted to be a—well, a part-time poet. I didn't ever think that it was possible to live from poetry. But I was going to be a part time poet, and I wrote down fifty topics that interested me. These would be the things I'd write poetry about for the rest of my life. And that's my first bit of writing that relates to anything published. And my writing from there on, as I say, fills all these filing cabinet drawers. What was the question again?

AJ: I think it was New Arcadia, wasn't it?

GM: No no, we've passed on from New Arcadia.

FROM AUDIENCE: *O, Dem Golden Slippers*

GM & AJ: *O, Dem Golden Slippers*

GM: Be alert, Antoni.

AJ: I've got my next question in my head, so . . .

GM: *O, Dem Golden Slippers* is in—uh, what remains of it, is in the unfinished . . . I'm talking now about another of my archives: the Literary Archive, which has twelve drawers. There's *Tamarisk Row, A Lifetime on Clouds*, eleven—uh, up to the one I'm writing now, is number eleven. And there's another drawer, full of unfinished and uncompleted things. And *O, Dem Golden Slippers* was a novel I started—or a long work of fiction I started in about '88 or '89, when *Inland* had been published, and I just couldn't finish it. It went out like a, an estuary or a—it branched out in all directions. Parts of it were published in that wonderful magazine *Scripsi* that disappeared some years back. And, uh, I gave up—and in fact, after giving up on *O, Dem Golden Slippers*, I gave up on writing. I never—I've never been—I've never felt it my duty or obligation or in my best interest to just keep writing. If I don't want to write, I stop writing. If I've got nothing to write about I stop. And, uh, so I stopped for several years after *O, Dem Golden Slippers*. But again, for those who know *Barley Patch*, that book, in a way, grew out of *O, Dem Golden Slippers* and I thought, well, if I was answering a question like that—why did I stop writing *O, Dem Golden Slippers*? What should I have done to make it a better book, whatever— there's a whole lot of references to my unfinished book in there. So I'm a messy sort of writer who gets it right in the end, almost by the wrong route or an accidental way round.

AJ: "Circling and circling," Gelder and Salzman say in their book. You're a writer who circles and circles.

GM: Well that's okay, yeah.

AJ: This writer, Jean-François Vernay. [Holding up book.] A book published in France last year, it's *The Panorama of the Australian Novel—1831 to 2009*.[4]

GM: He's a very tall man—did you ever meet him?

AJ: Yes I did. It's coming out in a couple of weeks, in translation. And Jean-François was very disturbed for you to be publishing fiction when he's written in this book that you will not write any more fiction. So he was most disturbed. He says he'll fix it in the next edition, but he was really, sort of, quite overwrought.

GM: In other words, with all due respect to the gentleman, he thinks it's a writer's duty to write—the reason we're writing is so he can write clever books about us.

AJ: Yep, absolutely.

GM: So we'd better do the right thing by him.

AJ: Now, on page 179 of *Barley Patch* you say, "What remains to be reported about my having decided to write no more fiction." Now, what would you like to say about that?

GM: Page 1 . . . ?

4. *Panorama du roman australien des origenes à nos jours 1831–2007* by Jean-François Vernay was published by Hermann Éditeurs in Paris in 2009. An English translation by Marie Ramsland, titled *The Great Australian Novel—A Panorama*, was published by Brolga Publishing in Melbourne in 2010.

AJ: Page 179. "What remains to be reported."

GM: Well, that's—

AJ: In italics.

GM: No, that's, that's . . . You've got me a bit confused. That's, if you read it in context, is simply saying what's left to put into this book.

AJ: Yep.

GM: Um. Well, it leads me to say that even when I was writing *Barley Patch* I thought this would probably be the last thing I write. Because I couldn't think of anything else that I wanted to write about. And I only write, as I said before, when I feel impelled, or driven, or—uh, not driven for the sake of my readers, but driven for my own sake, my own natural curiosity. What might come of this if I start writing about it? So, well, I can't directly answer your question because it only relates to the—you'd have to read the rest of the book to answer it.

But, the, um, of course there was a significant personal event that took place in February 2009, which was the death of my wife after a long illness with cancer. And I'd started just before she, we found she had cancer and I'd started a novella, about thirty thousand words, called *A History of Books*. It's fiction, but that's its title. And when I finished that, six months after she'd died, things had calmed down, I sat down and finished and thought that's it, again, nothing more to write about. But I've since started another one, a shorter piece. So you just don't know. I think, perhaps, in the next book, I'll delete any references to stopping writing . . . Put at the end, To Be Continued.

AJ: Now, Gerald, what would you say to the person who says, mistakenly, that this is not a work of fiction; it's a memoir. What would your response be?

GM: Well, it happened. And it happened in connection with the Adelaide Festival, last year. Ivor Indyk, the publisher—the man behind the Giramondo Publishing Company—rang me to say that the book *Barley Patch*, which had been entered in the fiction category for the Adelaide Festival, which is worth thirty thousand dollars and prestigious, and—none of my books have ever won a major prize in Australia. I've been awarded the Patrick White Award, I've won an Emeritus Fellowship, but no single book of mine has ever won a Premier's literary award, the Miles Franklin—in fact, I've never even been shortlisted for the Miles Franklin. But I thought, this is it, this'll be the book that will win. Not that, I mean, I don't lie awake at night thirsting for these things but if the opportunity was there, naturally I could look forward to it. So I thought, well, *Barley Patch* is in with a chance in the Adelaide Festival. But why he rang me was to say that they didn't think it was fiction. That it really shouldn't be in the fiction category. And then, I'll answer that in a moment. But what happened as a good result of that: the judges, to square off with him perhaps—I don't even know who they were, so I, I'm not making any judgement about them—but they recommended that the book be entered in the In . . . there's a category called "Innovatory Writing." You only get ten thousand dollars but that's better than a poke in the eye with a burnt stick, as they used to say. And it won the award. And I had the opportunity—I don't know whether the judges were in the audience, they probably were—but when I—I like making very short speeches at these sorts of things. And I got up at the festival at February this year, out in the tent there, and I said, well, I thought of many things when my first book was published. I thought, now I'm a writer and I've got . . . I never thought, among all the fanciful and hopeful thoughts that I had, never did I think that forty or fifty years later I'd be standing up at a thing called the Adelaide Festival, and accepting a prize as an innovator, at the age of seventy-one. Or whatever I was. And this—it stung me a bit to be thought, well, you know, it's, uh, I really think that any writer has the right to claim that a work is a work of fiction if it's published as a work of fiction. And for somebody to turn around and say, "That doesn't seem like fiction to me," well, my answer simply is that it *is* fiction.

And you ask me, well, how much autobiography is in that? Well, I don't know. There are—there are statements that I would—that came directly from the self that's sitting here in front of you, and there are statements in there that I couldn't possibly make, unless I were alone in a room in a writing sort of mood, and, that, um, if you challenged me with some of the statements I'd say, "No, I don't really believe that. That's not part of my personality." Because you must know, any of you who've tried writing, that it's—you become a different person for the time being. You draw on parts of yourself that you'd never expose or . . . It's not telling secrets. I'm not saying that they're shameful things. But there are parts of you that you don't even know about yourself, until you sit down and start writing. And that's why some people suppose—and especially since it starts out with the first-person narrator being a writer. They suppose it can't be fiction; it's autobiography.

Anyway, I got ten thousand dollars and a prize out of it. But it did sting me to think that—and not only that, if that were my first book, well then, fair enough, they might say, well he's a new bloke, we don't know anything about him, he writes this strange sort of writing which may not be fiction. But that was my ninth book and I must, I mean, they surely give me credit for knowing by now what's fiction and what's not. Anyway, what else is—I couldn't think of anything else to call it.

AJ: Yeah. Uh, Alain Robbe-Grillet's got a book which he dubs "fictional autobiography." It's called *The Mirror Which Returns*.[5] And that notion of fictional autobiography is interesting in itself.

GM: Ah, I think I've said enough on the subject, but I . . . So, there's an old joke that somebody told me about a guy in a university. The lecturer for . . . Somebody had to give a lecture on a high-powered critical subject, and he was sick or he couldn't—he called the other guy and said, you go ahead and do it for me. And the other guy said, "I can't lecture on that subject, they'll ask me all these questions." The lecturer said, "You'll satisfy any questioner if you use in your answer the words 'in a sense.' So if somebody says, 'Do you think this

5. *Le miroir qui revient*, 1984. Published in Jo Levy's English translation as *Ghosts in the Mirror* (London: John Calder, 1988).

is—?' 'In a sense, yes.'" So, if you ask me, Antoni, if somebody says, "Is that fiction or autobiography?" I say, "In a sense, yes."

AJ: Well, following up from that, I want you to go back to your days lecturing in creative writing. I want to know how many writers are in the audience? Hands up, please.

GM: What do you mean by "writers"?

AJ: How many writers? Writers published or unpublished. You consider yourselves as writers. Thank you.

GM: I wouldn't have dared to ask that question. It's none of my business. So I didn't put him up to that.

AJ: No. But Gerald, what I want you to do is give advice to writers. Now, what's your advice? What do they have to do?

GM: Well, that's easy. Well you just, you don't give up your day job. And I'm serious. I managed to write part-time, except for three years, back in the 1970s, I got three successive one-year grants from the Australia Council. They weren't in fact—they didn't help me all that much. I managed to write one book over the three years. But filling out the forms and trying to finish within a year what you said you'd finish so that you could apply for the next year's grant, it was a big strain actually, and I was almost relieved when the third time around they didn't give me one. And for many, many years I had no contact with the Australia Council. Except, of course, they generously subsidised the publisher of the books.

But I always managed to write in my spare time. And sometimes there was precious little of it. Uh, and I feel that the strain—and I'm only speaking for myself, but you asked for advice . . . The strain—and I used to say this to the students—the strain of writing to make money would have been so much that I would never have completed half of what I did. And besides that, you're free—or freer—if you're supporting yourself by some other job, even a part-time job—you're freer to write what *you* think you have to write. And you don't have this dreadful task of trying to guess what publishers are looking for. Or even harder still, what readers are looking for. So, I mean, you might have expected me to say something like, you know, write nice long paragraphs or write short paragraphs, but my most *heartfelt* answer to that is that you treat yourself as a part-time writer who is free to follow their own path.

And that, going back to the task of, the question "What are editors looking for?" I forget where I read it—it was in an American handbook for writers. Editors say, often, what they're looking for. But quite often, what they're looking for—they don't know what they're looking for until they see it. In other words you, if you're going to be successful, you might be successful by showing an editor—or a literary agent, and then an editor—what they never expected to see, but what they recognise as meritorious and worth publishing. So it's a stupid and futile thing to look at last year's bestseller and say, "Ah, that's it!" and then try and write your version. Or to read in the *Saturday Age* or the Saturday *Australian* some statement by a publisher that crime fiction is all the go this year or you can write a literary masterpiece with a crime fiction framework, and then you say, "Well, now I know what to do." No, you don't. You follow your own path. You follow your own impulses, your own creativity, for want of a better word. And then, if it's any good, it'll get published.

The story of my getting published was a near thing. The first book I finished was far too long. It was *Tamarisk Row* multiplied by about one and three quarters. And I showed it to a man who won't speak to me anymore. We fell out rather badly, then we patched it up again and later we fell out again. So this is the last time, because we're a bit too old to be patching up a third time. So his name was Barry Oakley. He was a novelist in the '60s and '70s. A literary editor of *The Australian* for a while and, uh, a good friend of mine in my young days. He's older than I am, about eight years older. And he'd been published. And so, he was the only person I knew in Australia, personally, who'd been published. And I dared to show him, well, asked him to read bits of *Tamarisk Row*. I couldn't ask him to read the whole thing. He read, oh seventy or eighty pages, and he found a lot of it not to his liking, but a lot of it he found excellent.

And he just mentioned this to Hilary McPhee who was just starting out as an editor of—she was looking for Australian fiction for Heinemann Australia. And this is going back forty years, to 1970 or '72. And Oakley just mentioned to her that there was a book by a man called Gerald Murnane, *Tamarisk Row*, that was worth looking at. Didn't say it was worth publishing. And she liked it, and she told me I'd have to cut it down, which I did. And when I sat in her office for the first time, and I only found out years later that this was almost the first book she'd edited, and I thought she was a wise, experienced editor, and we were both pretty nervous with each other, I guess. I sat in that room, and I happened to notice, in the corner, a pile, and I don't exaggerate, a pile so high, as high as the chair I'm sitting in, and it covered an area of about, from me to the front row, and it was all parcels, and it was a terrible thing to think that all these parcels were the unsolicited manuscripts and typescripts of people wanting their first novels published.

You see, the rumour gets around quickly, if there's a publisher looking for Australian fiction, and suddenly a tidal wave of unpublished manuscripts descended. And I thought, if Barry Oakley hadn't mentioned me to Hilary McPhee, *Tamarisk Row* would be lying underneath that three-foot high pile and would probably be lying there another fifteen years.

So, that was how—well, I mean, I'm only guessing, but I always think it was a lucky day and a near thing that Hilary read that. And after that, well, it wasn't hard after that. And by the way, I'm wandering but this is all, I suppose, interesting— I've been to four or five publishers, I've never made money for any of them, didn't lose much money, but they couldn't make me into a commercial success. And, uh, five, ten years ago, Ivor Indyk pressed me for, almost drove me to get that collection together for *Invisible Yet Enduring Lilacs*. Most of it had been published in magazines but not in book form. And I know now what I thought I knew, but didn't really know properly, when I was a teacher: the encouragement and the stimulus a person can get from knowing that they're likely to be published, as opposed to writing something and just hoping and having your fingers crossed, or getting rejections and continual rejections. Because knowing that Ivor was very interested in my work was a wonderful encouragement—I'm sure you know this, those who've been published . . . It's a wonderful thing to think you're almost certain to be published. So thanks to Ivor Indyk. I always make an acknowledgement of him. I tease him sometimes—when I launched *Invisible Yet Enduring Lilacs* he was covering his face and flinching because I made this joke about every time I used to give a talk or a speech, he'd ask me, "Can I have that for publication? Could you type me up a version of that for pub—" He was always pressing me and, "Could you go home and find something like that that you want published?" And suddenly I realised that he was really interested in everything I wrote.

AJ: Yeah, and was he forthright in terms of the editing? Say with *Barley Patch*. Did he tell you what to do, or did he give you a lot of free rein?

GM: Well, again if I—we had—it's silly to say that's something's funny, but not to be able to quote it and give you an example. But some of the funniest things I've written have been exchanges on the margins of my galley proofs with Ivor. Ivor saying, "Isn't this a bit over the top?" And, ah, "What—" No, I can't think of examples, but I showed it to another person and she said, "They're some of the funniest things I've seen." He tried to—all in good fun—he tried to tell me I'd gone a little too far in one direction, and well, there is one passage. It's not really a good example. There's a page, um, I suppose you might almost call it a sort of sexual fantasy, where the narrator confesses to seeing images of image-aunts and image-cousins on image-beaches with their image-buttocks partly exposed by their image-bathing shorts. And Ivor said, "You don't need to write like that about images." And I said, "You just wait," I said, "till you read my next book." I said, "You'll have your image-this or image-that up to here."

AJ: That's right.

GM: I was referring to *A History of Books,* that I've mentioned before—and it's going to make some people just seethe, I suppose—but it's—the, the expression image-this or image-that, the whole thing rests on the foundation that everything in the text is an image of something. So, I warned him. But that's only a slight example. But, he's—and I put him right on a point of grammar.

AJ: Did you?

GM: Yes, I did. He didn't know that the verb—it's four lines from that poem "The Fairies."[6] "They have kept her ever since, watching till she wake, on a bed of flag leaves, the deep beneath the lake." That's roughly it. Now, and the narrator of the text then goes on to say, "But the verbs in this stanza are in the present tense." Now the verb is —there's really only one verb the others are participles—the verb is "have kept," and Ivor wrote on the copy, he said, "But they're not, they're in the past tense." And I said, "Ivor, grammar lesson number one." And he, well, unless he was half asleep, "have kept" is the present perfect. It describes an action or reports an action completed in the present and having begun in the past. He didn't seem to know that, so again twenty years from now someone will realise that I knew more about English grammar than the publisher of the Giramondo Press.

AJ: That's amazing, probably nobody else has picked up Ivor for grammar.

GM: You're not here, are you, Ivor?

AJ: No, he's not. We share something in common. We both have a love of *National Geographic* from the 1940s to the 1950s. Now, could you tell the audience, please, where does your love of those images come from? What do those images do for you? How do they spark your imagination?

GM: Well, not quite the way perhaps you think, but it's the old story I suppose—and this is something that's always interested me, and many of you—most of you would have had similar, or conducted similar little investigations in your

6. By William Allingham, 1850.

own lives. Why is it, or . . . Am I so interested in X or Y for no other reason than that I was exposed to it an early age? Now, the one thing that comes to me, apart from *National Geographic*, is horse racing. Had my father not been a gambler, had he not brought the racing papers home, had he not trained a horse in the back yard for a few years in Bendigo, would I have been as interested in racing? I actually, there's a good answer to that. My brother had been exposed to exactly the same interests and he wouldn't cross the road to watch the Melbourne Cup if it was free across the road from his house, so the two of us were similarly exposed and only I took up on horse racing.

Going in to the *National Geographics* . . . Dad used to bring us home—Dad was a minor public servant and he used to bring us home—a school library would be throwing out some magazines or some old books and he would, Dad would visit, in the course of his duties he would visit the schools to inspect the rolls for attendance, the defaulters, people who were truants, who didn't go to school. And he got friendly with the teachers and he'd bring home, he brought, sometimes a collection of glass marbles, which is important to me. My first marbles were confiscated from poor little kids in Bendigo, fiddling with them under the desk. The teacher'd take them off them and at the end of the year, she'd find these marbles and give them to my dad, tell him, "I'm not really entitled to own them, but I do." Well, *National Geographic*. He brought home a couple of *National Geographics* in about 1944, '45, and that was the start of my interest in foreign countries.

AJ: Yep.

GM: Hungary, Finland, Malta, all these, and in particular America. I think in all, in about four different books I've mentioned West Virginia, because many of you would know that I don't travel—I travel within Victoria, but not outside Australia, anywhere much beyond Victoria—so I've never been to America, never will. But when I think of America I always think of West Virginia, because it was the first part of America I read about. And in West Virginia, and in the article on West Virginia there is a picture of a woman, and I think it's mentioned in about three books. She was just pictured—one of those women like the ones in your pictures. And you can get on to your aspect in a minute. She's got all these glass marbles coming out of a machine, made for industrial purposes or to sell to kids for toys. And it just fascinated me. I didn't, and I thought—I was five years old—I didn't know where marbles came from. They come from West Virginia. They're made in the mountains of West Virginia. And I, I still, trust to those funny little changes of thought that occupied me as a kid. My first interest in Hungary grew out of some pictures of—a picture that was mentioned in one of my books, I've forgotten which—might have been *Inland*. A great big stuffed dummy, made of hay and cloth, a kind of mock bridegroom. It's a wedding in Transylvania, a Hungarian part of Romania. And I just stared at that. I still don't know fully why it fascinated me. But here was this wedding feast going on, these peasants standing 'round in their Sunday best, for the wedding, and this great big dangling dummy figure, hanging above them, they'd drawn two poplar trees together.

But back to your question. Um, would I have—well, I wouldn't, the answer is no—but I don't know to what extent my first interest in *National Geographics* was just because dad put them in front of me. I certainly wouldn't have . . . there'd be fifty pages missing from my fiction. And then why he's brought that up is he's got something—hold it up, Antoni. Now I'm doing the interviewing.

AJ: Yep. [Holding up a book.]

GM: Antoni fascinated me years ago with a collection. You explain it.

AJ: It's a collection of images from *National Geographic*. Unfortunately the images are falling out of the book now, but it's called *In Search of Lost Time*, which is the Proust thing. And you take the images away from the text, and they look very, very strange. But, Gerald, maybe I'll give that to you, and if you could maybe just flick through for a little bit. But they are uncanny, aren't they, the images.

GM: Well the thing—ah, I'm not in the right mood to, sitting up in front of an audience, to react as I did, but when Antoni first showed me, what we noticed was the strange cheesecake images of women, and—not all of them—and then men in suits, the woman was always in—not all—but the woman was quite often lightly clad, and the man is in a suit.

AJ: There was an ominousness.

GM: Yes.

AJ: The woman was holding pineapples and the man was in a suit.

GM: Yes, and—that was, of course—I'd prefer to rely on my impression. I haven't seen this since—what was that year? '80 . . .

AJ: Yeah, '88, or '87.

GM: I've never forgotten it. That he—I mean, it's not my *National Geographic.* I sort of shuddered a bit when I saw this. My *National Geographic* was just a kind of fairy-tale world over the seas, of places where I'd never been. But this was a sinister world where a kind of, um, a sinister world where people pose—and of course, he's taken all the captions away, you don't know what they're doing. You get quite alarmed by the time you get to the—you want to know what the end of the plot is.

AJ: It's the Freudian uncanny. It's the return of something we sense. And because there's no verbal text around it, it's allowed to play on our imagination. Visual images coming into our preverbal imagination.

Now Gerald, you won the Melbourne Prize. Let's give Gerald a round of applause for winning the Melbourne Prize. You're tipped every year to win the Nobel Prize.

GM: Well, I get nominated. I mean, and this brings up the question—it's a bit of a—I shouldn't, you know, sitting in front of an audience, sort of complain about anything much. I've got nothing much to complain about. But if you said, "Go for your life, I give you permission to complain about something," it's that: the difference between the reception of my books in Australia, which—it's okay, I don't lie awake at night worrying about it. But it startled me when the Swedes discovered me. When I say the Swedes it was one man. He's a retired professor. He's not even a Swede—he's half Norwegian—his name is Harold Fawkner. He's half Norwegian and half Scot. But he lived most of his adult life in Sweden. And he was standing in a bookshop, in about 1986, and *Inland* was very unsuccessfully published in England. A Faber edition. The only good thing about it—the edition there had one of the best covers ever designed for one of my books, a hardcover *Inland*.

And he picked this book up, and he read it, and he wrote—he sat there and wrote a hundred pages, a kind of essay, a dense . . . I couldn't get through it—a dense critique of *Inland*, which he said was one of the most remarkable texts he'd ever read. And I'm not talking about some crank. I'm talking about a senior academic and a master's and PhD in literature in Sweden. And he started a single-handed campaign to get me published in Sweden. We've written a lot of long letters . . . I used to do what I did to Ivor in the margins of the galley proofs. I got sick of him writing sometimes, and used to be almost sort of, you know, have these sort of playful arguments with him, and try to bring him back to earth. Because it made me uneasy, because there's all this great weight attached to a book, which I knew was an important and good book, but it just, it was almost unnerving to be praised so much by such a man. So I'd say, Look, I only put that because of this or that. I tried to just calm him down a bit. Anyway, *Inland* was published, not very successfully, in Sweden, because it was a smaller literary publisher. But later on, a major publisher picked up—what did they do before *Velvet Waters?*—just lately, *Barley Patch* has come out in a Swedish edition, but there was another one—oh, *The Plains*. So *The Plains* and *Velvet Waters* have been published in Swedish, and they get reviews—I have to rely on Swedish translations, English translations. One of the major newspapers, a leading critic, described Gerald Murnane—probably thought I was about thirty or forty—as one of the most interesting writers in

World Fiction at the moment. Now, no one in Australia has ever said that, that I can recall. I'm sure I would recall it if they'd said it.

And what I think is this, that you can't help it but in Australia—and it could be any country—we've got a kind of, a pecking order. We know that these writers are up the top—I'm somewhere up there, I'm okay, but I'm not at the top. But the Swedes—this man, the Swedish academic community—they just, they don't know the pecking order in Australia. They just know this writer or that writer. And so they're not bound—they just react to the book itself.

And I find that really cheering. And a bit irritating, that it doesn't always happen, because of course, I know what writers are like. John Powers, my poor late colleague, he used to say, "Gerald," he'd warn me about the students. "They will never let you off. They will be greedy for your comments. Eager and greedy." And John always used to predict that he'd be lying on his deathbed in a hospital, and the nurse would find out that he was a teacher of creative writing, and say "Would you read this, and tell me where I should get it published?" But anyway, John died suddenly of a heart attack, so he was spared that.

But back to the pecking order, and the—a couple of years ago, a couple of Swedish academics nominated me for the Nobel Prize. And they do it every year. And what comes out of it, who knows? And I don't even think about it. But again, I doubt whether anyone in Australia—Peter Craven perhaps, if he were given the opportunity, would nominate me—but my place is, sort of, not up there, but sort of, up over that way, sort of north, northeast of the pecking order. And that's okay, as I said three times. But it just startles me sometimes when I think, now, the Americans . . . Three times—twice, *The Plains* has been published in America. No interest in it. I remember noticing in their *Publishers Weekly*. "This is not a work of fiction, it's a work of philosophy." And, you know, that's not bad for a guy who couldn't do philosophy, to write a work of philosophy . . . How did that start? About talking about the Swedes?

AJ: Yeah, it did. It was actually a preamble into another question. We didn't quite get to the other question. But, in your Melbourne Prize speech, you were talking about your love of Melbourne. You'd lived in so many different parts of Melbourne. But there's a rumour now that you've left Melbourne. So what would you like to say to that?

GM: Well, not permanently. Not necessarily permanently. I lived in Melbourne from—I was born in Brunswick, or Coburg, and I lived in Melbourne—we went away to Bendigo, Warrnambool—came back in 1950. End of '49. So I lived in Melbourne for sixty years without living anywhere else. And virtually forty years of it in the one suburb, in the northeast. Then after my wife died—and I wasn't, I mean, we were trying to prepare for it, it wasn't some sort of desperate, you know, emotionally fraught decision, I thought . . . One of my sons has a house in a remote country district in the far west, and I'm living there on a trial basis. And another one of my sons is minding my house in Melbourne. So I haven't necessarily severed my connections with Melbourne, but I'm liking it so much where I am over near the South Australian border that I'll probably stay there for the rest of my life.

So yes, I've—but my wife and I used to visit this remote place. It's over in the Horsham district. And we used to visit it, look after it. My son left it to us as a holiday house. And it's a strange thing, living in a small community. And they know I'm a writer—I didn't want them to know—I didn't care if they knew, but I wasn't going to tell them. And there's a funny story. I took a teacher from the school. There's a big school, one to twelve, a hundred and twenty kids, they come in buses all around. And I took a teacher from the school into my little work- and sleeping-room, little apartment as I call it, and all the filing cabinets were around and I said, "These filing cabinets, in each drawer is one of my books." And the name of the local football team there is called Border Districts. And that's the title—I loved the words—they just suited the title of the book. My book has nothing to do with football, or even much with that district. But I just wanted the title *Border Districts*. And he, I know he didn't believe me. I said, "Stephen, well it's not about this town or the football team," and he just walked out. And now, at the golf club, which I've joined, they say to me, "Look, don't put me in your book about our town." So I've got—they really are wary of me in a respectful sense.

AJ: Ah, we're going to throw to questions very soon. I've got one or two more questions, so think of your questions, please. Ah, Gerald, in all your books, they're about yearnings, longings, fantasies, memories, daydreams.

GM: Do you know something? Well, you know, he's right. But do you know something else that only occurred to me a few years ago? And I only state this. I don't offer any explanation or any reason for it. I sit in front of you as, not so much the—well, I'm the author, I don't deny that—but I always say I'm the public face of Gerald Murnane. The person talking to you now. I'm not—I don't feel as if I really wrote those books. If I were sitting alone on a quiet afternoon, I'd get back to feeling the way I was when I wrote the books. But I say to you, that I've had a happy life—I hope it lasts a bit longer yet—but I don't want to be found dead, slumped over a typewriter, my old typewriter. I'd sooner be found out on the golf course or somewhere. So I don't go on writing forever. But I have very little to complain about. I've mentioned a few small complaints. So I'm not one of those bleeding hearts or racked, tortured individuals who can't see what the world, why we exist and why people suffer and there's very little of that in my books. There's more humour, really. And some people have found the humour in between the lines.

However, it's a funny thing that almost every one of my works of fiction, whether it's long or short or whatever, the last section usually describes a male narrator, or character, alone. And reflecting. Not distraught. Not wracked— well, in *Inland,* he claims to have wept over a grave. But the grave, the person in the grave, he didn't even know, he only knew the name, there was no one he knew. So that's something to think about. And that's, I don't, I speculate about . . . But the essentialness of a lot of my fiction is solitariness. So even though I'm the most gregarious of people, the person who writes those books seems to be solitary. And his reflections are mainly on, not so much solitude itself, but a solitary view of the world. And what would it be like, this person is saying, what would it be like if I weren't so alone, or if I weren't so solitary?

AJ: Yeah. And your landscape is a mental landscape.

GM: Yes, yes. I'm not a good observer. There's a wonderful statement that I've carried with me for years since I've first read it when I was teaching, about a French writer called Alfred Jarry. He was a surrealist and he wrote a series of plays that I've never read. One of the pioneers of surrealism, and he died of alcoholism and he only lived to be about thirty. He was a cyclist in the days when cycling became popular in the early twentieth century. And he used to ride around the landscape around Paris, with his head down over the handlebars, and somebody rebuked him and said, "You're a writer and a poet, you should be looking round you. Observing the scenery." And he said, the answer he said, "One must have a very poor opinion of one's subconscious if one tells it what to take notice of."

And that explains me. I've never directly looked at anything intently. Things just—something will put its hand up and alert me and wave to me if it wants to be noticed. My landscapes are not, I don't know the names. I think I know the lemon-scented gum, the only gum tree I know, 'cos I planted one in the back yard. But I don't describe landscapes with any knowledge of them. They're just scenes in the mind. I think it might be getting on for question time.

AJ: I have, but, ah, that's just in case the audience doesn't have questions. We've got permission to go five minutes over, which is very generous, which is terrific, instead of being kicked directly out on the hour. So we've got fifteen more minutes with Gerald. Who's got a question? Yes, there's one there.

FROM AUDIENCE: You've mentioned that you had a list, when you were a boy, of fifty subjects. Can you tell us some of the things that were on that list?

GM: Well, just before I do. During the years when I wasn't writing fiction, I, as I said, wrote a lot of autobiographical writing. And one of the things I wrote was about thirty thousand words expanding and explaining, because most of them are just names of places, for example a street. Simple things. Trying to recapture, just code names for moods or—see, I believed, I was only seventeen for heaven's sake—I believed that poetry . . . I don't see much distinction between what I was trying to write when I thought I was going to be a poet, and what I ended up writing, so I'll just say writing, meaning any sort of creative writing. I thought that it was the duty of the writer to convey to other people things—as I almost said before—things that one normally didn't convey in social intercourse. So, if I were walking to my parish church at the age of sixteen one cold morning, and where is it, it's in *The History of Books,* I drew on this memory. And I saw that the sky, a bit of pink cloud in the sky, it's early morning, and the first sign of the warm days of spring. Some—just an ordinary mood of hopefulness or optimism might have come over me. But I thought, that's the sort of thing I must write about. Never did, but wanted to. So the entry would simply just be, you know, Clayton Church, September '55. It wouldn't mean anything to you. But it was a code word for that kind of . . . Once I walked past a—in the same area, that's why I'm thinking of it now—I saw two little kids playing. And it almost—it still remains a strangely painful thing. They weren't poor or underprivileged as we'd say now. They were just two little kids, but their clothes were—obviously battling people, paying off a little three-bedroom weatherboard in 1950. And the kids had a look of extreme joy on their faces. A boy and a girl, a brother and sister. They were just playing horsey. One was being the horse and one was being the . . . And I couldn't believe, I just felt a strange kind of compassion for them. So I just wrote down, two children playing or something like that, and I've never forgotten it. And so you wouldn't get any enlightenment if you were to look through those notes. You would need me to explain, as I have explained. You'll last the twenty years that you'll have to wait. You're young enough to last. You'll be able to read these things one day.

AJ: And a question up here.

FROM AUDIENCE: Gerald, you mentioned that you moved and so moved into a new environment. Do you find that that's impacted on your writing at all?

GM: No, no the room . . . I've always liked to write in a particular, just a nice, quiet room with the blinds down, and the place I'm living in is made of Mount Gambier stone, and the high windows you can't see sitting at the desk, I can't see through the windows, which suits me very well. I've got books and cupboards around. But I don't write about my surroundings. There's always this time lag. I don't think I'll live long enough to write anything about my wife's illness and death. I've written it all in diaries and things.

But just about, well, my son fell seriously ill in 1977. And it was five years before I fictionalised that experience, in something that's a sadly neglected piece of fiction. This piece is in *Landscape with Landscape*. It's called "The Battle of Acosta Nu." Everything's almost, the medical details of that are exactly as they were in real life, so to call it, except that in real life the son is revived after his heart stopped beating, but in the story he doesn't, he's not revived. But I mention that because, the time lag was five years. If as you speculate I've been affected or my feelings have been greatly altered by the move, it won't find its way into writing for another four or five years. It's just the way the processes work.

AJ: Gerald, do you feel connected with the great Australian nineteenth-century tradition of Henry Lawson, Barbara Baynton?

GM: No. No, no, I feel as the plainsmen feel, that they don't really belong in Australia. I love this country—I mean, I say that, but I always feel proud on election days when I see the "how to vote" people talking to each other, instead of, you know, killing each other or shooting at each other. I take little interest in politics or grand social themes and things. That's for other people to worry about. I couldn't think of ever living anywhere else. But my idea of Australia is a place where you can pull the blinds down and nobody bothers you. You can go and do your writing or your reading, and that's my Australia.

Not a country of shearers—I mean, in the hotel where I drink two nights a week, there's shearers and farmers and things all around. But I don't think they're necessarily any more interesting than any other sort of Australian.

AJ: Thank you. Question here.

FROM AUDIENCE: Gerald, I was thinking about what you were saying about your racing interest. And when you were saying that I was thinking about you were saying your brother grew up in the same environment, and he's not interested in racing. Well, he became a priest, is that right?

GM: Yes, he's a priest in New Zealand.

FROM AUDIENCE: I was just thinking about the religious . . . There's a certain sort of connection between order and disorder, if that makes any sense . . . And I was thinking, the racing stuff seems to be about a sort of order and religion seems to be about a certain order too, and yet you're also playing around the edges of disorder, if that makes sense.

GM: It's an awful lot to comment on. It's all mostly, what you say makes excellent sense. I'll just throw in a new sort of, use it as an excuse to make another comment. What I'm writing at present, people—it's funny, I've been to many and many over the years, many and many a gathering like this, and I used to joke, a bit cynically I suppose, they always want to know how much of your fiction's autobiography. That's why I devise that saying "in a sense, yes, in a sense, no." And the other thing is "what are you writing now"? And no one's asked that question, but *I've* mentioned it. And the thing that I'm writing now is almost like a meditation. It begins with the narrator catching sight of a little coloured glass window in a Methodist—an old, it's called, Wesleyan Jubilee Church in the little town where I'm living. And my writing deals with coloured glass, religious belief or lack of religious belief. What I'm saying is the subject of religion, or the sorts of things that people who are religious believe in, has never left me. What do you believe? I'm a sort of a non-materialist atheist. You look up Richard Jefferies. Who's ever heard of Richard Jefferies? One of the greatest neglected writers of all time. I'm reading him again now. Richard Jefferies's beliefs would be mine at the moment. He described himself as a sort of a non-materialist atheist. And the other writer, just while I'm thinking of it—I came prepared—I'm reading a lot of nineteenth-century stuff at the moment. I'll get back to that in a minute. And George Borrow. Who's heard of George Borrow? Another wonderful writer. Sadly neglected, I've read the—and I'll probably read them once more, *Lavengro* and *Romany Rye,* before I die.

But the religious thing. I can't think without that framework. It stays with me. That was Elizabeth who asked that question. Lis and I are correspondents. We've hardly ever met, I think, this is about the nearest we've ever been to each other. So we write to each other, and we put a lot of things into the writing that we probably wouldn't talk about if we met. But that religious thing, I'm glad you brought it up. And the matter of what's—it's in *Barley Patch,* too—what does a person think of when they think of God? Do they see a colour? Or, there's a character in *Barley Patch* who says, "God is an oblong blur." And there was an Anglican minister who once was asked—it was a factual thing, I read it in a book—"What do you think of when you visualise God?" And he said, "An oblong blur." And that absolutely fascinates me. What takes place in people's minds. So I'm still interested in all that sort of stuff. And my brother took the more conventional way of living his beliefs out.

AJ: Five minutes only to go, and it looks like . . . All right, up the back first, and then there's a gentleman here.

FROM AUDIENCE: Just a quick question to Gerald about—you mention in the start of *Barley Patch* twenty books that you might be able to recall. I think you recall eleven or twelve, didn't go on to explain the rest, that might have had an effect on you. And you have a memory of those, or the narrator at least mentions these . . .

GM: I'm glad you changed, that's okay.

FROM AUDIENCE: And, uh, obviously the preamble to that is sort of, almost sort of knocking the literary world's expectations of being able to rattle off the greatest books of the century. Of these sorts of feelings, or images, or colours as you were mentioning, that you do remember from particular books yourself, which book would stand out most for you personally? You mentioned the nineteenth-century stuff that you're into now . . .

GM: Probably, partly because of its size, it would be *Remembrance of Things Past.* But I wouldn't like to nominate one book. I mean, the book that's mentioned over and over in *Inland,* the Hungarian book that I read first in English, *People of the Puszta,* that caused me to write a whole book as a sort of tribute to it. I just, I won't nominate anything but Proust, perhaps, but I will tell you that, I share with the narrator very much, this sort of almost, it's not, wouldn't be too strong to say dismay. And I did, when I was writing that—what's your name, the questioner?

FROM AUDIENCE: Craig.

GM: Craig. When I was writing, and I did write *Barley Patch*, even though I'm not the narrator of it. When I was writing that passage I went for a little walk around the bookshelves—I was writing it where I lived then, in Macleod—and I was amazed, and as I said, almost dismayed, at how little I did remember of books—so-called great books—and in *Invisible Yet Enduring Lilacs* there's an essay called "Some Books are to be Dropped into Wells," in which the narrator says that he read the whole of Cervantes's *Don Quixote* and he only remembered one scene. That's an exaggeration for fictional purposes—I can remember a bit more than that—but very little. So, but I often wondered what was I doing, all those days, when I'd sat for hours and hours with books in front of me. And yet, you ask me about something like George Borrow, or Richard Jefferies, tiny little details have stayed with me for forty of fifty years. It's just this fascination, or this fascinating business, of what a human being needs from books. And what they don't need from books, in many cases. Now, there was a question here.

AJ: A last question, because we're coming to an end.

FROM AUDIENCE: Quite a few years ago, Peter Craven said that you were a minimalist writer. I think that that's true. I'm not sure what a minimalist writer is.

GM: Well, well I don't—you would understand from previous answers I don't think of myself as anything in, in those terms. But he also wrote that my—I think he used the word "philosophy"—is the sort of philosophy you get from kicking over stones. And seeing what was underneath them. And that made sense to me. I thought that I really haven't experienced a great deal in my life. I've been a father and a husband and I've seen my son die almost in my arms, and my wife die. And I've had all these things: been in love and been rejected and been accepted and all this, but I've never travelled and I've never had—I've had a limited, probably a less than average experience, and yet I've written—what is it now—eleven books. So, if that's being a minimalist, that's what I am. But it's not just having to do with very little, it's making much of very little. But that mightn't quite be what he meant, but that's the way I understood it. How about that, eh? We'll finish there.

AJ: That's fantastic, and we've got fifty seconds to go. Gerald, fifty seconds. What would you like to say to this group? You'll probably never see them as a group again? So, Gerald, what are your final words for this group?

GM: Well, we've heard all this before, politicians always say it on election night, but I *am* humbled. *I* mean it.

Transcribed by Hayley Jach, and with thanks to Steve Grimwade,
Director of the Melbourne Writers Festival

JOHN GRISWOLD

Looking for Writers Beyond Their Work

America's personality was once riverine, and all roads led to the wharf. Mark Twain writes, "When I was a boy, there was but one permanent ambition among my comrades in our village on the west bank of the Mississippi River. That was, to be a steamboatman."

But rivers no longer occupy the same place in our national consciousness, and towns like Hannibal, Missouri, where in the mid-1800s up to a thousand boats landed every year, were cut off like oxbow meanders when railroads, interstates, and then airplanes came along.

No boats were expected in Hannibal on April 21, 2010—one hundred years to the day after Mark Twain's death—or for the rest of eternity, near as I could tell. Even the resident *Mark Twain Riverboat*, a 120-foot sternwheeler built in 1964, sat idle and dark. Two policemen walked quickly through the narrow waterfront park, glancing over at someone shouting in the distance. Soon the shouting man and I were the only people on the bank as far as I could see in either direction.

He was fishing below a work barge tied off to some mutilated sheet-piling. He loaded up a giant hook with glop that I took for peanut butter but may have been his secret-formula catfish bait, and swung the rod hard and fast. The bait went flying off the hook and splashed down separately at a distance. He shouted an obscenity, reeled in, scooped up two fingers more of the glop from its jar, formed it carefully around the hook, and cast again with the same result. More savage cussing, more bait, another cast, same results.

I stood next to him companionably as the obscenities rained down, their thunder rolling across the Mississippi all the way to Jackson Island. Others might have felt uncomfortable in the situation, but you see I've *gone* fishing myself, once. Twain wrote in his notebook in 1898, "If I cannot swear in heaven I shall not stay there," and for a split second I wondered if it was *him*.

* * *

Why do we go looking for writers beyond their work? They are, after all, *unpleasant* people.

I know, for instance, a writer who was mixed up in a university phone-sex scandal; a writer who still can't drink Cuba libres because it makes him want the cocaine he used to do when he drank them with Mongolian prostitutes; a writer who replies to greetings with farts; a writer whose pedagogy involves giving students vile nicknames; and a writer who used to eat dirt.

And that's just Facebook friends.

In the film *Amadeus,* the composer Salieri sneaks into the room where Mozart writes. Salieri lifts Mozart's pen from its pot of ink and stares quizzically at it, as if it might provide a clue to how, in Salieri's words, "music, finished as no music is ever finished," "the very voice of God," came from, "That! That giggling, dirty-minded creature I had just seen crawling on the floor!"

This perfectly dramatizes our puzzlement over the gap between art and artist.

* * *

The centenary of Twain's death was also the 175th anniversary of his birth, and the 125th anniversary of *Huckleberry Finn.* I drove out to Hannibal to catch the ceremony at his boyhood home, where a time capsule would be buried in the presence of a Mark Twain impersonator, a beauty queen, and a dozen Tom Sawyer and Becky Thatcher "ambassadors" dressed in hokum-wear. I knew Twain would have enjoyed the ceremony, if only for the chance to soundly cuss so many so efficiently.

The interstate west of Springfield, Illinois, quickly narrows to an old state road ribboned with tar. In spring the bare soil across much of Illinois is monochromatic because it's been tilled uniformly by computer-controlled machines in fields that extend flatly to the horizon. But just west of the capital, the first low hills emerge, and the plowed dirt begins to look less corporate.

Trees grew along the route, the tender mist of their leaves punctuated with redbud blooms, and marsh weed and cattails grew in the ditches. None of this was allowed to exist along major highways in the east-central part of the state, where I lived, and seeing it made me happy. Drainage creeks twisted through the fields in tight green serpentines, miniatures of the lower river on which Twain piloted as a young man. The sunlight changed too, so inexplicably that it's tempting to refer to old theories about miasmal exhalations of the earth.

A sign marked ninety degrees west longitude: "1/4 way west around the world." Exits led to the hometowns of Stephen Douglas, John Hay, and John Nicolay. Lincoln was clerking at New Salem, Illinois, thirty miles from Hannibal, when Sam Clemens was a toddler cutting teeth. Grant worked in St. Louis and upstream at Galena, and General John Logan was born three hours south, near my hometown. I stopped at a Dairy Queen in this cradle of the American Civil War and bought the best chargrilled burger with cheese food and crunchy tomatoes I'd ever had.

Closer to the river, road-cuts exposed sandstone and limestone, and the highway crossed a long floodplain surrounded by distant bluffs. I experienced a microsecond of confusion. The landscape stood before me, irreconcilable with Twain's prose and my own memories, yet irrefutable. At least crossing the Mark Twain Memorial Bridge was no longer the terror it was when I was a kid and my mom wrestled the steering wheel of her little car, its tires pulling and shimmying, on the deck plates of previous bridges, while I looked far, far down at the boiling brown god.

On the Missouri embankment there was a fifty-foot high portrait of Twain in the medium of colored gravel. The road twisted around a hill and down past gas stations and a tanning salon into the center of Hannibal, where a trim business district contained the Mark Twain Dinette, Mark Twain Family Restaurant, Twain Tours with Twainland Express, Mark Twain Book and Gift Shop, Mrs. Clemens Shoppes, and Pudd'nhead's Antiques, Collectibles and Crafts.

Twain's boyhood home was there too, a small clapboard house that looked taller than it was wide, with other period or reconstructed buildings in a block's radius: a reconstructed version of the Blankenship home (the boy was a model for Huck Finn), a period building being called the Becky Thatcher House, the drugstore building where the Clemens lived for a while, and the courtroom where Twain's dad was a justice of the peace. Two blocks away on Cardiff Hill, where Twain played pirate as a boy and real bootleggers and other criminals lived, the town had installed a statue of Tom and Huck, a small butterfly garden up the slope, and a lighthouse on top, used not for navigation but to honor Twain.

The ceremony turned out to be respectful and sedate, mostly citizens of Hannibal gathering to honor one of their own, with few tourists and no broadcast media. Even the EarthCam pointed at the front door of Twain's home wasn't working.

The Twain impersonator took the microphone and did two or three well-chosen bits from Twain's repertoire. He invoked Twain's line, "Let us endeavor so to live that when we come to die even the undertaker will be sorry," which was poignant after he'd read the *Hannibal Courier-Post*'s obituary for Twain, published the morning after his death. The child ambassadors described what they had learned as Toms and Beckys, and one little girl spoke movingly about becoming president and alleviating the misery of the poor. I had only to turn my head and look up the steep incline of Hill Street to see the mix of dilapidated and well-kept houses that reflected the widening disparity in America, worse perhaps than in Twain's Gilded Age. Proclamations were read aloud from the governor, the US congresswoman for the district, and the mayor; 2010 was proclaimed the Year of Mark Twain in Hannibal, Missour-*uh*. After the ceremony people drifted back to their workplaces and into restaurants.

Feeling sad, I took a photo of a horse wearing a hat. Then I walked through the park to the river landing and along the decline of the wharf, the cobblestones so worn their edges stuck up like stone knives. I tried to cast myself back to 1853, when Twain left home, but two steel trestle bridges spanned the river now, railroad tracks paralleled the wharf with a levee beyond them, and there were masses of overhead wires, satellite dishes, and advertising signs.

Yet the river was utterly placid and smoothly flowing, even glassy, and purling the only hint at the mischief of which it was capable. Hannibal boomed after Twain left, then the boom days ended, and now Glascock's Landing felt very close again in *spirit* to how Twain described his town, in *Life on the Mississippi*:

> After all these years I can picture that old time to myself now, just as it was then: the white town drowsing in the sunshine of a summer's morning; the streets empty, or pretty nearly so; one or two clerks sitting in front of the Water Street stores, with their splint-bottomed chairs tilted back against the wall, chins on breasts, hats slouched over their faces, asleep—with shingle-shavings enough around to show what broke them down; a sow and a litter of pigs loafing along the sidewalk, doing a good business in watermelon rinds and seeds; two or three lonely little freight piles scattered about the "levee"; a pile of "skids" on the slope of the stone-paved wharf, and the fragrant town drunkard asleep in the shadow of them; two or three wood flats at the head of the wharf, but nobody to listen to the peaceful lapping of the wavelets against them; the great Mississippi, the majestic, the magnificent Mississippi, rolling its mile-wide tide along, shining in the sun; the dense forest away on the other side; the "point" above the town, and the "point" below, bounding the river-glimpse and turning it into a sort of sea, and withal a very still and brilliant and lonely one.

Twain returned five times as an adult. From his notebook of April 1882: "Alas! Everything has changed in Hannibal—but when I reached Third or Fourth Street the tears burst forth, for I recognized the mud. It at least was the same—the same old mud."

The mud of Hannibal has been largely paved over but still rises in the brick of the buildings sprawled over the hills. It's a decent metaphor for how great writers become part of the edifice of a nation, though Twain had doubts about what portion of him would remain.

"We struggle, we rise," he writes, "with the adoring eyes of the nations upon us, then the lights go out . . . our glory fades and vanishes, a few generations drift by, and naught remains but a mystery and a name."

"Fuck!" the disgruntled fisherman yelled over my shoulder.

* * *

In his essay "Writer and Region," Wendell Berry says: "There is something miraculous about [Huck Finn's voice]. It is not Mark Twain's voice. It is the voice, we can only say, of a great genius named Huckleberry Finn, who inhabited a somewhat lesser genius named Mark Twain, who inhabited a frustrated businessman named Samuel Clemens."

This phenomenon is made possible by a technology—black squiggles on white paper—that stores ideas and verbal images so we can see and manipulate them over time by the process of revision. What we love in a writer is this *recursive* voice, the most concentrated form of that person's best awareness, which can be kept in print, shelved in libraries, and stored in a digital cloud that smiles down from heaven. At its best it's like having a sane, just, brilliant friend who can never die.

But the distilled intensity and sometimes near-perfection of recursive work also explains, I think, the deflation we sometimes feel meeting artists. The *work* has been shaped over time with the aid of a thousand self-critics; the person who *wrote* it crunches dill pickles in his maw while talking to you on the phone.

The final disconnect is that unlike its art, the human animal is mortal. Your friend's work may have encouraged you to see and feel, but he or she is always waving good-bye from the fantail of a departing ship.

"Even Beatles die," writes poet Valzhyna Mort.

I can't reconcile that.

* * *

Too often, so-called American innocence—in politics, religion, science—is no different from cynicism. Twain's great gift was to find a way to reconcile knowledge and innocence, what Picasso meant when he said, "It takes a lifetime to become young."

It's not fashionable to speak of greatness of spirit, so let's say Twain was an innocence broker and that that quality in his work hypnotizes us, like birds before a snake. I refer of course to the child narrators, the attention to "innocents" staggering abroad (his best seller in his lifetime), the prose that has us believing *he's* normal but surrounded by odd and colorful characters, the personas of the naïf and the put-upon victim, the spotless white ice-cream suits, the image of the loving family man performing skits at home with his beloved children.

Call Twain avuncular if you like, but he put these qualities to work battling imperialism, racism, vivisection, cant, hypocrisy, sham, and injustice. He could also be viciously angry, cornpone, and hilariously filthy. Lecturing at a Stomach Club dinner on the topic of masturbation he reputedly said, "A jerk in the hand is worth two in the bush." By becoming in his work a whole human being, he shows how to love our muddy experience and gives us hope that *people* can be whole too.

* * *

One of the dangers of confusing the writing and the life is that the author's stuff becomes as suffused with meaning as his books. The Mark Twain Museum, separate from the boyhood home, is modern, cheerfully lighted, and contains an incoherent mishmash of objects that's still interesting and even moving: the death mask of Twain's only son, a little boy shown in a photo sitting up in his stroller; items of Twain's clothing; a pipe with the stem worn away by his teeth; two dozen paintings and sketches by Norman Rockwell for an edition of *Tom Sawyer*; a reproduction pilot's wheel; furniture from various households; and period newspapers.

The front page of the *Hannibal Morning Journal*, Friday, April 22, 1910, says Clemens was "bad in the morning at Stormfield" (his last home, near Redding, Connecticut) but "seemed in good spirits" and recognized his wife's nephew and niece.

"Unable to talk too much, he asked the nurse for his glasses. When he was given them he picked up a book which for many years had been one of his favorites, Carlyle's *French Revolution*, and read several pages of it. This exertion was too much for his fast-failing strength, and he relapsed into a comatose condition, which verged into complete unconsciousness from which he never recovered."

It's fitting that a display in the museum quotes a passage from *Innocents Abroad*, in which Twain complains about the ubiquity of holy relics in his travels in Europe and the Middle East:

"But isn't this relic matter a little overdone? We find a piece of the true cross in every old church we go into, and some of the nails that held it together. I would not like to be positive, but I think we have seen as much as a keg of these nails."

There are other kegs of Twain's nails on display a few blocks away at the other sites, and the gift shop at the boyhood home *sells* a few near-relics, should you want to take one home. In one corner I found: Wild Huckleberry Gummi Bears, Wild Huckleberry Pancake Mix, Wild Huckleberry Cocoa, Wild Huckleberry Honey, Wild Huckleberry Syrup, Wild Huckleberry Chocolate Bar, Wild Huckleberry Jelly Beans, Wild Huckleberry Sampler, Wild Huckleberry Pinwheels, Wild Huckleberry Stix, Wild Huckleberry Taffy . . . and Missour-uh Chocolate River Rocks.

There were also books by and about Twain, steamboat models, jaw harps and pennywhistles, and all manner of other geedunk and geegaws. In response to my questioning, the two older southern ladies who staffed the cash register patiently explained that the huckleberries were not local but grown deep in the Ozarks. Of course I'd seen right through that, so I was pleased with myself when I found the jam to be delicious anyway, that my boys liked their T-shirts, and the postcards I bought of Twain, cartooned by *Calvin and Hobbes*'s Bill

Watterson for the *Mark Twain Journal,* looked fine in my office. I began to plan another visit to pick up a few other things. Maybe a marble head.

We try to get *closer.* My friend Rory is rumored to have two bricks he took from the yard of William Faulkner's house, Rowan Oak. Rory's a big guy who lettered all the sports and for one afternoon flung cloth bags of flour for a living, but it's *rumored* there's a five-foot Faulkner scholar somewhere gonna kick his *ass.*

* * *

Sometimes it feels as if each of us is sunk in our own crystalline well. We think we know each other through the glass landscape until some event reveals how impossibly distant we are in that proximity, how another's singing was actually keening.

And yet. Once at a dinner I sat across from a poet and felt over the course of a short, broken conversation her enormous intelligence and consciousness focus on me. Such moments almost make the hard breaks of mortality bearable and drive us to search for more such experiences.

Then she walked out of the restaurant and kicked a dog. The dog was metaphorical.

* * *

One of Twain's favorite words was "lonesome." He uses it eighteen times in the great moral novel *Huckleberry Finn.* The novel *Tom Sawyer,* a boyhood fantasy by comparison, has only five mentions.

* * *

There were many events celebrating Twain on the centenary, the biggest of them the release of volume one of his unexpurgated memoirs, which he insisted not be published until one hundred years after his death. Despite the book being a $35, four-pound, 500,000-word ramble, by Thanksgiving it had gone back to press six times, and the publisher still couldn't meet holiday demand. All this renewed interest made us feel closer to Twain, a presumption he would have appreciated, ham that he was, and been amused by.

As Twain prepared to leave Hannibal for the last time in his life, Tom Nash, a childhood friend—now deaf—approached him.

Twain writes: "[Nash] was old and white-headed, but the boy of fifteen was still visible in him. He came up to me, made a trumpet of his hands at my ear, nodded his head toward the [other] citizens [who'd gathered to say good-bye], and said, confidentially—in a yell like a fog horn—'Same damned fools, Sam.'"

LUIS CHITARRONI

Five Silhouettes

GEORG BÜCHNER

The house was prosperous and only arson could have made it interesting. The family consisted of the father, the mother, the two daughters, and that permanent houseguest, Herr Muschtag, who would address him whistling the first part of his last name, as if he wanted to extinguish it. The pain had started in Strasburg and had followed him, hammering at his temples more efficiently than even a gendarme could manage. Herr Muschtag cleared his throat, pointed innocently at him with his pipe, and asked him if he had seen "The Musical Forest." As if he knew what he was talking about, he answered him that no, he hadn't had the opportunity. Pleased, Herr Muschtag brought over the bronze cage, put it on the shining tabletop, and peered into the bars, smiling. Inside there were four bears, each one with an instrument: two violins, a viola, and a violoncello. On the head of the tallest bear rested a raven or a crow. The pain consisted of nostalgia, dejection, the weak vertigo caused by his trip and these difficult hosts, his cranial nerves. Herr Muschtag pulled the lever stuck between one of the angular bars, and a certain change, a portent, was produced in the cage's interior, as if the air had shrugged its shoulders. Then, with painful exactitude, the bears began to scratch out a melody. The crow sang a sad and faltering song that said there was no consolation in its cell and that gentians don't last as long as mistletoe. Georg Büchner smiled. You could hear the trembling of snow in that voice. He was twenty-four years old and didn't know if the pain of death preceded death, was death itself, or came after death, inspired and ultimate.

He remembered Minna, her blush, her footsteps, the narrow corridor in which the portraits of ancestors resembled those of the servants more and more each day. Scenic instructions. The last butler, who had mistaken him for a messenger, had said, "I need to recover it before Monday or else . . ." And in the next act he sunk his hands into the open body of a rabbit. "Have you ever seen anything like it, Herr Büchner?" It was Herr Muschtag now, his eyebrow arched, his fists stained with gravy. The candlelight shuddered beside him. No. Minna's very dark mouth in the darkness, still in the darkness. In the darkness, the toads and the water beetles. Dytiscidae. Dark in the darkness of the muddied water. No. And Ludwig, his brother, who pulled one out and made it enter into the light. "You see it?" he said: the divided chitinous body, the brilliant elytra. A fable whose words may have been these fragile animals, the final animal a grateful whisper; the penultimate, an interjection . . . the pain, the real pain would begin after death, and Herr Muschtag would have to know it. He smiled in thanks. An homage. To the ingenious man of letters, to the Professor of Comparative Anatomy at the University of Zurich, who had to flee because of certain juvenile rages. Herr Muschtag, again: "Tell me something, young man, what would you say is missing from these . . . animals . . . that would make them simply . . . human?" He didn't know. In a letter that he wrote, in between two words, an accent, a blotch of ink: this was what life did with the truth. Insert a paragraph. And wasn't Herr Muschtag perhaps ideal, with his captious rhetoric and adequate truths, as a model for Camille Desmoulins (or vice versa)? Something was missing: the continuity didn't belong to nature but to history, but between them both someone was inserting a paragraph. Was it him?

"I have heard that you are interested in puppet theater. Is that true?" asked Herr Muschtag, always incredulous. He must have gotten it mixed up, just like the crow's accent had mixed himself up in turn. Perhaps the national language was nothing but that: an oscillation between von Kleist's blank verse and a peasant's stutter. But no, it wasn't puppets or marionettes that interested him. Animals, automatons. And the beetle's body had remained floating on the viscous surface. Abandoned. Useless. End of the experiment. And afterward, he would die, shutting his eyes. But before that he had to say good-bye, had to thank for his hospitality this restrained and agitated gentleman who had watched him among his wife and two daughters, amazed that he'd had so many things in common with this private tutor. That gentleman was always *among*. Among his snail collection and his handwritten notes on Spinoza's *Ethics*, in French, that meridian language . . . He went back to thinking about the empty eye sockets of snail-adorned skulls. How many more things did he have to see to be sure that *one* was enough to stop everything else? Not Nature, Art taught. To breathe through your ear. The two girls curtsied. Herr Muschtag approached them for the last time. He heard their calm whisper. He turned around. In front of him were the stagecoach and the road. The mistress of the house had tight eyelids and an astonishing mole: she would never allow her household to be interesting. Behind her, the girls made a racket in Italian that Herr Muschtag rushed to correct. Good luck. He watched vapor coming out of the horses' snouts, a limp hedgehog that turned into a bundle of spines. Things began to bore him. Between one and another there had always been too much blood, too many words. The bronze cage, Minna's mouth, his hands covered in rabbit entrails, the final beats of mechanical life in the crow's mouth . . . Unlike the captain in *Woyzeck*, eternity didn't disconcert him. He made a decisive farewell salute at the height of his temples, which still hurt. Now he heard a lumbering melody, rehearsed, result of some provincial composer's ambition, an omen of the days that would have to come. No stars in the sky, only clouds. Perhaps someone at those heights would dare to imitate Lenz. Then nobody would be astonished to hear that there was music there in addition to heat, a music similar to that which was missing between things, a music that would help the Earth's dead to breathe—those that, like him, didn't hear anything but the silence of blood and words. Suddenly, close to the cartwheel sunk in the cold earth, the hedgehog found its tracks in the bushes. He walked into the darkness as if he were slipping, determined and obedient, into its hand.

Georg Büchner was born October 17, 1813 in Goddelau, Hesse-Darmstadt. He studied in Darmstadt and later in Strasbourg, to which he had to flee, pursued by the Grand Duchy. He had a difficult life because of his illnesses and active participation in his era's revolutionary movements. Shortly before his death, he found work teaching comparative biology at the University of Zurich. As an anatomist and biologist, he is well known for his studies of cranial nerves and barbel fish. He wrote the plays *Danton's Death* (1835), *Leonce and Lena* (1836), and *Woyzeck* (begun in 1836, but incomplete at Büchner's death). Also a bit of exemplary prose, *Lenz*, based on J. F. Oberlin's diary, about the life of Jakob Michael Reinhold Lenz (1751–1792), "failed poet" and contemporary of Goethe. He translated Victor Hugo into German (the plays *Lucrèce Borgia* and *Marie Tudor*). His girlfriend, Minna Jaegle, was with him the day he died, February 19, 1837. The preceding story is just a bit of narrative license, which the author of these silhouettes has conceded himself with more audacity than talent. The life of Büchner could certainly make a good short story, but Büchner himself—or Lenz—would have to write it.

ENRICO DALGARNO

It was while I was looking for information about George Dalgarno, whose *Ars Signorum* (1661) so interested Leibniz, that I stumbled upon his surname's namesake. The last name unites them, or else simply—pantographically— traces an innocent spatial acrobatic across time. They say that the spiral is a spiritualized circle: well, George Dalgarno (c. 1616–1687) and Enrico Dalgarno (1848–1911) evoke a less spiritual but equally elegant figure, a lemniscate whose point of crossing might lie in the two centuries which separate them.

I should clarify that the work of each is as unknown to me as that of the other. At the same time, one and the other both pass almost invisibly through the course of the various great ideas of their time; one and the other both propagate readings that are difficult or impossible, as if one's apprenticeship to their work were only an unappeasable appetite, or an unsought and intuitive aptitude; one and the other both, finally, represent a crucial sort of annoyance—or monotonous sort of pleasure—within those regimes of banality and revelation that are dictionaries and indexes of names. Philosophy and art history seem to get along fine without mentioning them directly, but perhaps it isn't totally gratuitous to force their casual potentiality into a proper relationship with the help of Luciano Albioni's interpretation of the second Dalgarno in *Bozzetti per la scenografia del Millenio* (Torino, 1988), wherein Dalgarno appears alongside others, like Fidrmuc and Trebitsch-Lincoln, similarly lost to the art of biography. Although Albioni's book, treacherously, was intended to illustrate a hypothesis concerning Dalgarno's precursor, and the differences between them, perhaps it's best that we not waste *this* superficial description of Dalgarno's work by describing another.

Enrico Dalgarno was born in Padua, son of a bulky businessman who denied him his surname (Gobetti). "Dalgarno," is, nonetheless, a gift from the paternal side of the family: his pugnacious father's mother's maiden name. (As if Borges, subjected to the unpronounceable law of Tlön, had become Haslam.) The Scots ancestry (and, accordingly, his relation to George) seems less remote in leagues than in lustrums: Albioni mentions an uncle who taught German to Enrico, and who wrote a "hagiography" (?) of John Knox, ending his days in Edinburgh. As for Enrico, he studied in Padua and Rome; in 1873, he was named Professor of Aesthetics in Bologna; in 1876, he published a study "mapping the rhetorical correspondences between authorship and astronomy," based on the investigations of Giovanni Schiaparelli, who, according to Albioni, would later exercise considerable influence on Rensselaer W. Lee (*Ut Pictura Poesis*), Erwin Panofsky (*Idea*), and Jean Paris (*L'espace et le regard*).

But *the* work that concerns us began later, when Enrico Dalgarno prepared an extensive essay about Rembrandt's self-portraits. Albioni explains: "Rembrandt's self-portraits lead Dargarno to a crossroads that perhaps (not even early) psychoanalysis could have avoided. He came to the conclusion that the task of a man of letters (he never considered himself anything else) is to write (or to learn to write, throughout the course of his life) his own life." In a peculiar interlude, tyrannized by pleonasm, Albioni tries also to stammer out something about "a religion of listening"; there is also, however, a direct quotation from Dalgarno that doesn't seem unworthy of its commentator: "I am at once prey to synteresis and the confessional." Couches, at the time, as has been said, were still no more than an innocuous Viennese comfort.

Thus Enrico Dalgarno took on the mission of writing his life, from innocence to prolepsis, as many times as necessary (if each one of these "lives" were mandated by the appearance of a particular muse, as Albioni conjectures, nobody has yet confirmed this).

The first of the four "biographies" that Dalgarno was able to complete is, according, as always, to Albioni, who managed to consult the original, "a pictorial biography." In it, Enrico tells how he discovered voluptuousness while gazing at Veronese's *Allegory of Love*, tells with what precision the "precise sensation of the time that passed" (but what else could time do?) as he tried to copy the foreshortenings of the Great Masters was then recorded in his memory, and speculates as to what sort of currency it could possibly be appropriate to remunerate artists for creating works of art that "are humanity's only practical patrimony." Intoxicated by this idea in particular, Dalgarno persevered with his work: his second biography is "economic" in nature. Dalgarno wrote it in Davos, just after finishing his study of Rembrandt, and it was published posthumously under the title (editor's choice) of *Mirano in vari oggetti un solo oggetto* (1948). Albioni, who has a weakness for unpublished materials, doesn't spend much time on it, remarking that it only contains ideas that Dalgarno would develop more thoroughly in the remaining biographies. At this point, it's important to clarify that each one of these biographies is neither a continuation of the previous work nor an introduction to the subsequent; that is, Dalgarno's life's work is not an extended autobiography in four or five volumes. The "pictorial," the "economic," the "emotional," and the "pathetic," all represent separate and autonomous works; they are each "a life" in themselves (narrated from birth until the moment in which the preterist decided to take up his pen).

Economics, however, is a common factor to the four biographies that are known to us, or so synthesizes Albioni. Dalgarno describes the coins in use at each important stage of his live and composes his self-portrait in such a way that the obscure circumstances (or ill-luck or destiny) that resulted in his disinheritance will be made evident to the reader. Albioni also suggests that this constant attention paid to the author's liquid assets anticipates a class struggle *sui generis*: a conflict waged in secret between the "dispossessed" and the enfranchised, between the artistic *amateur* and the *amatore* of art. Two citations from *Ghirlanda bruna* (the so-called "pathetic" biography, the only one published in the author's lifetime, in 1911) seem to permit such an insinuation (the italics are Albioni's): "I always prefer the condition of the suspicious guest, *who may hide an object of value among his clothes*. That which I observe in the houses of the others was and is my only treasure, a useless possession that I am obliged to transport it from one place to another while those others, like the Archduke Leopoldo Guillermo, do nothing but exhibit it. [. . .] *The seventeenth century has laid the groundwork for all of us to know what we are like.* Some of us will be painted smiling, enjoying an atmosphere and a connivance *apart*: others already have in their Land a king, however tame he may seem, and kings do not smile. We will only be *valuable* when *they* display us in the gallery where their *children*, well-built and upright, can likewise remain serious." The modest publicity of these concepts had (yes, now the italics are my own) to have influenced Max Raphael (*Tempel, Kirchen und Figuren Studien Zur Kunstgeschichte, Ästhetik und Archäologie*) and John Berger (*Ways of Seeing*), says Albioni, but his enthusiasm for nosing out the "influenced" seems to be directly proportional to the pleasure he takes in withholding any specific examples.

Dalgarno's third biography, the "emotional" (also unpublished), is the most literary. In the apotheosis of his associative delight, Albioni compares it to Schnitzler's novels, Gertrude Stein's experiments, and the Triestean *Giacomo Joyce*. It dedicates itself simply to recording the author's emotional register, doing away with continuity in favor of distraction, with entries organized according to nothing more than a vaguely poetic intent. I will transcribe the two passages transcribed by Albioni: "Rehearsal. Old age abounds. A brief border of happy flesh whose indecency can or should excite me. Regarding what? Life passes, passes. Again and again I'm not able . . . to make my surprise plausible. They look at me, astonished, the men of lineage, the arbitrators of finances and standards. They don't know that in order to tell a love story, one must know how to say 'I,' though in my case it isn't necessary. [. . .] I am at once prey to synteresis and the confessional. Absolute hearing, the law of forgetting weakened by amnesia or by our ancestors' good memory. Kings who change hands. But if anything really gets through, you should invite me to the pronoun clinic."

Thus stands Enrico Dalgarno, who met Rilke early on and knew, in his last years, Rilke's Italian translator, Giaime Pintor. Thus too the two or three clear things we know about him, and that for his part he knew or didn't want to know something about a precursor likewise obsessed with names, and the way in which people hear them or don't hear them.

GERARD MANLEY HOPKINS, S.J.

Solemn, Father Negreira approached the mirror as if the reflected image might take some time to coalesce. Each day began with this not so useful ceremony. "The young priest's formal rigor, his gift for languages, could easily please the devil . . ." he took advantage of the pause to rub a colorless cake of soap onto his face. "Yet it's open to debate whether or not formal rigor pleases the devil, don't you think, Father Tweedy?" he asked. "It's difficult to come to a conclusion based upon observation of the demon's works alone, but, yes, I would say that there is a certain systematicity to evil. As for the poems you speak of, there is no rule in our order preventing us from reading them as mere exercises," answered Father Tweedy. Negreira's silence obliged him to continue. "Father Hopkins hasn't given us any other standard by which to read them, after all." "Much like exercises," Father Negreira ran over a rough patch of foam with his razor, "they are, ultimately, irrelevant, I'm afraid." He exhaled. "*Painstakingly* indecipherable." Father Tweedy pointed at the two raised hands on a crucifix. Meiosis: a liturgical moderation of emphasis. He said, "Difficult to read, it's true, but written devoutly. Father Hopkins's behavior has always been exemplary. The Order . . ." "The Order," interrupted Father Negreira, "can't condemn him for practicing an activity consisting of contemplation. Or do I mean a contemplative activity? Even so, I'm not sure of the advisability of such an activity: practicing it is equivalent to setting aside certain clear priorities in search of those states of mystic contemplation," here he wiped off the foam from the metal edge, "already condemned in the work of the heretic Miguel de Molinos." Father Tweedy took a step closer to his interlocutor; even before he spoke, he felt out of breath. "The various hierarchies of error spanning from Satan to Miguel de Molions are diverse and unfathomable to us . . . you and I shouldn't dare to judge a man who shares our ignorance." "The difference between a maniac and a sane man without sense is that the former will always find a group of followers among other reprobates . . ." Father Negreira turned his head the better to shake the stare of this insignificant little man whose reasoning was never quite clear to him. "While the latter . . . he won't even find success in a mental hospital." "Success?" asked Father Tweedy. "Meaning what?" Father Negreira began to dry his face, then he asked, "Have you read Keats, Father Tweedy?" "Yes." Father Tweedy granted the poet's distinguished profile a moment of admiration. "But I think that your esteem for me is far too generous if you believe that I have formed an opinion on everything I've read." "Have you ever, sir, been afraid of losing your faith?" asked Father Negreira. "Indeed so, there was one occasion, when I happened to be passing through a convent in Scotland . . ."

Father Hopkins was curled up near a door on which a small sign prescribed "Meat only once a day. No tea except upon rising, and then without sugar. No writing poetry during Holy Week or on Fridays. No sitting in chairs, save when there is no other way for you to work. Ash Wednesday and Good Friday, consume only bread and water." Since he had arrived, he could only rest by walking. Walking, an art. Condemned. To look at things with the intention of really seeing them, in all their precision or ambiguity, with all their imperfections. "Piebald," a word appropriate for a pony, not for a stream. Pinto stream? Uncertain words and imperfect things, the rules by which all things differ . . . Where was Duns Scotus? Since he had arrived, the water and Advent had been killing him. Would he ever master Gaelic? The water gave him diarrhea, spasms of pain. Before whom would he prostrate himself in this pain? The fast, which was approaching . . . what? Those minuscule mouthfuls of air taken by the beats of the earth—their mottled, overo coats—always close to strictly necessary food. What was necessary for someone *like* him? Not he himself, he wasn't necessarily in play. The streaks of God's great clouds. Then what was necessary for a lemming? Lemmings hurled themselves into the sea. Looking. Fearing. Hearing. Lemmings and lemurs, they probably knew more about death. They were alive. Again he felt his stomach cramp, a pain that seemed to spread the pallor of death through his insides, and then, if not without a certain systematic grace ("evil, evil"), turning him inside out like a glove, so that *his outsides* also paled. Would his true outside seem acceptable to the things he looked at? "Mr Hopkins lacks Bishop Berkeley's persuasion, but we must note in his sentences an aesthetic of calm that his prosody then violently bewilders . . ." Poetic appetites. Beloved Bridges had been confused more often than not. Literary nits. The darkness of the path to the place of light. The light, the torrents of light he'd found pouring over these swift things—petals, pikes, parrots . . . True beauty? And that woman: "If beauty resides in form, would you, sir, say I am beautiful?" The simple words they would read clinically in order to recognize an agonized talent. To possess beautiful forms. A few had been in his arms. Beloved: that gracious participle revealing the ethics of the past. Should he tell her? Beloved Milicent and Katie, beloved Bridges. Inverness, Inversnaid. Words that are names. Accentuating the distinction. Spelling out the differences. Accents, dashes, striations. Writing for that. Far afield of these elegant paradoxes. "The Frenchman said the marriage-tie was in every case a bad thing, for if the married tired of each other it bound them together against their will, and, if they did not, it was superfluous." Now, as soon as he recovers, he must return to his papers. Latin and Greek. Thanks to the knowledge of others he was becoming prematurely old. He looked at the edges of his fingernails, that which entered into them, dirtying them. And again the ascent of pain, the spiral of nausea. The echo of temperaments, another proof of futility, as if youth's coveted form never uncovered anything but enigmas. "To the happy memory of five Franciscan Nuns, exiles by the Falk Laws, drowned between midnight and morning of Dec. 7th, 1875." A shipwreck. Even if they didn't want to understand, it had been because of this that it had been written, so that the ages would have signs, accents, differences. Excellence, the proportions of the norm, come from a force that expresses them and triumphs asserting itself over the resistance and difficulty of the material that limits them. Henry Purcell, his divine genius. Now feeling the music. Listening intently to this wave of power and gathering the energy to rise.

Father Hopkins leaned out the window. At this hour, everything became onerously unnecessary: the vague twilight, the vapor, the stars' distant discipline. Beautifully unnecessary. Above all the resistance and difficulty, the night began to have a face.

Father Tweedy concluded his story. As he was talking, he'd had the feeling that he had nothing of substance to add to all the other testimonies he'd heard from those in danger of losing their faith. His words, however apt and precise, couldn't provide a proper description of the apt and precise significance of his experience. Maybe he should have insisted. He said: "Perhaps within a few years we will better understand what Father Hopkins meant to say. Words also need time." Father Negreira nodded; he felt that the meeting had come to a close. He thought about the era in which they had to live: a vast circulation of facts and names that ambitious history would know how to capture, dispensing with generalities like these rites, these confidences. From Father Tweedy's story the image of an antique painting lingered. The painter, he remembered, had paid special attention to the saint's lips, murmuring a sentence or a prayer there in an illuminated face. He had learned to see this in the closed mouth of men. The Hesychasm. Negreira gestured for Father Tweedy to take his leave, and followed after him. "For the joy of God and men," he said in a very loud voice, as if initiating a sermon dictated by his image in the mirror, "you and I need not be threatened by expectations." The morning was splendid.

Father Negreira and Father Tweedy are fictitious; no amount of coincidence with reality could make them less inoffensive, gratuitous, or fatuous. Gerard Manley Hopkins (1844–1889), Jesuit priest, is, after Donne and Shakespeare, the English language's greatest poet. Accepted into the Catholic Church by J. H. Newman, he faced the misfortune of his poetry encountering not merely miserly, but actually adverse times. It was the epoch of Pater and Arnold—whom Hopkins venerated—but given his experimentation with "sprung rhythm," and his syntax so similar to the mumbles and raptures of living speech, he strayed far afield of the conventions of such excellent "melodic" poets as, for example, Swinburne and Tennyson. His punctuation and meter, capricious as they may seem, link him to Donne, another surly experimenter of the indescribable; the imagery and his skill in verbal games have contributed to the comparison, often superficially, to Dylan Thomas, another poet both more studied and more casual.

The "beloved Bridges" of the text is the poet Robert Bridges, Hopkins's friend and executor, who corrected and helped to publish, years after Hopkins's death, the latter's work; Katie and Milicent were Gerard's sisters; Inverness and Inversnaid are both places in Scotland that Hopkins visited (he dedicated a magnificent poem to the latter); the French paradox comes from "On the Origin of Beauty," a text of the poet's in the style of a Platonic dialogue; "To the happy memory . . ." is the dedication of *The Wreck of the Deutschland*, a long poem by Hopkins that stands as one of his principal achievements in "sprung rhythm"; "Excellence, the proportion of the norm . . ." is (probably) paraphrased from a letter to Coventry Patmore, a poet who, turning on Hopkins, later said that his friend's versus were "veins of pure gold imbedded in masses of impracticable quartz"; the setting—described without recourse to Ignatius of Loyola, as is probably evident—comes to some degree from the anecdotes found in a book whose title, if I remember correctly, is *G. M. Hopkins: A Commentary*, but whose author has entirely escaped me. Hopkins was, in addition to a poet, a composer and draftsman.

WILLIAM GERHARDIE

Of Víctor Eiralis's face, I retain only a cloudy memory. In 1981, when I saw him for the first time, he was making his way as a copy editor while I believed myself to be losing mine working as a "journalist." He walked into the office, found a chair, sat with its back between his legs, and said, "Tell me, sir, does your writing always come out this bad the first time, or do you have to really work at the worst bits?" He seemed like a character out of Onetti. Since then he's always called me "Pavese," an epithet of which I could never quite be proud, because he immediately gave me an explanation that didn't have anything to do with lyrical or narrative talent. He told me he'd noticed I had an irresistible tendency toward suicide.

Later, something brought us together in a bar. Something that wasn't exclusively hate, but which had a good amount of hate mixed in with the mere spite that animated his cumbersome rejoinders. "I live caged by failure," he told me then, "but you, sir, are even worse: you live caged by error." Maybe his failure lay in his insisting on addressing me as "sir," or in thinking that we were all as hardheaded as he. About my error, however, he was entirely confident.

But when our failure and error became insufficient—or perhaps only indistinct—he discovered something far worse: with the smug defenselessness of the misguided, I had begun to admire him. Víctor Eiralis refused this bribe, but he gave me a silhouette in return.

On some occasion or another, falling into an exasperating old tic of mine, reserved for friends, I spoke to him enthusiastically of a certain exiled Russian writer. Víctor Eiralis boasted of being the only Russian literature expert in Argentina. He looked at me indulgently. "Yet another idiocy, Pavese," he diagnosed, smirking. "That cretin is an invention precisely for shameless idiots like you. Do yourself a favor, seeing as you claim to read English: Gerhardie. He'll go right over your head, of course, but that hardly matters." And he named some books by William Gerhardie, and I assumed he was simply embroidering an already unconvincing fabrication.

Afterward (and I'd continued not to believe him), he went on to speak to me at length of Gerhardie, clarifying that his last name was actually meant to be spelled without the final *e*, but that William himself had added it in order to emulate the Masters: Shakespeare, Dante, Racine, Goethe. All of this information came to me caged in the smell of juniper, and apart from further enriching Eiralis's spite, it didn't do much for me besides round off the implausibility of this Gerhardie nonsense. How about if I start to spell my name Chitarronie?

Now that Michael Holroyd (a trustworthy authority: biographer of Lytton Strachey and Bernard Shaw) has, however, allowed *God's Fifth Column: a*

Biography of the Age 1890–1940 into circulation via Hogarth Press (nothing to do with our Great Mother, mind you); now that Julian Symons (that almost criminal arbitrator) gave William Gerhardie eight cramped columns in the *TLS*; now that my idiocy has at last equaled my error, now that age and promise can no longer affect Víctor Eiralis, maybe it would be *useful* to dedicate a few lines to this writer whom I thought had been made up.

William Alexander Gerhardie was born in Saint Petersburg in November of 1895. (The year was always very important to him: it was the year in which they imprisoned Lenin and Wilde, the two writers who most influenced him). Like his father—the inventor of an infallible "system" for winning at roulette, which the son would practice in Monte Carlo with disastrous results—William was always a grinning dunderhead, an optimist; he was also a womanizer and whoremonger. Yes, those vain fixtures of the night really made him shiver, made him believe that every female body must, sooner or later, be possessed of the same sort of lust—both slow and sudden—he experienced himself. He never regretted regretting: his compulsion to lay hands on every woman he could was tantamount to recognizing the sadness of literature. And Gerhardie practiced literature with a harem owner's joy: he was a polyglot. In 1920, approximately, after surviving the horrors of a phantasmal war, he went to study at Worcester College, Oxford. From then on, he turned into something of a spy in the house of gossip. He heard the voices of Arnold Bennett and Agha Khan, of Lloyd George and Bertrand Russell; there was always something that interested him more: the crimson nails of adultery, the run in a stocking from some lost work of love. He spoke English with such hasty, choppy nonchalance that his North American tailor celebrated even Gerhardie's anthropometric peculiarities as though they were epigrams.

If Conrad transformed from a Pole into Shakespeare, albeit peppering his margins with grumbles of protest, warped words, the ashes of sense, Gerhardie changed from a Russian into Firbank, albeit with Dr. Chekhov's consent: gardens, hot springs, witnesses in galoshes. *The Polyglots, Futility, Resurrection, Memoirs of a Polyglot* are some of his books, and are indeed better (all of the critics now concur with Eiralis) than Nabokov's, purer in their impurity.

Gerhardie allowed his work to obscure "the difference between art and life" to which he'd never paid much attention in any case; he wrote that D. H. Lawrence was as "unable to satisfy a woman" as Hitler was "unable to bestraddle a horse"; he died peacefully in his Hallam St. apartment in 1977.

Two more anecdotes about Eiralis. The last time I saw him, it had already been a good while since we'd both changed our lines of work. He came out of a screening of *Amadeus,* and wasn't alone. I think it annoyed him to be seen with an ugly woman. "Pushkin wrote this same thing more than a century back, and the director of this piece of garbage is simply imitating his style, Pavese." Then, adopting the stance of some stone immortal experiencing a very intimate satisfaction, he said, "Let me let you in on a bit of good advice, a friendly motto: it'd be better for you to begin to fail before your error lets you think that you've achieved success."

The second-to-last time I saw him, we said our good-byes. He, he told me, had stopped working because "he had met a rich woman." Prosperity didn't do anything for his looks. He was more bloated and withered than ever. He sat in his cowboyish way and talked at me for a while. We both had been slaves, he said, but I would be one forever. Unfortunately, I would never realize it. At some point, after looking at my face in the mirror, *I* would simply feel disgust. Nembutal, pills. No, it was clear that *I* would not be able to die like a man.

I (without italics, please) tried then and there—as I'm trying now—to write something at the typewriter. Pretty anxiously. Until it looked like he had fallen asleep. Then I said his full name out loud—it sounded unreal. He opened his eyes and looked at me as though seeing a copy of the original (me) after having found that we'd loaded the carbon paper backward. I'll never know if he really had fallen asleep. "I dreamed that you were intelligent," he told me, "and that I hadn't had the bad luck of meeting you."

This was yet another occasion I thought and dreamed replies that are now unnecessary to write down.

Translated by Sarah Denaci

S.D. CHROSTOWSKA

Seven and a Half Studies

The Good, the Bad, and the Beyond

The beauty of the new fragmented novel is that writers can have it both ways. These books pay deference to complexity, that deity of the lit critic, but they are also marked by an intense devotion to plot, pacing and other elements of traditional craft. Highbrow and lowbrow elements are pleasingly blurred. Experimentation proves that it is compatible with accessibility. I am attracted to these books—and I suspect others are as well—because of their skill in serving such conflicting masters, and without obvious compromises.

—Ted Giola[1]

Those moved to evaluate aesthetic objects on ethical grounds very quickly realize that nothing is simply "good" or "bad" (and not just because it is made so solely by thinking). The introduction of *additional* categories attests to our acuity and discernment. Let us take *novels* as our example, for there can always be found a critic who follows the stocks of tradition yet does not fail to invest in the new and comely. We must straightaway mark the *good "bad"* novel for special distinction: successfully revolutionary, unsettling bourgeois prescriptions for success and mainstream values. Conversely, there is the *bad "good"* kind: the oh-so bourgeois, promoting and reinforcing mainstream literary values. And who cannot name at least one *good "good"* novel, that badly bourgeois work surrendering to and failing even by the standards it follows? It still deserves consideration,

1. Ted Giola, "The Rise of the Fragmented Novel (An Essay in 26 Fragments)," *Fractious Fiction*. 17 July 2013, online at http://fractiousfiction.com/rise_of_the_fragmented_novel.

if only for honestly trying. But as its author, do not expect a shortlist anywhere; the two positives, *good* and *good*, make a very strong positive *in our assessment* because such books represent the dismal failure to guard these tired standards. And finally (if such hair-splitting can have an end) there is the *bad* "*bad*" novel: failed, still however creditable for trying to be revolutionary; in this case the two negatives, *bad* and *bad*, also make a positive, however weak, for there is much to recommend the work, even if in the end it confirms the strength of the bourgeois grip on art. These labels we have proposed can be reversed to reflect the opposite bias. Thus, the *good* "*bad*" can be called *bad* "*good*," or simply *bad bad*; the *bad* "*good*" easily turns into *good* "*bad*," or *good good*, and so on. (If any of this is at all confusing, you may first need to sort out your loyalties.)

But we are not yet through. There is additionally the question of degree, and some books merit a stronger response. The *worst* ones, those beyond *good* and *bad* (or "*good*" and "*bad*"), are those that betray both "sides"—for and against revolution, or for and against the status quo. These productions are exposed for trying to "serve two masters" by claiming to be revolutionary while beneath their unconventionality buying into bourgeois literary codes and conventions of thought and feeling. They are unfaithful sell-outs. The terrible failure of this *worst* of books is that both sides would claim it, were it "true," but under the circumstances neither wants anything to do with it. It follows that the most terrific success, and the *best* book of all, beyond the categories *good* and *bad* (or "*good*" and "*bad*") and their pileups, is one the two "masters" are prepared to fight over, each claiming to be the rightful one, without ever doubting the fidelity of what they are fighting over. As such, this *best* work is the likeliest to be torn to shreds—not by any rabid criticism but the most rapturous adoration.

Writing cannot bring back a dead father. It cannot lift you from the pit of despair, or the peak of self-love, to a selfless euphoria, the prairies of tenderness, the gorges of eroticism. Its lava must harden into obsidian. It is the sound of a rimed heart.

Where does writing lead? In the opposite direction; that is, if you are not already dead, you will be at the end of a sentence. Or, if you are not yet alive, you will be so when you reach that end. Such is the nature of sentences. Give or take a little, they are the nexus of life *and* death, their culmination. But only in a manner of speaking (we knew that all along). Writing is an exercise to ward off death—the ohm of decomposition. But this surely is not what all writers believe. Writing is *equally* an act *toward* death, delivering us to its doorstep. It is élan vital bound up with deathly longing. At best, writers can expect Elysium (they are the only extant pagans), at worst, immurement in a sepulcher. Everyone else, every amateur in the rosaceous bloom of inspiration, bathed in the frothy spray of fame (inverse of baptism or ablutions), engaged in the alchemical experiments of prolificacy, endorses their own writing with a hemorrhage of hocus-pocus, a calculus of cabbalistic metaphors, capped with audaciously auspicious prognoses—but, sooner or later, gets cold feet and skulks away. (No amount of enema will purge the pent-up energy thus produced, no amount of emetic cure the resulting pestilence.) The anathema and maxim uniting all members of the Republic of Letters: *Creative Overcoming Is Dead!* Yet the most creative impulse burgeons in that uneasy mélange of pessimism and optimism. It is in the nauseous malaise, the ennui and the loathing, that vivacity is revived.

What dire, desolate states has writing *not* brought me to? What excess of polyamory, what surplus of polyagony has it not fed? And yet, to write this is banal; it is dipping your fingertips in the immense black sea of nonsense. Even now, the scribbling gesture consoles. The two currents (perhaps even three) flowing through the activity of writing seem incommensurable. But are they truly disparate? Where there is happiness, there sadness also lies, but stiff.

Where sadness dwells, there, too, happiness is hatching. These are the sparse moments of least delusion. Only then does lightness coincide with, *does it become*, heaviness; but, as with the embryo, its future sex is already prefigured, or, as with the fetus, the quickening begins in a smarting of the womb. Which will prevail—weightlessness or lightlessness? (What will be their ratio—this to appease the ward of psychodoctors?)

There is a *sixth sense* (possessed by some) that has to do with writing life, which the soul awaits, with writing death, which identity awaits, with writing anything whatsoever, which challenges habitual patterns of thinking and sensitizes us to overlooked redundancy. It is what eradicates stunted figments, what displaces our perspective, remakes us as demons, and "leads us astray"—to then reveal a slitted *vista* onto another world, a *cornucopia* of new experience, which are for most writers what riptides are for bathers.

HOMODOMUS, OR MAN-HOUSE
/A STUDY IN ALLEGORY/

If a house were something that came into being by nature, it would come about in just the way that it now does by art, and if the things by nature were to come about not only by nature but also by art, they too would come about in exactly the same way as they do by nature. Therefore each is for the sake of another. And in general, art in some cases completes what nature is unable to finish off, but in others imitates nature.
—Aristotle

A man who only copies this universal building, and simply gets material from it for his own use, the man who does not build in and from his own personality, a little house of his to dwell in, so as to be at home within his own walls and under his own roof, where if he has not hewn every stone from the rough himself . . . he has not lived his own life and woven his own character.
—G. W. F. Hegel

What ruins are in the physical world, allegories are in the world of the mind.
—Walter Benjamin

Solid and unrestrained, his limbs do not protrude from openings in his frame. The man-house, or *homodomus*, should by no means be taken for what he is not: the *contents* of a house—the family or tenants, all manner of household appliance and furniture; he has little in common with them except cohabitation. He can neither be reduced to them nor distributed among them. Similarly, he does not belong, in his immanence—in the simplicity of his angles, the imperfect measure of his walls, the caved-in slant of his roof, the unplumbed depth of his foundations—to the dreary district where he stands, that congested community of homes and those inhabiting them. He is shut out of it, shut in himself, keeping altogether to himself. As a result, on the neighborliness scale he ranks mediocre. Notwithstanding his condition or, if you will, his *ethos*,[2] it happens, and frequently—not to say in daily order—that the man-house is merely the house of a man without a family.

The *homodomus* is form, *Gestalt*, and content, *Stoff*—simultaneously, in unison. I should caution you against mistaking *content* for mere *contents*, for the latter are entirely subordinate to the former. The being of the man-house is an active filling and fulfilling, both of which senses inhere in the concept of *Gehalt*, or substance—not a pluperfect fulfillment, or, if so, then only potentially. The *homodomus* cannot be deemed a paltry idea, the residue of outmoded philosophy, the odd antiquarian relic.

To the German philosopher,[3] *homodomus* stands for the act of *poiesis*. He is the foundational existential event, man's presencing. His existence seems to abut

2. Greek for "dwelling," "habitation."
3. who held that "poetry, as the authentic gauging of the dimension of dwelling, is the primal form of building," and that "the poetic is the basic capacity for human dwelling," and that, in the words of one commentator, it is *poiesis* (Greek for "making," "creating") that houses being. Strictly speaking, a house is only a case; it is the home, permeated by Spirit, which makes for freedom.

on *allegory*, the fulcrum of which is given to the fledgling Catholic as a dove-colored wafer. Allegory courses through the poetic bloodstream. It circulates in our bodies, frail as they are, nourishing us, and leaves us unencumbered. We recognize it as instinctively as the maternal breast.

Intriguingly, it is in the *homodomus* that the manifestation of modern philosophical allegory is strongest. What, then, does allegory conceal from us? Itself—through its infinite, elusive self-mirroring. This is why, in reality, the *homodomus*, thus vacated (thought a façade, used as a front), inconceivable (who wants to interpret vacant interiors ad infinitum?), wins no sympathy from his cognates, the rows of ordinary houses, these environs pregnant with neighborhood which *it* withstands, to which it superficially belongs, but from which it stands apart.

Who, or what, rather, is the *homodomus*? Autonomy, cohesion, unity. Form and content without antimony. Too often, however, a conflict arises between form and its contents. The peripeteia can take one of two directions. Either: form forsakes contents, leaving their shapeless, unidentifiable mass in the material world, virtually without the right to presence (akin to a gentleman without headgear). Or: contents evacuate, depriving form of its utility (this may be likened to an old iron robbed of its soul). In both cases the *Gehalt* ruptures—form and content having dissolved their bond—leaving behind the orphaned, amorphous, self-styled contents. Nonetheless, the allegory of the man-house endures among us, born to build for life a home in the wilderness.

Of Parables

"Can a parable say something new?" I ask myself, full of consternation, moments before the curtain reveals me—the final participant of the 1st Annual Unknown Parable Authors Festival. With the question still gnawing at me, I step onto the stage, back straight, shoulders back, neck craned, head erect, adjusting my hair, and smoothing my beard one last time. At these signs, the curtain parts to reveal the audience stirring in their seats.

"Ladies and gentlemen," I begin, "In the name of all our participants, I'd like to thank you for coming out here tonight—on this death-dealing winter night, with the mercury still falling—just to hear our stories. When I was backstage just a moment ago, I asked myself a fundamental question and was at a complete loss for an answer. It is with all the etiquette required of this occasion that I would like to conclude the festival by putting this question to you. *Can a parable say something new?*"

"Sir—?"

"Yes, please—"

"I believe it can . . . I believe so . . ."

"Thank you. Madam—"

"Yes and no; I think parables represent timeless messages in new ways."

"All right, fair enough, thank you . . . And Miss—"

"I would have to say no, definitely *no*. In my opinion, the meaning of parables is the oldest truth or structure of belief, and among the most ancient cultural artifacts, such as archetypes, myths, and topoi . . . It has been said that parables are older than reasoning, older than argument. Though the meaning of each and every true parable seems at times naively simple (and certainly the parable *idiom* has plenty to do with this impression), its meaning never is *simple*, for we learn to understand a parable as time goes by, so complex does it prove itself to be. We learn that it is not to be taken at face value. Individual life, understood in terms of parables, goes something like this: what once seemed obvious in a superficial way then begins to seem obscure, and, after drawing us further into its obscurity by mystifying our sense of logic, finally yields to illumination, becoming obvious in a profound way. But this austerity of form and depth of content are nothing new; we've intuited the synthesis all along, though we cannot reconcile its terms—cannot *comprehend* it even if it is staring us in the face. Could anyone dispute that parables are *in their duality* unthinkable? Therein lies their power, and beauty. This is why parables have a special place in the vitals of humankind; although they may become more lucid with time, they can never be thoroughly lucid, so that just when we think we have understood, we realize the profundity of our error. We remember them without knowing them. They draw on dilemmas and morals from the very dawn of civilization. I would argue that, since then, they have only been retold, translated, countless times, in one form or another, in more or less similar words. It is as if their core meaning was always already present in the universal mind, woven into its fabric. It seems that the stuff of parables has been around forever, like the blueprint for the Tower of Babel . . . Take, for instance, your question; it is also, as it were, a parable."

"How so?" I blurt out, incapable of concealing my surprise—"I haven't thought of it in that way . . ."

"Let's say that the tellers of parables have always faced the dilemma of whether what they were saying was true. This is the age-old question hidden behind the one you posed. Despite the common currency of truth—that is, wisdom, and particularly the wisdom of parables—behind every wise saying there always lurks a doubt: will my words win me (or anyone who receives them) approval from the future?"

"Right, now I understand. As eloquent as your answer is, Miss," I reply, "you are in the wrong. You have, it seems, saved the integrity of our *authors'* festival—by telling us a parable that has never before been told: that parables do not know themselves!"

Midwife
/a maieutic parable/

She lived in a modern city, far from the village of her coming into the world, where she waxed for twenty springs until, thus risen like dough in her youth, a portmanteau-trousseau to her name, she rode off into the panorama: the heights, the smokestacks, the mechanism of a metropolis. Frankly, a story (much like the present one) could be told in a single lapidary sentence (much like the one above), *were it not* that a statement cannot ever equal a story. One statement will not suffice for the whole story even by paraphrase or periphrasis. And yet, despite the possibility of relating, in multiple related statements, a story so parsimoniously dropped into four lines, there is really (ostensibly) neither need nor reason for us to do so. And yet, a need *does* make itself felt, and a reason *does* enter into the equation. What to do? Clearly, something must be set down. The bottom line is: we would be excused, *were it not* for the title. Is it not a certain need that suggests a title—and is suggested by it—that peremptory word or phrase foisted, imposing, on the statements below into which *it does not fit*? Either way—fleshed out ahead of time or fashioned (organically) during the writing—the title is overbearing (we may say: as the head is to the heart). It resists erasure, is immune to being tampered with. Lest we forget: no title is fortuitous. Lest we forget: titles have no place *in* stories *even as they shape them*. A title is no stylistic flourish—no flair of an eager pen—no requisite if anachronistic foible of the creative process— no "final touch." It is a crown. It affects the nature of the woman left to guesswork in that first, laconic sentence. It hints at something beyond the circumference of the already-known (a situation at once tense, pervasive, and evanescent). It commands a continuation: something took place that could not make it into that pithy statement, though it assumed a place, as it were, overtop a life that, still far from any story, is only *the heart of its source*. Led by a title, we may notice renegade statements which attempt to elude the story in consigning it to the unknown, which work by omission and delay, displaying infidelity to their principle: *sentences should be made to tell* (yet how faithful they can be to stories without titles!) Let us reach consensus: if a title, then a promise, then a purpose: to tell of something worthwhile that a narrative will, in part at least, accommodate, and in its turn come to alter. To recapitulate: *if it were not* for a title, this need would not arise. The title not only entitles; it obliges and constrains. And yet, contrary to appearance, titles are not immutable. They are prone to being undercut; take, for example, the title given above. Let us, then, leave our protagonist to her novice devices. "When I was nineteen, I dreamed of my birth. Midway between the womb and the world—already alive and still unborn—I saw the first flash of light. I thought: what a miracle birth is! That is how I remember it. I don't know if it was my own birth I was dreaming, or if it was a memory, but it was as lifelike as if it were me being born. When I awoke, I was astounded at my size, my thoughts, and I had the urge to be present at a real birth. I remember it was Caesarean. This is how I resolved to become a midwife . . ." Not a long account, all told, but how different from the opening lines! Flowing from the mouth of her who lived it, coming full circle, to the title's stead.

No Outstanding Work
NULLE ŒUVRE EN SUSPENS [4]

qu'ils ne souffrent pas et que je souffre, non pas seulement dans l'esprit, mais
dans la chair et dans mon âme de tous les jours
(that they do not suffer and that I do, not only in my mind, but in my flesh,
and in my everyday soul)
—Antonin Artaud to Jacques Rivière (1923)

Do I, the young poet asked the editor of the *Nouvelle Revue Française,* have the right to think (*le droit de continuer à penser*), *the right to speak*? The work he had sent in was not the result of inspiration but of spiritual jolts (*saccades*) that tear the words to shreds (*lambeaux*). Salvaged from the void, wrenched from chaos and composed in this ruined state as best he could, primitive to the extreme. *Et cependant je ne suis pas bête*, and yet I am not dumb, not a beast. He demurs: you are judging my work by today's standards; judge me instead by those that are absolute (*du point de vue de l'absolu*). What is art other than this wresting of a soul from the absolute darkness that reigns in man's breast, man's skull; what standards *other than absolute ones* can be brought to this human art without doing to it a civilized from of violence?

4. For the first fragment, the full sentence reads: "Voilà encore pourquoi je vous ai dit que je n'avais rien, nulle œuvre en suspens, les quelques choses que je vous ai présentées constituant les lambeaux que j'ai pu regagner sur le néant complet" (Antonin Artaud, *L'Ombilic des Limbes* [Paris: Gallimard, 1968], 21). Subsequent references are to ibid., 19–47. All quoted text (original French and translation) is rendered in italics.

Rivière is, understandably, fascinated. He gradually comes around to seeing this writer, who has no work on him he hasn't shared, no work on standby, as an exception to the droves of poets who have always, on a backburner, some uninspired something or other, fanning the flames of their mind instead of putting them out. He reads Artaud's difference from the *phenomenon of the age* as it asks to be read: as a true illness (*une véritable maladie*) and, as such, a source of *authenticity*, touching *the essence of being, the very cry of life*. Artaud's near-indifference to the *literary plane*, to *literature properly speaking* (that weak, self-obsessed *phénomène d'époque*) guarantees his sanity and literary sainthood. Having thus gone *below to gaze at the underside of art*, at his correspondent's *deep and private misery*, Rivière comes up not with a better appreciation of Artaud, but with Artaud-as-principle: *One must be no longer able to move, to believe, in order to perceive.* The source of timeless art is utter desiccation. Absolute judgment is cruel only to those who do not suffer.

CALLED LITERATURE
This persistent naming . . . we call literature.
—Paul De Man[5]

The odyssey of naming, which took us from speech to writing between the Scylla and Charybdis of the encyclopedia and the novel to Literature and then the logosphere, is at an end. Why? Just because! Things heated up, literature was brought to a boil, to a *word reduction*. It no longer rears its head in any discursive domain that claims demystifying powers. It is now part of the cold soup we drink daily, preferring not to know the ingredients.

5. Paul De Man, "Criticism and Crisis," in his *Blindness and Insight* (Minneapolis: University of Minnesota Press, 1986), 18.

THE POST-BOOK

You are aware that letters are of many kinds; but there is one kind which is undeniable, for the sake of which, indeed, the thing was invented, namely, to inform the absent of anything that is to the interest of the writer or recipient that they should know. You, however, certainly don't expect a letter of that kind from me. For of your domestic concerns you have members of your family both to write and to act as messengers. Besides, in my personal affairs there is really nothing new. There are two other kinds of letters which give me great pleasure: the familiar and sportive, and the grave and serious. Which of these two I ought least to employ I do not understand. Am I to jest with you by letter? Upon my word, I don't think the man a good citizen who could laugh in times like these. Shall I write in a more serious style? . . . And yet, under this head, my position is such that I neither dare write what I think, nor choose to write what I don't think.

—Cicero, in Rome, to Caius Scribonius Curio Burbulieus, somewhere in Asia, first century BC

The ancients have spoken—on how a *letter* should read. Artemon, a compiler of Aristotle's correspondence, held that, to sound right, it "ought to be written in the same manner as a dialogue, a letter being regarded by him as one of the two sides of a dialogue," Demetrius the Stylist tells us. This same Demetrius, precursor to Cicero, held his theoretical own: the letter, in fact, "should be a little more *studied* than the dialogue, since the latter reproduces an extemporary utterance, while the former is committed to writing and is (in a way) sent as a gift."

Such "gifts" to familiars, friends or friend-to-be, "should abound in glimpses of character," building rapport, interpersonal bonds. They are to "obey the laws of friendship, which demand that we should 'call a spade a spade' [or a fig a fig, τὰ σύκα σύκα] as the proverb has it." It is not necessary to bear one's soul in a letter. To reveal one's hand is enough. But for goodness's sake no tergiversation. Honesty hand to face is easier than face to face.

As regards style, Demetrius is explicit: combine "graceful" with "plain." He recommends elevated diction to show regard for those being addressed. "The heightening should not, however, be carried so far that we have a treatise in place of a letter," a formal discourse headed "'My dear So-and-So.'" More *studied* than the dialogue, then, but not to the point of *study*. Studied, but short of "stilted." Not too high, not too stiff, and definitely not "too long." Uttering even "sentointious maxims and exhortations seems to be no longer talking familiarly in a letter but to be speaking *ex cathedra*."[6] Friends do not take well to lessons from friends. They are receptive to "expositions" of "simple subjects in simple terms." The path of plainness is unadorned and brief. For beauty, take the path of elegance, picking "expressions of friendship" and a "good many proverbs" along the way. "The only philosophy admissible" in letters is "common property and popular in character." Thus, make each *proverb* count. (*Let your letter wait for the post, not the post for your letter*. When rushing to post, consider that haste *makes waste*. What's that? *A true friend is like a privy, open in necessity*? Well now… Just between friends, *who has no head needs no hat*… Godspeed, then, be on your way!)

Such is the freedom allowed the letter form, a very long time ago.

*

Too long and *stilted*? Isn't that what most books are nowadays? Like clowns on wooden poles that try too hard and take too long to make us laugh.

So you write that you want to write on? But cannot abide the circus acts? You say there are many like you? And that you sent an open letter to the publishing gods? You're asking where to hide from professionalization? How to escape the literary profession of faith? I know nothing beyond this: on no public forum, in no public form.

6. Demetrius, *De Elocutione*, trans. W. Rhys Roberts, 4.223–235, trans. mod., my emphasis.

Cicero's letters sought no publicity.[7] Those between Abelard and Heloise came out centuries after they were exchanged. Byron collaborated on Moore's "life and letters" of Byron. Those between Michel Houellebecq and "BHL" had nothing but publicity in mind. Their authors think themselves notable people. And notables' letters ought to see the light of day.

Exciting new correspondence of Bad Boy (our novelist) and Big Bore (our philosopher)! Watch these giants have it out in private! How would they be as pen pals? Take a peek! Buy the book!

Far from mutual antagonists, they formed a united front against a common enemy. As the whipping boys of French letters, they knew to capitalize on mutual sympathy, against all expectations. Without poison-pens their duel became an orgy of commiseration.

"Our letters have become one of my few joys," writes Houellebecq to Lévy. Reflecting on the practice second hand: "Schopenhauer notes with surprise that it is quite difficult to lie in one's letters (current thinking has not progressed on the subject . . . : there is something in an exchange of letters that fosters truth, participation—what?)." Letters compel them to let their hair down—what's left of it anyway. But their exposure to the public transforms this letter-exchange into *co-confessional* writing.

Real books, sole-authored and published, loom large as the true if for the moment neglected demiurgic vocation. Playing literary adviser to Lévy's philosopher-prince, Houellebecq hopes "these letters will have reminded you of the pleasure of secrets indispensable to the success of" a real book! BHL: "Books are not a mirror but the girders of the universe, and that's why it's so

7. Though late in his life, as his personal letters became collector's items among his friends, he began entertaining the possibility. But they would have to be further prepared: "It is better that I look through and correct them. Only then can they be published" (Marcus Tullius Cicero, *Epistulae ad Atticum*, trans. Evelyn S. Shuckburgh, 16.5.5, trans. mod.). They were, however, only after his death.

important that there should continue to be writers." Besides, mirrors don't serve dissimulation. How exciting, ultimately, to be caught in the "writer's paradox," which is to say, the *novelist's*: "I'm deceiving my world. I'm not who I appear to be. It's marvellous to be taken for another and all the while, hiding behind this mask and this borrowed identity, to take on the features and steal the soul, the heart, the life of my contemporaries." Calling his own "taste for secrecy" "pathological," BHL admits to planting "lies that are false and false clues that are true," like a "secret agent . . . losing himself in the panoply of his masks and ruses."[8] But for things to get this exciting, some-*world* first has to care.

The outcome of this confessional levity is not a vow to "authenticity," which anyhow for Lévy's opponents betokens "absence of style and talent."

> I'm emerging from this dialogue serene, happy with the same sort of relief, I imagine, that the criminal feels after his confession.
> My impression is that, instead of endangering myself, I've been liberated and that I'm ready to reengage with that adventure of the novel that . . . I've been afraid to return to. . . .
> It's the best effect our correspondence could have had on me.[9]

Alors, now back to publishing—back, that is, to the book! What else did you expect from correspondence already under contract? At Hermes's altar they stood . . . (like two tourists at Delos). And you thought they'd *worship* at it too?

*

Project Gutenberg sorts literature (like Cicero letters) into "heavy" and "light," which no empiric would let us equate with "high" and "low." "Light literature,"

---

8. Bernard-Henri Lévy and Michel Houellebecq, *Public Enemies: Dueling Writers Take on Each Other and the World*, trans. Miriam Rachel Frendo (New York: Random House, 2011), 282, 288, 119, 289.
9. Lévy and Houellebecq, 293.

part *belles-lettres*, is never so "low" as to be kicked around by the unwashed in the mud, like a ball, "heavy literature" never so "high" as to put as in mind of tailed comets or winged Icaruses on their starry trajectories.

The true "man" of letters cannot be told apart from the tiller of a field. The fact is that the same earth has been turned over many times before by plows much like his. The sowers who follow him want no part in pulling the plow. These are the literati. They reap all that they have sown and leave nothing behind. They eat well and even profit by it.

Who is it that scatters seed *between* the furrows? Letters are just this growth that those wanting the crop harvested and sold take for ugly weeds. But these growths are neither wild, nor ugly, nor useless, imitating weeds to live out their life cycles. No one will bother to pull them so long as they do not compete with the corn for a place in the sun.

*

The familiar letter, long bound by rules of decorum, indentured to information, is old news. Even Madame de Sévigné's, which still stands as model of French prose, was subordinate to the art of human affairs. Despite their charm, eventual editors make clear, their historical rootedness and density of personal reference prove that "literature of that kind cannot stand alone."[10]

Somewhat newer is the novel's epistolary romance, the letter being that handy artifact of private life and divulged secrets, sensational revelations. Indeed, the literary letter has not outgrown its reputation as *pute du roman*.

The steamy *Letters by a Portuguese Nun* (1669), Richardson-Fielding's *Pamela-Shamela* (1740–1741), and Rousseau's *Julie* (1761) were easy sells. Freed from

10. *The Letters of Madame de Sévigné to Her Daughter and Friends* (Boston: Roberts Brothers, 1889), iii.

formal constraints, the genre became a medium for the artist's statement—announcing thereby its distance from art. Even hostility to art (Rousseau's "Letter to d'Alembert" on the theatre (1758) comes to mind). Not long after, letters would accommodate laments over the loss of correspondence: "the republic of letters is only a market in which one sells books. Not making concession to the publisher is our only virtue," wrote Sand to Flaubert. The pleasures of letter writing could now appear more vividly. "Your letters fall on me like a rain that refreshes, and develops at once all that is germinating in the soil." And Flaubert to Sand: "Our letters crossed again. That proves beyond a doubt that we feel the same things at the same time in the same degree."[11] Proust's own fondness for private letters echoed this overinvestment decades later (in 1903, 1909, 1917):

> If I hadn't all these absurd letters to write I should really like to write you a proper letter, where you can say the things that you can't say face to face.

> You have written me a letter which is a work of art; and it is neither signed, nor in your handwriting, but couldn't be by anybody but you.

> [t]his "epistolary relationship" about "business affairs" which you carry on with me with such stupendous correctness and so much feeling, is just as witty but gives me more pleasure than Voltaire's correspondence.[12]

Given epistolography's role in his love life, one imagines Kafka would concur. Described somewhere as a "voluptuary of letters," he eventually turned on the form (in his exchange with Milena):

> you know how much I hate letters. All my misfortune in life . . . derives, one might say, from letters or from the possibility of writing letters.

11. *The George Sand–Gustave Flaubert Letters*, trans. A.L. McKensie, online at http://www.gutenberg.org/cache/epub/5115/pg5115.html.

12. Marcel Proust letters, online at http://www.yorktaylors.free-online.co.uk/letmenu.html.

People have hardly ever deceived me, but letters always have, and as a matter of fact not those of other people, but my own. In my case this is a particular misfortune which I do not want to discuss further, but it is nevertheless also a general one. The easy possibility of writing letters— from a purely theoretical point of view—must have brought wrack and ruin to the souls of the world. Writing letters is actually a communication with ghosts, and by no means just with the ghost of the addressee but also with one's own ghost, which secretly evolves inside the letter one is writing or even in a whole series of letters, where one letters corroborates another and can refer to it as a witness. How did people ever get the idea they could communicate with one another by letter! One can think about someone far away and one can hold on to someone nearby; everything else is beyond human power. Writing letters, on the other hand, means exposing oneself to the ghosts, who are greedily waiting precisely for that. Written kisses never arrive at their destination; the ghosts drink them up along the way. It is this ample nourishment which enables them to multiply so enormously. People sense this and struggle against it; in order to eliminate as much of the ghosts' power as possible and to attain a natural intercourse, a tranquility of soul, they have invented trains, cars, aeroplanes—but nothing helps anymore: These are evidently inventions devised at the moment of crashing. The opposing side is so much calmer and stronger; after the postal system, the ghosts invented the telegraph, the telephone, the wireless. They will not starve, but we will perish. . . . Incidentally, "they" are also exposed by the exceptions, for it sometimes happens they let a letter through untouched, and it arrives like the light, kind handclasp of a friendly hand. But probably that also merely appears to be so; such cases may be the most dangerous of all, and should be guarded against more carefully than the others. On the other hand, if this is a deception, at least it is a complete one. [13]

13. Franz Kafka, *Letters to Milena*, trans. Philip Boehm (New York: Schocken, 1990), 223.

In the same letter he recounted sleeplessly composing an imaginary letter to a friend, then receiving a real one from him the next morning. But this is merely a strange coincidence, not that intimate correspondence of personalities that a coincidence of letters would merely register. To Kafka, the ghost letters "are real; they aren't just wearing sheets." They are the means of love as well as the face of his beloved. "In their entirety as well as in almost every line, they [Milena's letters to him] are the most beautiful thing that ever happened to me," even if later he fears they "always contain a worm."[14] And, as Milena would write soberly, with Franz clearly in mind, "letters complete the work like a map completes the world. . . . [W]e search the letters for motivations, logical clues. . . . We do not expect any art from letters; we expect something *human*."[15]

Something human. Like Rousseau's six love "Letters to Sara," which may or may not have been written on a dare. Like Benjamin Franklin's autobiography that is part letter to his son, and which its author may or may not have wanted made public. Like Dickinson's "Master Letters," which survive as mere drafts, their addressee unknown (1858–1861). Like Vincent's lifeline of letters to his younger brother, family and friends. Like Nietzsche's *Wahnbriefe*, so-called (1889), one addressed to "Princess Ariadne," some signed "Dionysus," others "The Crucified"—improvements over "Your old creature," his valediction from a couple of weeks before. (Could his notion of letters as "unannounced visits," "impolite incursions" to be followed by a bath, be behind the expressive freedom of his pen?). And let's not forget Kafka's undelivered screed to his "Dearest Father" from 1919, or Artaud's exchanges with Rivière several years on.

We have seen islands of literary realization through letters. Seneca's *Moral Letters to Lucilius* (first century AD). James Howell's *Familiar Letters* (1645–55). Heine's *Ideas—Book Le Grand* (1827). Bettina von Arnim's *Goethe's Correspondence with a Child* (1861). Alphonse Daudet's *Letters from My Mill* (1869). Robert Walser's "Letter from a Poet to a Gentleman" (1914).

14. Kafka, 208, 150, 186.
15. Milena Jesenská, "Letters of Notable People," in ibid., 261.

Shklovsky's *Zoo, or Letters Not about Love* (1923). Rilke's *Letters to a Young Poet* (1929). Ernst Jünger's "Sicilian Letter to the Man in the Moon" (1930). André Chouraqui's *Letter to an Arab Friend* (1969), *récit visionnaire* prefaced by Shimon Peres. Chris Kraus' *I Love Dick* (1997). Even Jacques Derrida's *The Post Card* (1980). Even our two French clowns (2008). Even yours truly.

There is plenty to suggest an "epistolary turn" in contemporary literature. Peter Dimock's *A Short Rhetoric for Leaving the Family* (1998)—opening "Dear Des and General." Lynn Coady's *The Antagonist*, Barbara Browning's *The Correspondence Artist* (both 2011). *No One Writes Back* (2009) by Jang Eun-jin (from whom we learn that "if the address is correct, the route" by which letters travel, "is neither dark nor smelly").[16] And Dimock just did it again: *George Anderson* (2013).

*

Today, letter writing as practice, its history and elegance inseparable from parchment, paper and good penmanship, is obsoleted by electronic mail. Before we complain about the daily pile of e-mail, let's remember: we hold up our end of the flow. We dig ourselves out by responding to it all, swinging our "pens" like shovels—"stroking the plastics" hardly renders the strain of what we actually do. Even the computer groans, since typing e-mails robs machines of their mystique. We long to apply ourselves, try our hand at something old, which we call something new: using the keyboard to write longhand again.

Some of our work in this form is good, but its engineered ephemerality leads us to forget most of it. We archive these urgent missives (and they are becoming more urgent by the year). Time is short, and we produce copiously, in haste, simple subjects with sloppy phrases and obvious words. We often say more than we would say in person—but not for excess of reflection. Texts,

16. Jang Eun-jin, *No One Writes Back*, trans. Yewon Jung (Urbana-Champaign, IL: Dalkey Archive, 2013), 9.

if not e-mails, accommodate our impulsive blurts. Often we say less, with telegraphic abruptness.

We would gladly reconcile the two, *writing fast* and *writing slow*, at least some of the time. We imagine we can buy this time as long as we work out a new method within the existing one. Hyperconnectivity kills traditional epistolography even as it makes space for the e-pistolary on the path of frustration. Letter writing, done as regular exercise, improves concentration (and could, as was once thought, improve character). We might find ourselves dreaming of an extraordinary correspondence as sidetrack to our ordinary ones. Or of a Slow-Mail movement, a mass phenomenon. In a moment of revelation, we might turn to the letter and its wilted conventions to recover the art of written communication. And it is here that we stumble upon an alternative literary zone.

Besides, isn't it a peculiar and sick art that calls itself *letters* after having dropped letter-writing from its repertoire? To revive its spirit, if not its letter, Demetrius's pagan purism must go. We need a conspiracy of letters. Not just an "epistolary turn." A silent epistolary revolution.

(1999–2013)

JACQUES JOUET

Nine Suppositions Concerning *Bouvard and Pécuchet*

1. Suppose that you were to ask me here to say a few words, preferably heartfelt, about a mythical and apparently incomplete book, *Bouvard and Pécuchet* by Gustave Flaubert, I would note, right from the start, the necessity of rereading it, which for me would be my third reading, the first was forever ago and left no trace, the second saw me taking notes on the flyleaf, allowing me to track the changes time had wrought on the book, that's to say those in the eye of the reader, but then, supplied as I also am with a somewhat bittersweet memory related to the subject, I would want to speak about the day when Mme Annie Lebrun, on the *Panorama* program broadcast by France Culture (the show is no longer on the air), assassinated one of my books without first having read it, simply by virtue of having just heard an interview with myself, commenting on whatever it was I had just said by declaring that it was almost as stupid as Bouvard and Pécuchet being reunited, and this sentence, intended to be implacable, immersed me instead into that well-worn self-interrogation: how should I take this? *eh bien*, at the time, rather poorly; over time, rather well.

2. Suppose that you were then to ask me to dive into the body of the text, which is the least you could do, I would gladly start with its title, which today seems remarkable to me for a whole host of reasons, and particularly in that, while giving a novel the title of its hero is hardly anodyne in itself (*Madame Bovary* is not called *The Sentimental Dissolution* any more than *The Sentimental Education* is called "Monsieur Moreau"), to title a book with the names of *two* heroes is actually rather uncommon, and while I must remind myself here that you certainly won't neglect to throw *Tristan and Iseult* or *Paul and Virginia* at me, titles of heterosexual *couplaison*, I would retort that in cases where one has two males on one's hands, neither (upstream) Rosencrantz and Guildenstern,

nor (downstream) Thomson and Thompson, serve to eponymize the works from which they emerge, and that it's only following *Bouvard and Pécuchet*, it seems to me, that one can have Hesse's *Narcissus and Goldmund*, let alone Laurel and Hardy, although we must also bear in mind that while Cervantes did not title his book "Don Quixote and Sancho," Diderot, all the same, chose *Jacques the Fatalist and his Master*.

3. Suppose that you were to ask me, here, on the strength of the above reference to *Quixote*, to make an attempt to lay out the genealogy of my *personnagitude*, I would note, with the complicity of the Charles Huard etching reproduced on the cover of the Gothot-Mersch edition of *Quixote*, that I cannot help but imagine Flaubert lurking behind the figures of the little fat man and big lean man of la Mancha, deciding to give us, by way of contrast, a little lean one and a big fat one, always and again of la Mancha, if not quite the same la Mancha (because, you know, in French, we refer to the English Channel as *la Manche*, and of course Flaubert's heroes set up shop near Caen, where no doubt they could scent the salt of that passage), drawing in this way two very distinct and unforgettable silhouettes, the two couples rhyming quite clearly (and witness the vague echo: "qui-xote" / "cu-chet") in terms of the mental difficulties they risk in being exposed to books (which brings us back to Emma Bovary as well), which books should in all good educative conviction clarify one's views, but instead lead in the end into the mire.

4. Suppose that you were to ask me to push a little more at the envelope of this story about a couple who fell in love at first sight, I would remark that if we were to return to the deserted Boulevard where first they meet, we found find that these two characters are described not as big or small, per se, but, curiously, as "the taller one" and "the shorter one"; that is to say, they're measured one against the other, not on their own; likewise, they aren't in a master-servant relationship (in this too they are very modern), with the infantile truculence of Bouvard soon set up against the virtually sectarian snippiness of Pécuchet, all of it manifesting a remarkable double-mindedness and a potential for quixotic dialogue that appears

to me to take its source in the creative person of M. Flaubert himself—extravagance and colorfulness vs. exactitude; sexual extravagance vs. strict abstinence—not, I mean, in the service of a sort of autofiction, but rather to create an alternovel that isn't afraid to set foot upon the ground of potential autobiography, and in double entry, no less, which only assures us of its originality.

5. Suppose that you were to ask me now to further typify this novel, somewhat in the same fashion as Alfred Jarry when subtitling his various opuses (*Faustroll* is "A Neo-scientific Novel"; *Days and Nights* is a "Novel of a Deserter"; *Messalina* is "A Novel of Imperial Rome"; *The Supermale*, is "A Modern Novel"), I would be tempted to write, simply, that it's "A Comic Novel," without that preventing me from asking the question: what sort of laughter are we talking about? or, to put it another way, if Raymond Queneau defined the comic novel as a novel that smiled and disdained death, and instead Flaubert is mocking life and laughing out loud and simply despising death, where does that leave us? how did Flaubert manage to make a comedy that spares no one, not even books themselves—including his own—on behalf of the world; a comedy in which his learned gentlemen, "who were so famously well-read" are seen most often through a keyhole, or in any case certainly voyeuristically—"the two men, naked as savages, splashed each other with bucketsful of water. . . . They could seen through the latticework . . ."—a book in which the staging of, for example, Pécuchet and the priest's theological skirmish under the umbrella and the squall is just as hilarious as the notion of heating bath water with the very body soaking in it, an incredibly prescient and sensible solution to the energy problem, which is itself nearly as funny as a recent and very serious article I saw in the news on the necessary and ecological (for the ozone layer) reduction of the number of pet cows.

6. Suppose that everything had not already been said on the intellectual courage of *Bouvard and Pécuchet*, on the total engagement that animates our couple before their moment of temporary discouragement, I could then stress their more audacious side, those sweet-talkers, those boxers climbing into the

ring in quest of knowledge, and whose unavoidable destiny will be to take more than a few punches, because these are the risks of the job, but punches of what nature and thrown by whom? by the naysayers of course, who are legion, and who nourish the novel with a bevy of splendid secondary roles created by the hand of a master; but mainly by a nonspecific entity called life—the real, the concrete world, whose complexity laughs at the violence that is done to it in the name of scientifically, encyclopedically, politically simplifying it.

7. Suppose that my reading were to make further demands upon me, insisting that I elucidate the ways in which Bouvard and Pécuchet, despite their more than commendable efforts, are put down by the spiteful world, I would be obliged to highlight the terrifying or salubrious, as you will, skepticism of Flaubert, who offers us, on the page, the spectacle of a Novelist of Doleful Countenance reduced to the role of mere transcriber (don't copy each other, our good teachers used to tell us, you'll only wind up copying nonsense . . .), which is one of two things: either an austere but ultimately positive way of purifying the exercise of art from all the rhetoric of the "artiste" (it's in this manner that Charles Reznikoff copied, for example); or, rather, an act of desperation, deducing that the final outcome of the exercise of art is nothing more than a fatal and endless parroting of all the words that have come before, a work there will be no need to complete since it is, in itself, incompletable.

8. Suppose that you were to ask me here if I nurtured some admiration, regret, or sympathy for the incompleteness of *Bouvard and Pécuchet*, I would not only respond in the affirmative, but, more, would lay out an axiom stating that the incompleteness of any and every incomplete book, when it is extraordinary, is and was always, always, always deliberate (is it not, Messieurs Kafka, Proust, Musil?); this axiom permitting you to ponder—in no particular biographical order—death (but perhaps one *must* die in order to be seen as a great innovator of incompleteness?), and then not only why but *how* the incompleteness was, if I may put it this way, accomplished; for example, we can contrast *In Search*

of Lost Time, a "finished" book, which has an *explicit* (in the medieval sense) apparently intact—albeit a book still considered incomplete, as it were, on its interior (or, for that matter, perhaps complete, after all?)—while *Bouvard and Pécuchet*, for its part, would seem incontestably to have an *incipit* at its disposal, and yet to lack, explicitly, its *explicit*.

9. Suppose that you were to wonder at last if I don't still have a notion, somewhere in the back of my mind, to comment on the already too-commented-on first line of *Bouvard*, namely, "As the temperature that day had risen to 33 degrees,* Boulevard Bourdon was completely deserted," I would respond that in a private sale I recently acquired a previously undiscovered portion of the original manuscript of *Bouvard and Pécuchet* (I wanted to scan it in and e-mail it to you as a surprise, but the file that was on my computer inadvertently disappeared this morning thanks to a mug of cocoa getting knocked over onto my keyboard), which happens to contain no less than sixteen different versions of this *incipit*, which is certainly significant, and I wanted to give them all to you here:

> *version no. 1*: As there was a glacial temperature of −133 degrees, the Boulevard Bourdon no longer existed.
> *version no. 2*: As the temperature had dropped to −33 degrees, the water had frozen over in the lake at the Port de l'Arsenal below the Boulevard Bourdon, which was not very well-frequented anyway.
> *version no. 3*: As the temperature had dropped to −32 degrees, the skaters skated on the lake at the Port de l'Arsenal below the Bourdon Boulevard, on which the streetwalkers didn't dream of turning tricks.
> *version no. 4*: As the temperature had dropped to −13 degrees, the travel agencies on the Boulevard Bourdon were advertising camel-trips in the desert.
> *version no. 5*: As the temperature had dropped to 0, the Boulevard Bourdon wasn't buzzing with people.

* The Dalkey Archive edition (2005) translates this figure to 92° Fahrenheit.

version no. 6: As the winter was actually heating up a little, up to 3 whole degrees, the Boulevard Bourdon was a little less deserted than the seasonal average

version no. 7: As it was a very mild 22 degrees outside, and there had been no pollution warning for the day, the French National Assembly was completely deserted.

version no. 8: As the temperature that day had risen to thirty-three degrees, Boulevard Bourdon was completely deserted

version no. 9: As the temperature that day had risen to 33 degrees, Boulevard Bourdon was buzzing with bees.

version no. 10: As the temperature that day had risen to 35 degrees, the printers on the Boulevard Bourdon left words, sentences, and sometimes entire passages out of their composition work.

version no. 11: As the temperature that day had risen to 68 degrees, the asphalt on the Boulevard Bourdon had started to melt.

version no 12: As the temperature that day had risen to 69 degrees, the travel agencies on the Boulevard Bourdon were offering sled rides through the frozen north.

version no. 13: As the temperature that day had risen to 70 degrees, even the Boulevard Bourdon presbytery lost its luster and didn't remain cool, which had previously been its primary attraction.

version no. 14: As the temperature that day had risen to 72 degrees, the asphalt on the Boulevard Bourdon had finished melting.

version no. 15: As the temperature that day had risen to 89 degrees, the thermo-survival jumpsuits of the president, ministers, and deputies at last reached the end of their capacities.

version no: 16: As the temperature that day had risen to 99 degrees, the water was ready to boil in the lake at the Port de l'Arsenal below the Boulevard Bourdon, which had remained totally deserted since the great warming of the planet, which ended all life, even fish, on the premises.

Flaubert finally decided on the temperature that we know today, 33 degrees, which permitted him in a subtle and not-too-civilizationally-apocalyptic way to put the final situation at the beginning of the novel, namely the desertification demanded by the fury of the world reacting violently, as we've seen, to the impacts of the at once touching and pretentious efforts of human knowledge, such that the power of the world displaces and destroys the human species ("*totally* deserted"), de-fi-ni-ti-ve-ly hushing it up, applying a final solution to the knowledge or obscuritanism that drives the novelist to lead us to believe in the *incipit* when, obviously, this here ain't one of 'em after all, and that Flaubert chose, as a matter of fact, in the name of paradox, to start his book with a threat and with an *explicit* by anticipation, which is to say, to start his book with the end.

Translated by E. C. Gogolak

THALIA FIELD

Irrationality, Situations, and Novels of Inquiry

1.

On Plato's door: *Let no one enter who does not know geometry.*

You may find this inquiry difficult to trace. Slow to unfold. Never looping back to make sense of the trajectory. It's a fluorescence, though you may suspect this isn't about fiction, that fiction can't sustain such a grotesque and barbed peduncle. You may say that a novel is less a long-move cactus than something that flowers off the bat and spreads easily, reproduces regularly. You could certainly say this is written without a plan and already I should in all reason abandon it to this first failure.

Well, here I am again, looking back, but shooting forward, let's try another route, to attempt to prove (through one of the many wonders of proof) the irrationality of situations and by extension the novel of such. Is there anything rational (knowable) about a situation? Imagine (in a proof by contradiction) a situation that you'd call finite and knowable . . . (pause . . .)

Q.E.A. (quod est absurdum)

And so we realize that contemplating situations creates an infinity of everything we know and don't, above the waves and beneath: perspectives, acts, desires, thoughts of thoughts within acts, molecular routines that take shape, take sides, make multiverses from space-time, exchange energy, overlap, argue, rise, stall, cease . . .

Pythagoras: *There is geometry in the humming of the strings, there is music in the spacing of the spheres.*

The situation we thought we could imagine slips like a fetid leftover into an irrationality whose non-repeating infinities won't go away. No matter how entertaining or lyric or cinematic, there's an unglued ugliness making the whole equation hard to handle. Taming or cancelling or ignoring all the infinities is called the standard model, or normalization.

Pythagoras: *A thought is an idea in transit, which when once released, never can be lured back, nor the spoken word recalled. Nor ever can the overt act be erased. All that thou thinkest, sayest or doest bears perpetual record of itself, enduring for eternity.*

From the earliest words (a single noun, the pointing and naming, the autocorrection of spelling, from the blessings and trauma of single eggs adrift in the ocean) emerge magnitudes whose entanglements I can only begin to represent written out on paper-like substance and consumed in readerly order. All this in an attempt to paper over what we might call "situation A". Given that all situations thwart history, it follows that this AB, BC, CA, etcetera . . . provokes a growing complication of sides. The Greek word *historia* (ἱστορία) means "inquiry through research, and the writing that comes of it."

1.4

Let's consider Hippasus, a long-ago Greek in southern Italy, diligently making his name among Pythagoras's remaining gang. Did he see the beauty in his cohort's slogans, the perfection of simple geometry where numbers glow, the *arche* in ratios of solid agreement? Hippasus, perhaps a lover of roundness, of a square, of the polygons and crystals that mirrored his natural world, was filled sometimes with merriment but also perhaps with little patches of dread. Shaded, shadowed, bothered, did this unlucky Hippasus sense that something impossible had entered the estate?

Angle: Pythagoras's gang assumed all angles (of things, disputes) should be orderable, reducible (one question, one answer.) They liked pairs of rules and sides (of arguments, shapes) that could perfect each other through ratios of integers. But this was not always to be. Reducing to absurdity shows that the diagonal of a square with the measure of 1 produces incommensurable sides that are both even and odd. The square root of 2, the hypotenuse of the subsequent triangle (the diagonal of that ill-behaved square) thereby became the first irrational number, a number uncontainable, that spun off magnitude from the divinity of number, and produced a decimal that wouldn't repeat and wouldn't ever, ever, ever, end. Only death would stop it, or so they thought, as they tossed Hippasus into the sea as a traitor to all things which number, in its marketability, had done for them.

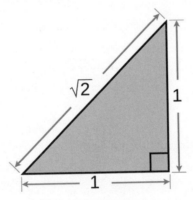

So this first instance of irrationality, proven as it was so easily, caused enormous disruption, blooming just before the death of our hero. But Hippasus is a stand-in hero; he's just a guess. History leaves so many guesses, and guesses are the first proof of the incommensurable unmappable inquiry (novel) where any diagonal crossing the situation, the shape of it, is unmatchable with any side.

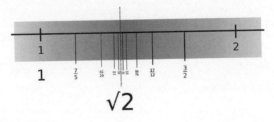

Pythagoras: *All is number.*

And so we conclude, with all respect to our ancestors, that the novel should be that imperfect geometry, that symptom of infinity that contains a hole.

1.41

Or Hippasus, having put a dodecahedron in a sphere, may have broadcast the irrational to his ultimate detriment, but neither has anyone to this day squared a circle. Irrationality for a while was his official secret. But collapse of the form called for, his rampant personality failure, proved how violence behaves proportional to its solipsism, and that stories of violence, violent stories, do nothing but beg the question.

Take any situation (personality, inquiry), halve it into two equal situations (arguments, personalities, inquiries), then halve it again, then again into an infinity of finely halved arguments (some call this "reality") and this cannot be *summed up* though it moves relentlessly, but futilely, toward zero. Likewise the world's inhabitants compete, for resources, power, love, using the most subtle weapon imaginable: communication. Competing realities may be the only reality (just as there are greater and lesser infinities) and stories gain advantage at the direct expense of others. The verbal combat, the smiling one-ups, the subtle status maneuvers, the many fractured ways grammar can put others in their places, and finally what that means: to be *put in a place*. This is the subtle violence in all stories. Being put in a place can be deduced as the ratio of one personality crossing a situation to the circumference of the whole situation, and is itself irrational (π).

Meanwhile, laughter is pleasantly irrational and might also have contributed to the death of Hippasus. Epictetus's Enchiridion: "*Let not your laughter be loud, frequent, or unrestrained.*" He, laughing, loses the thread, becomes useless and possibly dangerous. These objections compare laughter to cruelty, turning a situation antisocial. But the jostling, endemic in the slices of spheres, shows the comedy more exquisite for how seriously each joke is believed. Has anyone grown murderous from laughing? In masquerade and comedy, the laughter drowns out bureaucracy.

Chorus: recall an argument overheard from the top of the stairs. One sided or two, three or more, the battle seeps into restless sleep. In memory, in history, we investigate this incompleteness (this overabundance of overhearing) despite the inability to fully sum it up. Approaching the paradox of any story, we tease out the incommensurability of the other sides. In any ecology, each argument promotes its infinity through products, weapons, deeds, and of course, words.

Pythagoras: *Begin thus from the first act, and proceed; and, in conclusion, at the ill which thou hast done, be troubled, and rejoice for the good.*

Chorus: reconsider the ponderous agave that sits barren and after twenty years offers one enormous growth, grotesque and disproportioned, ugly, optimistic, awkward, and then dies. Non-safe dying too, the kind that stays dying. People ask, "If we prevent it flowering, will it live longer?" Sadly, no. Its not-being-there crumples in ruin, just as a giant squid's empty garment floats to the seabed heart-broken and spent. For the giant agave and giant squid send their fruiting irrationals as once-last tiny seed-babies on the wave.

This is my novel: Listen to side M. Then to side Y, which is supposed to be commensurate. The angles between add up, it is shapely after all. But side Q says one thing, slightly off, the story going haywire. The others try to compensate their own angles. The angles of the stories seem congruent, but never where the proof makes it easy. Segments are even. Segments are odd. Both can be deduced because it's not a triangle, or any determinate polyhedron. It is irrational to try to listen to everyone. It's more irrational to try to believe them all.

Protagoras: *Man is the measure of all things.*

Plato: *What I say is that "just" or "right" means nothing but what is in the interest of the stronger side.*

Rationality, for all its emphasis on the discrete, shows itself in an endless spectacle of violence, a melodrama of beggar's questions (circular reasoned) practiced before a private audience. In delusion of private voices, some novels gain celebrity estate, but forfeit unruly time and a messy world, their testimonies rigidifying as the slow boil starts, the water appearing preternaturally calm for awhile.

Plato: *Is that which is holy loved by the gods because it's holy or is it holy because it's loved by the gods?*

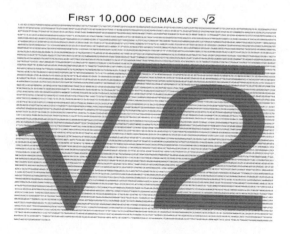

FIRST 10,000 DECIMALS OF √2

1.414

Consider a patch which contains the arguments of everyone wandering in, burrowed, fleeing, flying, infesting, pollinating, destroying, selling, recreating, symbiotically inhabiting or even preying on it—what immensitudes and microscopia! What bizarre riot of unheard-of forms! The closer we look, the more complicated and crowded the patch becomes, not only with creatures but creatures inside creatures joining and dividing until there's nothing living inside the living but energy moving in all directions. If our lenses could see even farther, we might glimpse the cosmos of untellable gravity: *alogos*.

Pythagoras: *It is difficult to walk at one and the same time many paths of life.*

Like irrationals, values are mostly *incommensurable*, with no common measure. This means that so-called rational choice, the way we might proceed, for example, onward toward success, toward greater [insert positive value here: kindness, popularity] is prim and paradoxical. Your scheme can never be used to make sense of mine, just as Aristotle cannot be understood in terms of Freud (at least not without laughter.) The dimensions of characters, their tangents and situations, are thus incommensurable, and not just in competing *ipse dixits*.

But back to our public sphere (disobedient, unmanageable), ultimately our curiosity, which is all we have to use like a microscope, a weapon, a shell, a fork, or any biological feature, to gain both nourishment and survival. To inquire, to approach a situation, requires the listening post, and the painful bloodless comic wound where past and present combine. Even the smallest fragment of language passes down just as form, preferences, money, hair color, genetics, or luck do, giving advantage or crippling handicap. Demon. Strata. Night amplifies a sudden agora to the ears. A starry field. Define universe U with a set I.

1.4142

A mathematician goes to the street and listens for ideas. He allows one thing to lead to another and proceeds in an unnerving investigation that comforts him only in a stolen nap. His fellows have convinced him he's a poor talent and later he goes to battle and dies of a wound. Or he goes to sea and is drowned for his work. What do the living know about keeping "this" and "that" apart in the maelstrom? If he was a writer and not a mathematician, would he have made the same gamble?

A set is *closed* if its complement (everything that is not in it) is *open*, but this means we can imagine an open set whose complement is also open, making the first set both open and closed, and therefore *clopen*. Your set is *clopen* if and only if its boundary is empty. Complement: everything that is not in set A. Boundary: everything used (passports, police, awards, agents) to be sure that people from off the estate are kept off.

Pythagoras: *The oldest, shortest words—"yes" and "no"—are those which require the most thought.*

Hence, the once-flowering, irrational novel—the one that refuses to be deduced. With no common unit of measure, the novel of inquiry has few family yet its reunions are fantastic. That's the carnival of the dead, their impossible howling cacaphony. *Clopen* in form and function—and also ripe, infected, a bit swollen, chunky, unassimilatable, circus-meagre, harried, brain-boggled but unafraid of blooming once and dying—the parts slither and stray, overlap unyieldingly to excerpting. Made finally of precious paper and distributed by hand, a wilder boundary than we can imagine, across the so-called garden wall.

It's an eavesdropper's, grave robber's project, publicly assembling taxonomic monsters from long-buried situations just as giant squid are only known dead.

A giant squid's life proceeds without human witness, in the dark unprocessed layers beyond the outer network. Only later, its anatomy can be parceled when it washes up too late, color drained, eye bigger than previously thought, from finding its obscure meals and running obscure errands. Gliding obscurely in the obscure rain, invisible in the water, its arguments and situations disperse in a sudden inky cloud.

1.41421

Cats, shapely, half-dead, adorn the *agon*, with their feral struts, shrugs, their lounging and love-fights. As interference breaks through interface, arguers stand on shoulders, squabbling in rough voices to ascend conundrums and "speak up," the poor, hard-of-being-heard, offstage. Annointed experts step in to moderate, other authorities accuse and refute, prove by numbers, take up celebrity. Rebels erase authority. Horses stampede from the barn. Then the space must be trucked off, or the accumulation desisted. Riot police. Invitation to "dialogue" that is nothing but privileged personalities in disguise. An agon unrelents, pulls up the tent corner stakes until the confused geometry takes flight.

Aristoxenus: *Whenever he heard a person who was making use of his symbols, he immediately took him into his circle, and made him a friend.*

The public space fills again as actors, "real people," even cats step in, a crowd of best-guess possibilities. The multitude of voices is the richness of the world, not its demise, the agon a moment of crystalized wonder.

Agave, dying, has an inflorescent afterlife and then decomposes. The death that seeds, signals the final death. Can you stop an agave from *flower*

ing
and keep it from d
ying
by

cut

ting off its

stalk

?

No!

the

pro

cess that cau

ses the plan

t to flow

er also kill

s

th

e plan

t

Or was he in exile? The secret that Hippasus shared was not for sharing, yet his inquiry is the one we repeat. We know the square root of two exists, there it is before us as a line on paper. But yet it also doesn't exist, because it's inexpressible beyond sign and symbol.

Making our way forward means reading the situation as it corpselike feeds us with dissolved fertility, hunking a reef, recirculating to the atmosphere to drench us. Library, graveyard, carbon cycle, why don't we actively shrine-up those who never knew us, showing ourselves to their blind eye. Invite them who can't read us to read us again and again. This season needs them to overwinter our words, like wasps the yeast that allows the wine, just as we overwinter theirs:

> A foolish consistency is the hobgoblin of little minds, adored by little statesmen and philosophers and divines. With consistency a great soul has simply nothing to do. He may as well concern himself with his

shadow on the wall. Speak what you think now in hard words, and to-morrow speak what to-morrow thinks in hard words again, though it contradict every thing you said to-day.—"Ah, so you shall be sure to be misunderstood." (Emerson, "Self-Reliance," 1841)

Grant us all misunderstanding, just as a giant squid's stomach bisects its brain. The leg slides into a tentacle where eggs circulate. Three hearts power up astonishing escapes. Nothing familiar. Jaw hole of razors; "We can only guess," the experts recoil, "what this might be for!" The squid gives birth from her leg, and only once, before she sails dead to the ocean floor. Who would accept this monster? Yet we are encouraged to watch Masai giraffes on the giraffe-cam from the zoo without leaving the couch. "If the giraffes are not in their enclosure, it might be a nice day." Give me the hidden, horrendous stranger.

Aristotle: *So poetry is something more philosophical and more worthy of serious attention than history.*

1.414213

The funny part is that Pythagoras never wrote anything in his lifetime, nor did his contemporaries write about him. We don't know what he said, did, or thought. We do not know if he was even a mathematician as there is no mention of mathematics in any early writings about him or his followers. The first accounts, written 150 years or so after he died, disagree extensively among themselves and only fourth–fifth-century (BCE) hagiographies call him a divine being, positioning him as the origin of Plato's philosophy. That his teachings were largely secret justified the lack of written texts, and allowed for the many buried forgeries "found" centuries later.

Thus a Pythagorean Situation; inquiry tangles. One says he ate some meat. Another: he was strictly vegetarian. Eudoxus: "he not only abstained from animal food but would not come near butchers or hunters." Aristotle: "the Pythagoreans refrain from eating the womb and the heart, the sea anemone and some other things but use all other animal food." Many say Pythagoras influenced Plato's metaphysics. Plato never mentions him. Aristotle only calls them the "so-called Pythagoreans" who may have known of limiters and unlimiteds, though this is likely a reference to Hippasus. In Aristotle's missing treatise on these so-called Pythagoreans, he may have described Pythagoras as a miracle-worker with a golden leg, who bit a snake and was able to be in two places at once. Aristotle says he prohibited eating beans, but Aristoxenus says "he valued beans most of all vegetables, since they were laxative."

Empedocles, on Pythagoras: "A man who possessed the greatest wealth of intelligence!"

Heraclitus: "King of the charlatans!"

1.4142135

Is such microtonal aharmony the fate of all situations? Sources are confused. Sides are taken. Each is right. They are all wrong. The towering peduncle may be magnificent but its appearance depends on its dying; its arrival marking the transfer of stored nourishment to the act of seeding. The flowering agave makes soap, pens, awls, paper, needles, sugar, string, medicine, rope, tequila, fiber, and a variety of food and drink.

Unending like it's the last thing I'll prove, let's investigate lines, points and angles. Maybe write inquiries that rehearse the carnival of situations, for novels invite ways to write up the performances. Let's write like death is ready to flower up through the head like a parasite breaking open each momentary obscurity. Let's write like all the voices live in our guts, a billion bacteria whose DNA have taken over most of our functioning. Write like the mysteries of everything that we think are not us are actually our mysteries, in wonder at everything that isn't anything like what we thought it'd be. Let's write assured that because inquiries are infinite, the possible novel is irrational.

1.41421356

WARREN MOTTE

Margins and Mirrors

Recently, I was invited to reflect upon the theme, "The Edge of Europe." I found myself more and more perplexed, not by the idea of the edge, but by the idea of Europe. I was surprised by my own reaction, I confess, because, although I am not myself European, I have long thought of Europe as something familiar rather than something foreign. I first visited Europe long ago, when I was a kid; I have lived there for extended periods off and on; I have been married to a European for thirty-five years, and we speak her language, rather than mine, at home; I have spend part of every summer there since the 1970s; many of my closest friends are European; my sons carry European passports; I have read a lifetime's worth of European literature; and so forth. But the more I think about it, the more I am forced to admit that the *idea* of Europe escapes me. As a construct, it's too embattled and too vexed. Its field of reference is too vast and too momentous. And its generality is continually called into question by its particularities. Undoubtedly, not everyone feels as uncertain about this notion as I do. And it is certainly not my purpose to suggest that everyone should.

I realized however that I'm far more comfortable with the other term in the theme I was asked to ponder, that is, the "edge." On the face of it, that may seem counterintuitive, for one might have imagined that any comparison those two terms would reveal "Europe" as the more stable and readily understandable of the two, and the "edge" as the more slippery and refractory. Yet I really don't see things that way. I have long felt that the term "edge" designates the kind of site where I live and work, and I have come to think of it as a pretty comfortable place. Let me explain, or try to explain, in a manner perhaps more interrogative than declarative.

I am an American and a student of French literature. That is, I have spent my career in a language and a cultural tradition that are not my own. Not mine by birth, I mean, and as if naturally. I recognize nonetheless that there is nothing *natural* about *culture*. Some aspects of culture are very intimately bound up in questions of choice moreover—at least for people who have the leisure and the opportunity to choose. And if I have chosen to focus upon a culture other than my own, that very choice has certain things to say about my attitude toward my own culture, about the "inside" and the "outside" of culture, about the gestures involved in moving from one culture to another and back again, and indeed about my freedom to choose.

It is tempting to suggest that people like me inhabit the edges of culture, *here*, merely by virtue of the fact that we have chosen to work principally in another culture, *there*. In a baseline perspective, that rings true. And even, to some degree, it describes the situation of people born into European culture who have chosen to make their career here in the United States, for though that culture may be something long familiar to them, they pursue it, for the most part, in a place which regards that culture as "foreign," and they do so, for the most part, for the benefit of students who likewise regard that culture as "foreign."

Yet I am persuaded that things are far more complex than that, in every single case. For one thing, the distinctions we draw between "central" and "marginal," "native" and "foreign," "same" and "other" are never quite as simple as they seem on the face of things—or indeed as we might in certain instances wish them to be. I'm thinking here, of course, of academic types like me, and of the academy that we inhabit; and I'm thinking, too, about the *culture* that interests all of us. I have argued on other occasions that the way we define ourselves as academics, and the way others define us, depend very much on perceptions. Like lenticular images (those infinitely seductive things that one used to find in cereal boxes), what one perceives changes radically as one's angle of perception changes. On the one hand, yes, we academics do seem to be on the margins of society, several steps removed from the hurly-burly of everyday life and its messy realities. We deal in metaphor and figure after all; we spend our days parsing arduous textualities that may have little to do with the *now*; we may even have friends (lord love them) who are far more conversant with the twelfth century than with the twenty-first. On the other hand, it seems obvious to me that a great many people would consider our situation as one of absolute centrality when compared to the sites that they themselves occupy in society—and indeed they would be quite right to do so. The reality of our situation undoubtedly resides in a place more mobile than we might have thought, and in a supple, relativistic conception of who we are and what we do.

All this is to say that when I remark that I'm comfortable with the idea of the "margin," when I suggest that I am quite happy to work on the "margins of culture," and when I think about my own relation to that site, I'm speaking about a place that is in a very real sense utopic, and one that in any case shifts dramatically in function of the differential manner in which we imagine it. Let us try to imagine it right now—and in the first instance at least, it shouldn't be too difficult to do so. And let me be clear about who I mean by "us." When I say "us," I mean people who are interested in literary studies. Deeply interested. Interested enough to spend a year, several years, or indeed a whole lifetime in that field, either as an amateur or a professional. And the more one strides through that field, the broader it may seem. Yet the feature that might strike other people is the narrowness of that field, to the contrary, a narrowness that seems to be more apparent every day, as our field becomes more embattled. All of us would recognize, I think, that literature does not enjoy quite the unquestioned cultural hegemony that it once did. And that the choice to study literature, today, is a bit different from the same choice, made in a previous generation. Whereas the cultural importance of literature was once axiomatic, it is a case that now has to be argued actively. And in fact, one can trace that argument, dressed in a variety of guises, and voiced in a diversity of tones, in contemporary writing. For my own part, I have recently spent a lot of time thinking about what I've called the "critical novel," in other terms, a novel that is aware of the tradition it inherits and that adopts a critical stance thereto; a novel that insists upon its status as a constructed object, rather than pretending to be *given*; a novel that sketches new possibilities for the genre, but does not always incarnate them; a novel that invites its reader, either openly or more subtly, to engage with it in a critical fashion.

That kind of novel argues actively and insistently a brief for the cultural pertinence of the novel. It does so under duress, in a sense, but that process is a healthy one, I believe, irrespective of the fear of cultural marginalization that provokes it. It's not such a bad thing, either, that we students of literature should be called upon to make the case for the importance of literature, rather than taking that notion for granted, when we find ourselves in conversation with people who don't feel as strongly about literature as we do—or indeed when we're talking among ourselves.

Clearly, we folks in French Studies must argue that brief all the more forcefully. For if the importance of literary studies is no longer a given here in the United States, how much more precarious is the status of *French* literary studies? It is true that French language and culture used to enjoy a certain cachet here in America, but it's safe to say that such distinction is no longer quite what it used to be. I suppose that everyone like me, in the course of our conversations with "civilians," has seen those people shake their heads as politely as they could when they learned that we are students of French literature. Upon occasion, we encounter people who are less polite. Not long ago, a dentist made it clear to me that he saw no reason for anyone to devote any time at all to literature in any of its forms. Exercising a truly heroic effort of will, I refrained from head-butting him. I cheered myself with the thought that I inflict less suffering on my clients than he does on his, all things considered. And I recognized, too, that I have almost as much loathing for his profession as he has for mine.

Any reasonable person would easily see, however, that that dentist's position in our society is more central than my own. And it's not that I envy him that status, I hasten to add. Quite to the contrary, in fact. For I am convinced that we in literary studies—if we are willing to exert another kind of effort of will—can take the notion that we inhabit the margins of things and turn it to our advantage. Far from something that limits us, we can reconfigure that notion as something that frees us and expands our horizon of possibility.

Sander Gilman, for one, has reflected upon what it means to be defined as a marginal person: "I am not neutral," he writes, "I am not distanced, for being an outsider does not mean to be cool and clinical; it must mean to burn with those fires which define you as the outsider" (17). Edward Said argues that the intellectual is always somehow exiled in our society, but that such a condition presents distinct advantages: "Exile means that you are always going to be marginal, and that what you do as an intellectual has to be made up because you cannot follow a prescribed path. If you can experience that fate not as a deprivation and as something to be bewailed, but as a sort of freedom, a process of discovery in which you do things according to your own pattern, as various interests seize your attention, and as the particular goal you set yourself dictates: that is a unique pleasure" (62).

Seen in such a light, the idea that we work on the margins of culture is distinctly less bleak than it might otherwise appear. For let us examine that margin, that *edge*, and our own relation to it. On the face of it, the edge would seem to be a vertiginous and threatening place. We teeter upon it, constantly in danger of falling this way or that. But the truth of the matter is that whatever way we fall, we fall *into* culture. Moreover, that fall is *itself* a cultural event. Because the amplitude of culture is such that it beggars the notion of boundaries. That's something that the people who dismiss culture refuse to understand, but that we who take it seriously see very clearly indeed. In other terms, the edge of culture is merely a fold in culture's vast fabric. We are free to dance upon that edge; we don't have to worry about falling off, nor about causing others to fall off; we may exploit the possibilities which that position puts on offer, in a stance that is boldly and pleasingly off-kilter.

In that very spirit, I would like to speculate more concretely about the kind of work we can do on the margins of culture. My own area of specialization is contemporary French literature, and more specifically, I am interested in the novel; more specifically still, I am interested in the novel of what some folks call the "extreme contemporary." That *field* (and I hesitate to use that word, because it suggests a coherence that may in fact be lacking), that field is itself a marginal one with regard to others in literary studies. For there are no guidelines, no maps, no familiar signposts there. Where other fields have a closely defined—and jealousy guarded—set of canonical works to focus upon, the critic of the extreme contemporary must decide for herself or himself what is worthy of consideration. And we don't always get it right. But getting it right is perhaps not the only point. Pleasure is also important in academe, I submit, though we academics are often encouraged to deny it. Play is important, too, in the most serious sense of the word. It is a privilege, moreover, to watch French literature unfurl, like a wave that crests and then breaks, and then to give some account of that process for the benefit of folks who did not witness it firsthand. That's the kind of stuff that I do, and I am well aware that most people—both those whom I've referred to as "civilians," certainly, but also people in my own profession—would see me as working on the edges of things.

So yes, I could give an account of that work, and try to demonstrate how I have come to appreciate the idea of marginality over the years. But what I would really like to do is to speak about another project that I have pursued, one that is a bit more quirky and off-kilter still than my work on the extreme contemporary. Allow me to explain, begging your readerly indulgence as I do so. And let me remark that, among all of the projects that I've undertaken in my career, this one illustrates most clearly the abundance of possibility that working on the margins of culture provides.

Many years ago, in the mid-1970s (a moment that seems positively antediluvian to me now), I began to collect mirror scenes in literature, that is, scenes wherein a subject glimpses himself or herself in a mirror. I began collecting them as an antidote to the doctoral dissertation that I was writing at the time. It was not that I was disgusted or bored with my dissertation, but rather that I felt the need to be doing something else, too, something "unofficial," and off the syllabus as it were. For a very long while, I kept this project closely guarded, thinking of it as a shameful secret activity for a scholar, like keeping a diary or playing on a softball team. Upon rare occasion I mentioned it to a few non-academic friends, and even to a couple of writer friends, but generally (with only a couple of exceptions) in passing and in veiled terms.

So, for the past thirty-five years I have been collecting mirror scenes as I read, and squirreling them away for some eventual winter. I should mention that I read bulimically, and always have. My readings are mostly (but not exclusively) contemporary works, and primarily fiction. The majority of them come from French and English literature, though I read quite a bit of stuff from other European national literatures, and from Latin America as well. They represent what I think of as a healthy mix of so-called "serious literature" and so-called "popular literature."

When I come across a mirror scene, I note its page reference, along with author and title, on a three-by-five index card that I use as a bookmark. After I finish the book, I transfer whatever nuggets I've mined to a master set of index cards, once again retaining only author, title, and page reference. Of course, lots of the books I read have no mirror scenes at all; some have only one or two; others have many. (The record, insofar as my own readings are concerned, is held by William Gaddis: I'm pleased to report that *The Recognitions* contains no less than eighty-three mirror scenes.) My guess is that I now "possess" (if that term has any meaning in this context, and I'm not certain that it does) something approaching 12,000 mirror scenes in roughly 2000 books, from, say, Homer to Jacques Jouet.

In all of this, I have obeyed two fundamental (though admittedly arbitrary and extremely idiosyncratic) rules. First, I have to come upon each scene myself, in the course of otherwise undirected readings. That is, I have never gone in search of mirror scenes, nor have I accepted them when upon rare occasion benevolent friends aware of my project have contributed them. Second, they must occur in books that I own, and have shelved in my personal library. For how else would I find them again, one day, with only page references to go by, in an age when editions change so quickly?—and I confess, too, with some chagrin, that I am as loathe to leave the comforts of my own library as Oblomov was to leave the comforts of his couch.

I finally did get off my couch, so to speak, impelled to do so by a need to account for my mirror scenes in some organized way—a need whose origin I was careful not to interrogate too closely. Invited about ten years ago to give a talk at a university on a subject of my choosing, I chose to talk about my mirror scenes, and about my own efforts to come to terms with them. In order to prepare that talk, I went back through my collection, for the first time in decades. Not systematically and exhaustively—there were simply too many scenes for that, I reasoned—but instead taking soundings here and there, and seeing what might surface. Flush with my newfound resolution to face these things squarely, I imagined a tripartite typology for mirror scenes. In the first type, the subject recognizes himself or herself unproblematically. In the second type, the subject finds recognition difficult, but ultimately possible. In the third type, the subject fails to recognize himself or herself. Allow me to adduce a couple of examples of each type, in order to flesh out those categories—and also, I admit, for the pleasure of revisiting passages that I have read, in the past, with pleasure.

Vladimir Nabokov's Timofey Pnin has no particular problem recognizing his own face:

> Peering at himself in the cracked mirror of the medicine chest, he put on his heavy tortoise-shell reading glasses, from under the saddle of which his Russian potato nose smoothly bulged. He bared his synthetic teeth. He inspected his cheeks and chin to see if his morning shave still held. It did. With finger and thumb he grasped a long nostril hair, plucked it out after a second hard tug, and sneezed lustily, an "Ah!" of well-being rounding out the explosion. (150)

Similarly, a character in Marie Nimier's *La Girafe* inspects himself with a clinical eye: "Catching a glimpse of my reflection in the hallway mirror, I regretted that I had not had the energy to shave" (199; my translation, as elsewhere, unless otherwise noted); and a man in Julio Cortázar's *The Winners*, upon reflection, likes what he sees: "He stroked his chestnut-colored mustache and looked with satisfaction at his freckled face in the wall mirror" (24).

In Bruno Schulz's *Sanatorium Under the Sign of the Hourglass*, however, recognition comes harder: "What do I look like? Sometimes I see myself in the mirror. A strange, ridiculous, and painful thing! I am ashamed to admit it: I never look at myself full face. Somewhat deeper, somewhat farther away I stand inside the mirror a little off center, slightly in profile, thoughtful and glancing sideways. Our looks have stopped meeting" (173). Think, too, of Salinger's Zooey Glass—Zooey Glass!—who refuses to look at his reflection in the mirror when he shaves. Upon occasion, recognition, when it is achieved, is translated through the gaze of another, as in Caroline Lamarche's *Le Jour du chien*: "Just then, by chance my glance encountered my image in the mirror facing us. I saw myself unembellished, without premeditation, I was astonished to see my expression, both determined and fragile, which took my breath away and dumbfounded me with admiration. Suddenly, I discovered myself as you saw me" (63–64).

The heroine of Emmanuèle Bernheim's *Stallone*, however, sees a stranger in the mirror:

> She was about to brush her teeth when the steam on the bathroom mirror cleared.
> And she saw herself.
> No. It was not her.
> She rubbed the mirror with the flat of her hand. This plain face, this shapeless hairdo, that couldn't be her. (26)

And Rilke's Malte Laurids Brigge grapples unequally with the mirror and with himself:

> Hot and angry, I rushed to the mirror and with difficulty watched through the mask the workings of my hands. But for this the mirror had just been waiting. Its moment of retaliation had come. While I strove in boundlessly increasing anguish to squeeze somehow out of my disguise, it forced me, by what means I do not know, to lift my eyes and imposed on me an image, no, a reality, a strange, unbelievable and monstrous reality, with which, against my will, I became permeated:

for now the mirror was the stronger, and I was the mirror. I stared at this great, terrifying unknown before me, and it seemed to me appalling to be alone with him. But at the very moment I thought this, the worst befell: I lost all sense, I simply ceased to exist. For one second I had an indescribable, painful and futile longing for myself, then there was only he: there was nothing but he. (94–95)

Now, in the course of collecting scenes such as those, I learned a couple of things. When I began, I told myself that I would write a book about them one day. And for many years, I continued to collect them with that goal in mind. I always supposed, I realize now, that if I sat on them long enough, like a mother hen on her eggs, something would hatch. The basic material, the *stuff*, is a treasure trove, an Ali Baba's cave, a middle-aged academic's dream. Yet the very richness, the diversity, and the multiplicity of the material made it impossible to deal with. How to begin? The informal approach I had adopted for my paper would clearly not suffice for a book project. No. I would have to begin with an exhaustive inventory of each and every one of those scenes, with a view toward elaborating a kind of *catalogue raisonné* in which each would find its place. Because to neglect even one would put the entire project in the wrong. But even if I answered the question of *how* to begin, I would not be much further forward. For the other prior question is *when* to begin. And that is a question which, for my sins, I had deferred for thirty-five years. I'm sure that you recognize the problem: it is always too early—or too late, as Jean-Paul Sartre and Marcel Bénabou have told us.

In short, as I worked my way through that paper ten years ago, I was forced to conclude that my project was impossible. As much as I was fascinated by those mirror scenes, and though I knew that I would continue to collect them, I understood once and for all that they escaped from me. They held me charmed, captivated, mesmerized in their grasp, as if *they* collected *me*, rather than the contrary, and the one shining truth of the matter was that writing a book about them was clearly and obviously impossible. I told my audience as much, and begged their indulgence for putting on offer a parable of academic obsession, with no possibility of satisfactory resolution.

Insofar as my need to account for my mirror scenes was concerned, I thought I had laid it to rest, by virtue of that very gesture. But in fact I had not. In the spring of 2007, drawn back to those scenes in a trance-like state by something that I cannot explain, I sat down for a couple of months and took notes on all the material in my index cards. I went over them from first to last, leaving nothing out, rereading every scene I had flagged since the mid-1970s. I culled the ones that seemed to me the most pungent, and I arranged them in very approximate, very abstract, utterly idiosyncratic categories. I then put those notes away, in the bottommost drawer of a filing cabinet, thinking once again that I had satisfied my urge to come to terms with my mirror scenes. I turned to other, more reasonable things.

But clearly it couldn't last. I revisited those notes, in mild rapture and as if inevitably, in the summer of 2008. And again in the summer of 2010. And yet again in the summer of 2011. Each time, I updated my notes with material from my new readings, and filed them away again. What resulted was a sheaf of notes sitting upon my desk, 160 pages of them. Therein resided a thousand mirror scenes, give or take, lovingly abstracted from my index cards, wherein lurked many thousands of their fellows. I stared at those pages, and they stared right back, accusingly. The only solution I could see was to act upon them.

So I did. And I can report that I have spent the time between then and now acting upon them, pretty much every day, and that the material result of that activity is a manuscript, and that that manuscript has been accepted for publication, with promise of becoming, in the near future, an actual book.

But not quite the book that I might have imagined—and this is where some of the more pungent consequences of working on the margins of culture have come home to me. For the categories that I postulated at the outset broke down under close inspection. Some of those breakdowns occurred at moments I might have foreseen; others occurred at moments largely unlooked-for. I can live with that, quite happily in fact. Because the sort of normalization that my categories would have provided (had they been utterly *categorical*) is not principally what I was after. Other concerns seemed more important to me, and more interesting: examining the way a given topos circulates in the economy of literature; tracing the conditions that govern self-representation in writing; reflecting upon how we readers project ourselves into the fictions we frequent; coming to (provisional) terms with my longstanding fascination with these scenes. And so forth.

I came to see that my mirror scenes served a deeply specular purpose for me, allowing me to watch myself reading, in a sense, and to infer from that activity a variety of general considerations about reading itself. Focusing on this material day after day, certain things became apparent. Things involving my profession, the objects toward which I direct my inquiries, the conditions of possibility of those inquiries, and the different positions I can take with regard to all of the former. More particularly, when I gaze into the mirror of this project, I see myself in different guises. A sixtyish professor, beavering away at a piece of scholarly writing. A person who lives a great deal of the time in his own imagination, giving full rein to that imagination. A committed reader, surveying the particulars of his commitment. A collector, perusing and arranging his collection in order to put it on view. A academic at work. A man at play. I confess that I'm more attached to the latter sort of image, for reasons that will be, by this time, massively apparent.

Pursuing this admittedly off-kilter project in a happily off-kilter fashion, free to do so at my own pace, playing by my own rules, and largely unconstrained by conventional academic protocol, I was finally able to understand what drove me. It was the persistent notion that somewhere in literature, just around the next corner perhaps, perfection lurks, as crazy as such an idea may sound. For I sense that my position with regard to these mirror scenes is closer to that of a lover than to that of a critic, and lovers can of course believe the most outlandish things imaginable, and believe them deeply.

I continue to see *intimations* of literary perfection here and there, as I search for new mirror scenes. I find them in characters, for example. Take Humbert Humbert, a man's man if there ever was one. Or any of Fernando Pessoa's heteronyms. Or Mr Bradly Mr Martin, who slouches through

William S. Burroughs's books. You get two for the price of one with him, and the fact that his honorifics are unpunctuated makes for low maintenance. Or Louis-Philippe des Cigales, the poet who is utterly unknown outside of the city limits of Rueil, but universally known within them. Or Fawn, George Smiley's misnamed and shockingly violent bodyguard. Or Ed Feasley, that paragon of intemperance and improvidence, a model for us all. "Chrast" (as Feasley himself might say, in his Hudson Valley drawl), why can't there be more characters like him in the books I read?

Perfect passages sometimes leap off the page at you, landing right in your lap and demanding to be hugged. Their wording, their rhythm, their tone, everything about them convinces us of their inevitability. They are as they are because they could not have been otherwise. Let me mention just two examples of that species. The first is from *Ulysses*: "Mr Leopold Bloom ate with relish the inner organs of beasts and fowls. He liked thick giblet soup, nutty gizzards, a stuffed roast heart, liver slices fried with crustcrumbs, fried hencod's roes. Most of all he liked grilled mutton kidneys which gave to his palate a fine tang of faintly scented urine" (57). The second (once again) is from *Pnin*: "Two interesting characteristics distinguished Leonard Blorenge, Chairman of French Literature and Language; he disliked Literature and he had no French. This did not prevent him from traveling tremendous distances to attend Modern Language conventions, at which he would flaunt his ineptitude as if it were some majestic whim, and parry with great thrusts of healthy lodge humor any attempt to inveigle him into the subtleties of the parley-voo" (139).

Perfection such as that is perfectly tonic. And it beggars my attempts to come to terms with mirror scenes, which serves to keep me both humble and amused. Yet quite apart from all that—or actually, and more accurately, smack dab in the middle of all that—I am absolutely convinced that the place to go looking for perfection (assuming that one should be so inclined) is on the margins of culture. A place that exists only by virtue of our wish for it to exist, and that we inhabit thanks to a conscious and continued effort of will. Not a place outside of things, not somewhere we've been relegated because of our fundamental eccentricity, but rather a place we *choose* to imagine because we are free to do so, and which in turns serves to put in evidence that freedom of choice.

Seen in that light, the situation of a student of literature is an enviable one. Speaking for myself, that recognition has helped me to understand more fully a few things that seemed obscure to me when I set out upon my mirror scene project. One thing I know, for example, is that my activity in this case is not directed toward any particular goal; it is largely disinterested; it is playful. I pursue it for myself in the first instance; but I do not exclude the possibility that it may eventually interest others, few though they may be, and as presumptuous as such an idea may seem. Furthermore, I know now that my fascination with these mirror scenes is both endless and end-less. That is, it is ongoing and uninterrupted, with no end in sight. If I felt an absolute need to bring my activity to a close, I guess that I could restrict myself to reading only those books that I've already read. Or indeed I could stop reading entirely. But I'm not likely to do that. More than anything else, it's a question of quality of life. And that's a very important question—even for an academic.

WORKS CITED

Bernheim, Emmanuèle. *Stallone*. Paris: Gallimard, 2002.

Cortázar, Julio. *The Winners*. Trans. Elaine Kerrigan. New York: Pantheon, 1965.

Gilman, Sander. *Inscribing the Other*. Lincoln: University of Nebraska Press, 1991.

Joyce, James. *Ulysses*. Harmondsworth: Penguin, 1969.

Lamarche, Caroline. *Le Jour du chien*. Paris: Minuit, 1996.

Nabokov, Vladimir. *Pnin*. New York: Bard, 1969.

Nimier, Marie. *La Girafe*. Paris: Gallimard, 1987.

Rilke, Rainer Maria. *The Notebooks of Malte Laurids Brigge*. Trans. M. D. Herter Norton. New York: Norton, 1964.

Said, Edward W. *Culture and Imperialism*. New York: Knopf, 1993.

Salinger, J. D. *Franny and Zooey*. New York: Bantam, 1969.

Schulz, Bruno. *Sanatorium Under the Sign of the Hourglass*. Trans. Celina Wieniewska. Harmondsworth: Penguin, 1979.

LILY HOANG AND BHANU KAPIL

The Colon
(from *An Asian-American Guide to Grammar*)

Recommended for all members of the ethnic avant-garde and those who love them.

The colon invoking list, invoking yearning, invoking our desire to want to please: you. Here, the sentence remains glass and looking into a cupcakery. Inside, sugary breasts piled high, touching, sensuating the mouth. So posed and juxtaposed, the colon emerges: just as expected: red velvet, plain old vanilla, dutch chocolate, german chocolate, carrot.

The colon is the mark of impurity.

The list becomes want, a list of wanted items. Most commonly, a list of things to buy, things to do imminently, things to do before expiration, things to want for later—for maximized eros, that despicable beast—traits to look for in object/person/place/event x, y, zed.

To have a list of negatives or cons is still a want: of opposites, of reflecting magic mirrors.

The colon: "a rope." How, on December 16th, 2012, in Delhi, a girl was thrown from a bus—and eviscerated there in the rape culture to be or come as it happened. Or in steps. On the steps and then the ground. Gang-raped by six men or boys, on a continuum—who used an L-shaped, rusted metal rod. To tug out—her intestines. Witnesses and bystanders—what were they doing? Nobody called the police for forty minutes—saw a "rope" hanging out of her body. The colon is what is inside: now outside. As a form of punctuation, it allows the reader to contract: around the urethral tissue, the fascial plane of the bladder's rich meat. To inhibit a fuller feeling—the peristalsis of your own smooth muscle, the space around the internal organs: intact or hard. Do you feel this: in your own body? The colon: "a rope."

The colon: of places conquered, flagged, made to own.

In India, students make anti-rape lingerie, wiring stitched into the wiring of a bra.

The colon: vagina and anus. They are not open. There is no blankness between the lines of the circles. They are closed, painfully.

The problem with the colon is yearning, the selfishness of it.
    The problem with yearning is yearning.
    Perhaps it is not inherent to the punctuation mark itself.
    But it is.
    Inside the mark is a wanting for more—a list of everything wanted until etcetera arrives.

I am interested in Foucault's definition of the genitive, but not enough to look it up. The colon marks a site of recursion: the instant that the wave hits and then goes back. Many worshippers were waist high in the water—a tray of milk, sugar and marigolds extended outward, an extension of the arms—like cyborgs—when the tsunami hit, and so I do not wish to use the word "wave" metaphorically when: these other images persist in the light culture of loss. I am not sure: that I want: anything: any more—in the way that you write of, Lily.

The word *survivor* is ugly, and my family is immigrant women survivors: of rape, of imprisonment, of colon cancer, of mental hopeless, of addictions, of

Otherness and tacky accents. I am all but one, the one that is my mother. Inside her body, cancer like punctuation, a million colons in collage, she smelled of diarrhea. That is the real ugliness, how easily I put it on paper: my mother's humiliation.

We are a family of *survivors* until my sister no longer. At forty-four.

If my sister were a sentence, she would not be glass. There would be no cupcakery and the sugary goodness of inside would be only saccharine, an imitation, that nasty aftertaste.

The colon stitches up the orifice. The colon bricks in the meat. But I think of it as survival, a way to manage thoughts, what it takes to get from one place: to another. To generalize. To generalize about bodily rupture. The colon marks the places in the sentence that have a breach, a physical one, too much touch. Who will love me now? I like to think of narrative as glossy, light blue and silver, replenished or strengthened by its scar tissue: which is syntax. The colon presents the arse of the sentence to the mouth of the reader: which is syntax. Too.

Please contact the editors directly if you are not able to write a memoir or a love letter without feeling a surge of anxiety. We can help with that. Commas are next.

ADRIAN WEST

The Fragile Shelter of the Declarative: on Edouard Levé

1. The left side of the face in the photograph— hence the right side in life, or what once was life, for its subject has committed suicide six years back—is ovular, with a swatch of stubble stretching into the shadow in the hollow where the sphenoid and temporal bones meet. The thinning hair is invisible against the black background, and the large lobe of the ear is disproportionate to its thin crest. The other side is gaunt. The mouth skews to one side, and one eye is slightly higher than its neighbor. Their stare is dignified and resourceless, and recalls those lines of Celan rebuking the lifting of stones and the exposure of those constrained to cower beneath them. The imperfection of the face is what renders it pathetic, in the strict rather than the derisory sense of the term, and calls up an idea I have never had the time to write about, that art is predicated on injustice, particularly in the conferral of dignity, and is a moral gesture directed toward the reapportionment of commemoration. The photograph, attributed to the portraitist Marthe Lemelle, is on the page of the Centre George Pompidou. When I begin to write, I am not aware that a similar image was split and its two halves duplicated to yield a pair of phantom twins, one chubby, one lean, in Edouard Levé's 1999 work *Auto-jumeaux*; nor do I recall that he had already remarked in *Autoportrait* on his own bilateral asymmetry. The vulnerability of Lemelle's image is purposely effaced in the distortion. Of his photographic work in general, Levé remarks: "There are no psychological relations between the characters . . . What I produce here, as in my other reconstitutions, is a referent without history."

2. In his essay on Edouard Levé, *L'esthétique du stereotype*, Nicolas Bouyssi, quoting Gilles Deleuze, observes: "The purely present object does not exist; everything present is ceaselessly enveloped in a 'fog of virtual images.'" The

purely present object I take to mean something like the above-mentioned referent without history, whereas virtual images would consist in the echoes of the past, the nagging doubt as to other presents, maybe more valid than one's own, and the propulsion, subordinate to but not in the least dependent upon the will, into futurition. The virtual—history on the one hand and telos on the other—lies at the basis of the distinction between subjects to which Levé's acts of leveling are openly hostile, as attested to in his photographic series *Homonymes* and *Amérique*, the one portraying common people who share the names of famous people, and the other unremarkable cities in America named after storied world capitals. Among the characteristics of "list-artists" like himself, Levé stresses the importance of "the refusal to establish hierarchies, to select, or even simply to choose."

This sort of programmatic statement tends to obscure under the cloak of aesthetic activism a sensibility that precedes and inspires it; in Levé's work this is the unbridgeable alienation from the sense of meaning in ordinary undertakings. The relationship of this affective state to Levé's documented depression and eventual suicide seems far from casual. Among the most marked aspects of his work is the removal of a necessary ingredient to a ritualized activity to accentuate the strangeness its ritualization conceals: in *Rugby*, for example, men are posed in postures of athletes at play, but expressionless, and without the ball; in *Pornographie*, fully clothed men and women are arranged in hardcore sexual positions. This is *ostrananie* not as an artistic gimmick or a mere mode of sharpening the spectator's perceptions, but as a reflection of lived experience.

"Putting two things together that are unrelated gives me an idea," Levé states in *Autportrait*, inviting comparisons to his Oulipo forebears and to Raymond Roussel, whom he admired deeply. Yet only a few pages before, he writes, "Virtuosity annoys me, it confuses art with prowess." And in general, there is a somber urgency in Levé's writing that is as far as possible in intent from the fluency and wit of Queneau's *Exercises in Style* or the mirth of Harry Mathews's *Singular Pleasures*. Levé has described his work as literary cubism, where the agglomeration of declaratives is analogous to the perspectival planes; but whereas cubism remains an idealism, a method of approaching an object whose transcendent substantiality is never questioned, Levé's refusal to impose order on his sentences calls into question any possibility of a unifying principle. Instead, there is a visceral paralysis before the semantic systems by which sense is made of the world.

3. The cordoning off of artistic narratives from other forms of verbal production is probably a mistake, insofar as the marks of psychological disturbance evident in the latter are characteristic of the form of the subject's thinking and are bound necessarily to affect the former. This is particularly the case with postmodernist writers whose writing is only classified as fiction for lack of a better term. It appears obvious that assertions as to the autonomy of the work of art such as were characteristic of New Criticism—which in any case have always struck me as expressive rather of an aversion on the part of their advocates to the broadening of their reading beyond belles-lettres than any defensible theoretical program—is inadequate to the analysis of a book entitled *Suicide* that draws on the details of an actual suicide and the author of which committed suicide mere days after passing the manuscript to his publisher. The same cannot be said for the suicidologist Edwin Schneidman's idea of the postself, his studies of the banality of suicide notes, or the enormous corpus of studies affirming the fundamental role of autobiographical memory distortions in depression. Recollecting on the one hand that studies of word and image frequency in autobiographical writings as well as in response to projective tests have shown robustness as predictors of future suicide, and on the other, that Levé himself describes suicide as a meaning-generative act, a gesture conferring order on the "incoherent" acts of the living, it is fruitful to consider to what degree Levé's writings and photographs portray the descent into a situation of psychological frustration from which suicide appeared the only reasonable exit. The aim of doing so, it should go without saying, is to enrich critical appreciation of his work, not to stifle it by resort to by reductive platitudes or Lacanian mystifications.

4. The first traces of Levé's artistic pathology lie in the works for which he was primarily known in France in his lifetime, his photographs. In 2000 he exhibited a series called *Angoisse* (Anguish), taken during a short stay in a city of the same name. The photos document banal, depopulated surroundings: a dismal dance club, a closed church door, a frowzy dining room with plastic tablecloths and deer heads on the walls, each described simply in terms of its location: Entrance of Anguish, Anguish at Night, House of Anguish, and so on. In an interview, Levé remarks: "It is true that it is a somewhat surrealistic village, because if you just add its name to any word—'fence of anguish,' for example—it all becomes interesting." In addition to the additive technique seen here and in *Pornographie*, where the subjects' clothing works to restore a sense of bare corporeality normally swallowed in the erotic fervor the pornographic image provokes, Levé also employs the reversal seen in the series *Homonymes* and *Amérique* and the subtraction of essential elements characteristic not only of *Rugby* but also of his second prose work *Journal*.

The photographs present a number of themes that will predominate in the writings that follow them: a dispirited, almost humorless irony, the avoidance of temporal succession or spatial specificity, ambiguity about pertinence and belonging, the abstention from or derangement of proper names, and an impoverishment of affect, rendered jarringly apparent in what Nicolas Bouyssi calls the "asemantic" faces of Levé's subjects. This mania for reticence strikes me as the photographic equivalent of the primitive language games proposed in Wittgenstein's later writings: by suppression of the details in which inquisitiveness is normally bound up, mollified and lost, Levé pushes the viewer toward the question of essences: of the what persists in people and places whose claims to their titles have been annulled; of whether a face deprived of expression or a body arrayed to a purpose for which the catalyst has been removed continues to have any sense at all.

5. Laurence Brogniez and Charlyne Audin state, in reference to Levé, "Enumeration tends toward a form of exhaustion." This exhaustion, which

should be taken to mean both the expenditure of available possibilities and the physical and psychological feelings of weariness, is present in Levé's writings from the opening sentence of *Oeuvres*, his first book in prose: "A book describes works that the author has conceived but not brought into being." A list of 533 possible art works follows, ranging from facile to ingenious to absurd: a camera is dropped from a window, filming its own fall; a large chair is surrounded by several small tables; a group lobbies to have salaries paid to zoo animals. Levé's eventual realization of a small number of these projects only serves to emphasize the contrast between the fertility of his imagination and the relative atrophy of his resolve, and the sense that it is extraneous to carry out what has already been conceived, a condition that bears at least a family resemblance to despair: an emotion shared by the figures in his photographs, aimless and only casually aligned to some whisper of purpose, transgressing the very idea of embodied being, which Merleau-Ponty defines as an inclination-toward.

Levé's second book of prose, *Journal.* returns to the subtractive technique featured in *Rugby*. It is divided into eight sections, including Society, Science and Technology, Classifieds, Culture, and Television. Each consists of news stories with the proper names excised, so that it is impossible to say where they took place, or when, or to whom:

> A woman, a senator from a liberal opposition party, was killed while driving through the streets of the capital, a week before the congressional elections. The police have accused the revolutionary armed forces. Three other people were killed in the course of the attack.

In the course of this writing, for the sake of comparison, I have reread a number of passages from the book alongside articles from several days' newspapers. An example:

> Lanza killed 20 first-graders and six educators with a semi-automatic rifle inside Sandy Hook Elementary School on Dec. 14. He also shot

his mother to death inside their home before driving to the school, and committed suicide with a handgun as police arrived.

Which of these two, I have asked myself, is truer? To pose this question is to inquire as to the purpose served by the proper name in discourse—the extent to which it discloses and the extent to which, under camouflage of disclosure, it is an instrument of suppression. The name of Adam Lanza in the second story serves as a provocation to the trotting out of commonplaces—be they sustainable or no—about the virtues and shortcomings of gun-control laws, the quality of mental health care in the United States, and so on, stock phrases pulled from the cultural ether that have the form, but not the inner texture, of discursive thought. In many ways, it can even be averred that so many news stories' highly morbid nature is related to the need for psychological immunization provoked by the "shock" of the modern age as described by Benjamin in his essay on Baudelaire, for a series of generally doubtful excuses why the disasters that surround us will nevertheless not close in. And perhaps in a larger sense, what is conveyed by news discourse is precisely a set of instructions for deferring the emptiness of the purposes embodied in the news-consumption experience.

Levé's "reconfiguration," to use his term, extends into spheres beyond the lurid. The Economy section is particularly dispiriting:

> An investment group has indicated that it will purchase the majority stake in one water firm for another water firm.

Though just short of 150 pages, the banality of such passages induces a chastening tedium. Thinking of the articles one reads every day that are formally indistinguishable, and differ only in being festooned with words like Yahoo, stem cell, the BRIC countries, and Kanye, one wonders: is it only in proper names that meaningfulness resides? And if Yahoo, stem cells, the BRIC countries and Kanye have no more lived poignancy for me than the absent referents that populate Levé's brief chronicles—if I have never been to the BRIC countries, never met or even listened to Kanye, have the vaguest idea of the nature of stem cells and know nothing, really, about Yahoo, beyond its unsightly purple logo—do these words not stand in then for mere symbolic values the essential qualities of which I am unacquainted with?

It must have been clear to Levé how trite the preoccupations of newspaper readers appeared when clarified in this way. To that extent, I believe *Journal* can also be viewed as a gesture of scorn expressing deep social alienation, the pain of not caring what others care about, or of not even being able to care, that is fundamental in, among others, the Durkheimian model of suicide.

6. It was during a 2002 trip to the United States undertaken for the purpose of photographing the towns later featured in his monograph *Amérique* that Levé, deeply depressed and convinced that his death was looming, compiled the list of 1,500 declarative phrases later published as *Autoportrait*. Though nominally inspired by Joe Brainerd's *I Remember* and its French analogue, Georges Perec's *Je me souviens*, *Autoportrait* has none of the delicate wistfulness of its forebears, and presents a vision of the self as a bare cumulus of statements ranging from prosaic to heartbreaking. Arranged haphazardly, with Levé's customary refusal of privilege or hierarchy, their effect is anti-evocative or even evocative of absence in a way that recollects the case histories of patients subjected to electroconvulsive therapy, who have, in place of memories of large stretches of their lives, a rote aphoristic knowledge gleaned from the statements of family and acquaintances. From the first page, procedural self-definition seems to stand in for the absence of the robust—even if demonstrably false—autobiographical intuitions that ground the psyches of ordinary people. For example, Levé writes of a time when he wished to see whether or not he was homosexual, and attempted to masturbate while imagining making love to a man. Framed differently, this anecdote could be amusing, but in *Autoportrait* it reads as one more indication of the author's inadequacy for selfhood.

The English translator of *Autoportrait*, Lorin Stein, remarks in an interview on a certain kinship between Levé and Montaigne. *Autoportrait* is an essay in Montaigne's sense of a sally or attempt without a foregone conclusion. This is of especial interest to the degree that the essay, with its generic indeterminacy, best records the imprint of the mind of its conceiver: a person's natural endowment of reticence, fluent wisdom, or boisterousness, unsuppressed by convention, show themselves in the essay in their wonted proportions. *Autoportrait* departs from a radical sense of unfamiliarity with the inner self and is characterized by a tendency toward the equation of intensive or ontic realities with their merely constative or numeric expression: in place of a textured discussion of the author's sexual life, there is a list of the places on a woman's body where he has come, the numbers of people he has slept with, the places he has made love. This clerical vacuity imposes onto the events of life the same feeling of extraneousness that inheres to artistic endeavor in *Oeuvres*: what is considered is not the momentary, irreducible surge of feeling, but the outer form and its logical propensity. A seemingly offhand comment about swingers' clubs is illustrative in this regard: "I appreciate swingers' clubs, which take the logic of the nightclub to its natural conclusion." Levé's perspective here takes the ritual of build-up, the *deceleration* before the completion of the sexual conquest, to be a superfluous distraction. The conclusions rendered up when the reasoning behind this statement are applied to life as a diversionary episode between birth and death are clear.

7. Recent research on depression and suicide has focused heavily on deformations of memory among the depressed. The cause-and-effect relations are far from clear, but it is established that the depressed encode memories differently from their non-depressed counterparts, often showing extreme deficits in event-specific knowledge with relation to happy moments in their lives and a tendency to the overgeneralization of happy recollections in relation to sad or distressing events, the episodic content of which is left intact. A group of researchers based in the Pitié-Salpêtrière Hospital in Paris have found there to be shortcomings in the autonoetic consciousness of depressed patients, so that their memories of positive events tend to be dissociated from a sense of self and remembered as though from a spectator's perspective; further, in many cases, the depressed rehearse their negative memories, so that they

become clearer, more elaborate, and more oppressive over time. The effects of these distortions are recursive. An initial negative bias in memory encoding over time tends to eclipse the possibility of producing happy memories and the self-assurance that relies upon them for persistence. With time, these effects alter the ordinary functioning of the brain, leading to physiological changes due to which the resumption of a happy life becomes impossible.

The preceding paragraph, though a hasty and partial summary of current findings, should be juxtaposed with the following statements from *Autoportrait*: "I live with a feeling of permanent failure, although I don't often fail at things I try to do"; "I have trouble remembering any truly happy moments"; "One day I told my analyst, 'I don't take any pleasure in what I have,' and I wept"; "My memories, good and bad, are sad in the way dead things are sad."

Edouard Levé handed in the manuscript of his fourth prose work, *Suicide*, to his editor at éditions P.O.L on October 5th, 2007, ten days before hanging himself in his apartment. The lugubrious nature of his photographs and writing aside, the act was not unexpected: he had been institutionalized several times, had attempted suicide before, and had even made a model of himself to have dangle from a noose for his photographic series *Fictions*, but the model broke and the image was never captured.

The ostensible subject of *Suicide* is a boyhood friend of Levé's who was the victim of a pedophile priest and who shot himself in the roof of the mouth with a rifle. The book is written as a letter to this friend, now more than twenty years deceased; but the conceit's tendentious nature quickly becomes clear. The dead man and Levé had not been close—indeed, Levé states that his friend's significance lies precisely in his having taken his life, and it is soon apparent that the "you" to whom the sentences are addressed is a pretext for Levé to converse with a version of himself abstracted by the barrier of death, a "pre-posthumous" self, to use a term he employed to describe his own works.

A marked characteristic of *Suicide*, largely obscured in the English translation, is the reliance on the imperfect tense, which lends a weary pallor to the past the narrator recounts and draws the subject's sorrows and his forceful truncation of them into sharper focus. There are no purely happy moments recalled in concrete detail. These positive summary memories, as they are referred to in clinical literature, thus have a nostalgic form that may contribute to the narrator's feeling of exile from them, his sense that happiness is bound inextricably to the extinct, and his association of longing with the possibility of his own disappearance.

The closing section of *Suicide* abandons the epistolary form, and is composed of a series of tercets limited, in Hannah Tennant-Moore's apposite phrase, to an inventory of "gradations of basic comfort":

> Red irritates me
> Black moves me
> White calms me

Reading it, I was put in mind of Shannon Stirman and James Pennebaker's essay "Word Use in the Poetry of Suicidal and Non-Suicidal Poets," which found a preponderance of self-references across the work of poets who had committed suicide and a sharp reduction in the use of the words "we," "us," and "our" in the writings immediately preceding their deaths. In *Autoportrait*, the word "we" appears twenty-three times over 112 pages, the word "us" three times, the word "our" seven; the figures for *Suicide*, a work of similar length, are fifteen, five, and one, respectively, and allowance should be made for the generalized "we" of such phrases as, "Death closes the series of events that constitutes their lives. So we resign ourselves to finding a meaning for them," which are more a manner of speaking than an expression of shared sentiment with others.

I also recollected a moment when I myself was near suicide, for hours could not stop the onward rush of images that showed me taking my own life, and had to repeat time after time Wittgenstein's phrase "Death is not an event of life" in order to get through the night. Beyond the lulling effects of mere repetition, such elementary declaratives have a sheltering quality; assertion may not be certainty, but at least it possesses the form a hypothetical certainty would take. The vacillation between the beckoning of living and death is a bitter humiliation that frequently depletes the psychological resilience necessary for continued survival. To his vanished friend, Levé writes, "Wavering made you suffer more than deciding did." The act of saying good-bye to oneself, the knowledge that the struggle to resist the enticement of nonexistence is done, may invoke an oddly pleasant assuagement of self-hatred. Perhaps only those who have stood at the edge of suicide recognize this as one of its most exquisite allurements.

JACQUES HOUIS

Transgressive Autofictions:[1]
Literary counterculture in 1960s Saint Germain-des-Prés

The '60s in French literature are primarily known today as the era of the Nouveau Roman and, at least in retrospect, Oulipo, as well as the era of a certain complicity between literature and theory, perhaps best represented by the journal *Tel Quel* and its founder Philippe Sollers. This literature was, of course, "experimental," joining the other major art forms of the century in breaking down the representational conventions of realism, from linear temporality to reliable witness. But none of the writers involved are identified with the counterculture of the '60s, with what might be called the essential '60s zeitgeist. It may be that the formalist and minimalist tendencies of these movements, representing a species of modernism, simply did not align with the baroque, romantic, or lyrical sensibilities of the decade or its radical tendencies. In France, the authors or the works that *did* failed to coalesce into a school or movement, did not play the literary game, and staked a claim only

1. Serge Doubrovsky coined the term in 1977 with reference to his novel *Fils*. Autofiction combines two paradoxically contradictory styles: autobiography and fiction. An author may decide to recount his/her life in the third person, to modify significant details or characters, using fiction in the service of a search for self. Scholar Arnaud Génon's definition ("Note sur l'autofiction et la question du sujet," *La Revue des ressources*, 8 January 2007; available online at http://www.autofiction.org/index.php?post/2008/10/13/Rubrique-a-venir3) gives us a good idea of how this very French concept plays out in contemporary critical discourse: "Whereas Rousseau proclaimed the originality of his project and the unique nature of his self, the subject of autofiction is created in the Other's words and inscribed in the wake of his predecessors. In addition to being virtual the subject makes himself textual. He is made in the image of the genre that exposes him. He is monstrous and hybrid. He is never one. He expresses the plurality we encompass. He multiplies the strata, is unveiled by the writing and annihilated by the fragmented form it takes. More than a new literary genre, autofiction is in fact the means the subject has found to call himself into question, to refuse the idea of a univocal truth and lay claim to his fracture." (Translation mine, as throughout this essay.)

to the status of transgressive outsiders vis-à-vis the literary establishment—hence their relative to near total obscurity. There were other factors as well: Certainly the strongly autobiographical tendency in our sample does not fit into the standard picture of the French literature of the '60s, although it does anticipate major trends of later decades. It will take some serious detective work and dogged scholarship to gain anything like a full picture of this French literary counterculture. However, if the small part of it I will be covering in this overview is at all representative of the whole, we may have to revise our idea of twentieth-century French literature, giving a bit more weight to these descendants of Rimbaud, Lautréamont, Artaud, and Genet.

Françoise d'Eaubonne

The "scene" I have been alluding to emerges from a small group of friends[2] who frequented the storied cafés of Saint-Germain-des-Prés in the early '60s: Nicolas Genka, Patrick MacAvoy, Jean Sénac, and Françoise d'Eaubonne. Of these, only the last named would achieve a measure of international celebrity: In 1971 she co-founded the revolutionary Front Homosexuel d'Action Révolutionnaire (FHAR); in 1974 she coined the term "ecofeminism"[3] in her book Le Féminisme ou la mort; she was also the author of more than fifty other books in a career that spanned the years 1942–2003, producing biographies, memoirs, science fiction and historical novels, film novelizations, essays, and poetry. D'Eaubonne's subject matter often put her at the forefront of countercultural writing: works pertaining to gay liberation and ecofeminism; the persecution of witches seen as "sexocide"; the gospel

2. MacAvoy and Sénac, MacAvoy and Genka, d'Eaubonne and Genka were close friends. D'Eaubonne and MacAvoy were friendly during the period in the early '60s when the writers frequented the Café Flore and Les Deux Magots in Saint-Germain-des-Prés.

3. Ecofeminism, or ecological feminism, is a philosophy and movement born from the union of feminist and ecological thinking and the belief that the social mentality that leads to the domination and oppression of women is directly connected to the social mentality that leads to the abuse of the natural environment.

of Veronica; biographies of Antoinette Lix, Qui Jin, Pasteur Doucé; a book-length essay about the reinvention of love through literature and music, etc. Unfortunately, only two of her books were ever translated into English, and neither are now in print.

Of particular interest to us among her many books is *La plume et le baillon* (The Pen and the Gag; Paris: Esprit frappeur, 2000), which concerns three twentieth-century victims of censorship: Violette Leduc,[4] Nicolas Genka, and Jean Sénac, all of whom belonged to her circle. Although only Genka suffered from official censorship, strictly speaking, d'Eaubonne shows how neglect, editorial timidity, and unwarranted critical hostility constituted a form of censorship in Leduc's case, while marginalization and eventual assassination silenced Sénac. MacAvoy's obscurity was more self-inflicted and therefore did not warrant a place in the book. Recalling Rimbaud, he gave up writing in his twenties, after being published twice by Julliard: at eighteen and twenty-one, respectively. His third book, for which he received an advance, was never published after the editor in charge of the project was fired. Later, he burned his manuscripts and, under the name Nala, devoted the rest of his life to playing the sarod, a stringed instrument used in Indian classical music. He is the only living member of the circle of authors featured in this article.

Even d'Eaubonne herself was the object of relative neglect, despite her sizable output and numerous contributions. The scholar Hélène Jaccomard, author of *Lecteur et lecture dans l'autobiographie française contemporaine: Violette Leduc, Françoise d'Eaubonne, Serge Doubrovsky, Marguerite Yourcenar* (Geneva: Droz, 1993), stated that "The precocious, fertile, and engagé writer, Françoise d'Eaubonne, might as well not exist . . . in the eyes of literary criticism. I mean herein to acknowledge the fact that the critics have neglected this unique body of work, as well as to acknowledge receipt of one of Françoise d'Eaubonne most original texts, her autobiography. Throughout three volumes of memoirs, not only does a colorful self-portrait emerge, but

---

4. As Violette Leduc's work is widely available in English and relatively well known in the Anglophone world, she is not among the subjects of this article, although she is far from irrelevant to postwar French literary counterculture.

also a quest filled with insights about this difficult genre."[5] The three volumes referred to eventually amounted to four, covering the 1920s to the year 2000 and totaling 1,135 pages, finally published as a single volume under the title *Mémoires irréductibles: De l'entre-deux-guerres à l'an 2000* (Paris: Editions Dagorno, 2001). Although these works could easily have been the portrait of an era, or a trove of gossip about the famous literary figures d'Eaubonne knew personally (which is how the books are represented by their publisher), the memoirs are in fact far more personal. As befits the writer that d'Eaubonne was, they detail the complexity of her efforts to be in the world. Throughout, she keeps asking rather than answering questions about what it means to be her—as though her activism had led her to be just as skeptical about her own assumptions as she was about those she found in the world in which she lived. As early as the first volume, written between 1963 and 1965, she is very frank about her sexuality. A subject that might otherwise invite prurience or simple narcissism here adds another dimension to d'Eaubonne's fascinating singularity: the co-founder of the Homosexual Front for Revolutionary Action, she was heterosexual, as she says, in spite of herself. A fiercely independent feminist, she was also acutely aware of, and disarmingly candid about, the dependency imposed by feelings of romantic love, feelings against which she nevertheless admits to being defenseless. The third volume of her memoirs, *L'Indicateur du Réseau*, subtitled "counter-memoirs," is organized topographically and alphabetically rather than chronologically, like the train schedule to which the title refers. Entries are organized according to Place, Age, and Length of stay, which allows an achronological approach focusing more on place than narrative. All four of the memoirs revisit the same experiences from the new perspectives granted by age and circumstance. To the extent they try to answer the question "Who am I?" they provide the same definition as André Breton in *Nadja*: "[those] whom I 'haunt'"; perhaps even expanding this definition to include one's "haunts." Composed for the most part during the '60s or in their wake, the memoirs also reflect the supra-literary

5. "Françoise d'Eaubonne: accuser (la) reception," *The French Review*, 67.3 (Feb. 1994), 486.

sensibilities of the time, as they were manifested in France. As Jaccomard puts it, "More so than a good many of her contemporaries, [d'Eaubonne] is in tune with French society and its ever-shifting political landscape."

Nicolas Genka

The circumstances of Nicolas Genka's childhood (born Eugène Nicolas, 1937–2009) are front and center in his works. His father, an engineer and a communist, married a German woman, also a communist, whom he met while he was an occupying soldier in the Ruhr after World War I. The family, which included Genka's three sisters, lived with the father's mother on a remote property in rural Brittany. They had thousands of books, but sometimes lacked the resources to light their lamps. While Genka's father turned to alcohol, his autocratic grandmother (a war widow and retired boy's school headmistress who dominated her son) forced her daughter-in-law, whom she hated on account of her nationality, to become a servant in the house. It was not until age seven that Nicolas realized one of the domestics browbeaten by his grandmother was his own mother. While Nicolas and two of his sisters attended school, his third sister Aline endured the same brutal treatment as her mother, perhaps because Aline had sought to protect her. Both were also beaten by the alcoholic father, who might as well have been carrying out his mother's wishes. Eventually, Nicolas's mother succumbed to madness. At the close of the Second World War, having lost three of her brothers, she was discovered on a train platform by Aline, toting a bag containing two onions and a crust of bread, bound for Germany and talking to herself incoherently. Enraged by this attempted escape, Aline stabbed her with a pitchfork, after which her husband locked her in the attic, where she remained with her infected wound until Nicolas informed the local authorities of her situation. After battling his abusive father and helping his sister Aline escape out the window using bedsheets, Nicolas found refuge in the home of his Russian uncle and adopted his last name. He later served as a medic in Algeria, moving to Paris when he returned to France, living off his army-discharge pay and doing odd jobs while he wrote.

His first novel, *L'Épi monstre*, was published in December 1961, when he was twenty-four, thanks to Christian Bourgois, then an editor at Julliard. It led Jean Cocteau to establish then and award it the Prix des Enfants Terribles Jean Cocteau. The book was an immediate success, selling ten thousand copies in a matter of weeks. The film director Pier Paolo Pasolini, as well as the authors Vladimir Nabokov and Yukio Mishima, contemplated translating it into Italian, English, and Japanese respectively,[6] but in July 1962, the Minister of the Interior banned any further sale, translation, export, or publicizing of the novel on account of its incestuous content. Soon thereafter, Genka's family homestead in Brittany was ransacked by "persons unknown." A new edition of the novel was tolerated in 1999,[7] though the ban was not officially lifted until 2005.

Genka's second novel, *Jeanne la pudeur*, published in 1964, met much the same fate. Hailed as a masterpiece and awarded the Prix Fénéon, it too was promptly banned, only to reappear reissued by Flammarion in 1999. Although certainly violent and scatological, neither book, it should be noted, is remotely pornographic.

L'Epi monstre tells the story of Morfay and his two daughters, Mauda and Marceline, who live in a big house on a hill, overlooking the village of Querlas. Morfay (*Mort-Fait*, or "death-make," also rhymes with *forfait*—"felony" and would seem to allude to the Celtic goddess figure Morrígan by way of her descendant, *la fée Morgane*, or, as she is known in English, Morgan le Fay) is

6. *Libération*, May 24, 1999, available online at http://www.liberation.fr/portrait/1999/05/24/nicolas-genka-61-ans-baillonne-dans-les-annees-60-pour-avoir-raconte-l-inceste-son-roman-l-epi-monst_273807

Actually, there is conflicting information about these celebrity endorsements. All sources indicate that the three writers were at least involved with Genka, and most report them as projected translators. Pasolini in particular promoted Genka, and the publicity for the eventual Italian translation of L'Epi monstre features language to the effect that Pasolini's dream has finally been realized. This is of particular interest because Françoise d'Eaubonne was convinced that François Malraux, the author and minister of culture under De Gaulle, so hated Pasolini that the director's promotion of Genka played an important role in the eventual ban.

7. Nicolas Genka, *L'Épi monstre* (Paris: Exils, 1999).

an alcoholic (like Genka's father) an ex-resistance fighter (like Genka's father), and an educated man living among illiterate alcoholic peasants he entertains with gutter wit in return for alcohol (like Genka's father). Mauda is clearly based on Aline, as she lives the life of a servant in the household. Marceline appears to be an amalgam[8] of Genka's other two sisters, Jeanne and Andrée. She is a free spirit who has left boarding school and come home after the death of her grandmother, remembered as *la dame aux gants noirs* (the lady who wears black gloves), a retired boy's school headmistress (like Genka's grandmother) who comes to her son's defense when he amuses himself to his wife's horror by roasting cats alive in the oven:

> "Take a look at what your fellow Germans roast in the oven! . . . Not cats! . . . They would have sent you there yourself, you deranged Rosa Luxembourg! Kraut Louise Michel!" [. . .] And Morfay went on to dress cats in doll clothes. While he waited for his mother, consumed with rage, to trumpet a formidable couplet: 'I don't really know what my son thinks; but you gave him murderous instincts,' he stuck matchstick suppositories into them that he then lit. (62)

In the book, the girls' German mother bears the nickname La Trine. And the circumstances of her life and death resemble those of Genka's own mother, Marianne:

> Mauda closes her eyes enlarged by the dark. "I didn't love her enough," she whispers to herself, "I didn't defend her enough. When she went crazy I put a hole in her thigh with a pitchfork: she wanted to go back to Germany naked under her 'cat skin,' with a suitcase in which they found just two old onions and a few crusts of bread, nothing else—I didn't want her to leave. Oh! I beat her too, he told me hitting her would put her in her right mind. But if it weren't for me she

8. Or even perhaps the female stand-in for Genka himself, who, if one account is to be believed, was raped by his father.

surely would have died sooner. When he locked her in the pantry, with spikes on the door, and she didn't say anything for days, I really thought we'd killed her."—She flashes on her mother's cadaverous eye sockets, the weightless body on the stretcher, the social workers bumping into Morfay, a rigid, harsh, unbearable Morfay: "Get rid of this rotting meat!" And the same Morfay three days later: "Ah! Those morons want to play rough with me! Get our mourning clothes ready."—The body of the person who had been La Trine was lying on a bed at the morgue. Her head was covered with a black veil, and this black square inside the white cube of the room gave Mauda a shock of the kind felt in the presence of a decapitated corpse. Her features could be distinguished through the veil—the half-closed eye, the open mouth, and when, most politely, the men who would nail the coffin shut removed the veil so that the corpse could be identified, Morfay hesitated, as if unsure. La Trine had become a horrible thing, a little skeleton badly dressed in bluish skin with dark circles that devoured her face. (97)

L'Épi monstre was banned under a 1949 law applying to publications for children, intended to protect minors. Although the book contains nothing that could be called pedophilia, incest is clearly an element present in the Morfay household. Through numerous allusions, it is made clear that Morfay and his older daughter Mauda have a sexual relationship, which seems to underpin the sadomasochism of their interactions. Mauda struggles to free herself from her father's domination but fails and ultimately kills herself. Her suicide concludes the last chapter of the first of the book's two parts. This entire chapter is characteristic of the Genka style, an apocalyptic, hallucinatory lyricism, which here seems to wed nuclear annihilation to the depredations of the patriarchal nuclear family:

Morfay will watch the windows turn green. "That's it, they've dynamited the planet. Mauda?"

Morfay will watch his daughter enlightened. "I see the plain in your eyes, and the heart of things, and farther. I see a dark point, it's the sign of the coming race. We're going to disappear. Engulfed. Disintegrated. We shall no longer see each other, my saint . . ." And Mauda will cradle his head in her heart: "You won't die, since I love you . . ."

The days will come wearing open cassocks, carrying crosses, tabernacles, all that insolent bric-a-brac; migrations of philosopher-manufacturers will come, carrying hidden veils and lawsuit material for nice pale rhetoricians, resolutely in love with Man and resolutely jerking themselves off with His destiny through their own and oneself; the maniacs of Christianity will come, the illuminated ladies whose periods are the stigmata and whose faith the thrusts of sex, the pederast missionary gentlemen, the little sluts will come, at their asses the servant princes, arms filled with the sunflowers of madness, the pyromaniacal old men will come, the poets floating on silk and opium, the lovers of the sow will come, the theoreticians of fortune, the surgeons of vanity: the laureates of the revolution.

[. . .] They will all traipse again through Mauda's Garden, they will all traipse again through Marceline's forest: "Halt childhood! Halt hope! We have seen Lot's daughter, she is going to rule the world!" [. . .]

Will Mauda, stricken with a saintly panic, see the fire at the end of her unconscious night? Will she finally wake up? Will she be stuck all of a sudden between her father and the crowd, will she understand the need to choose?

What if the gigantic trap of this love appeared to her suddenly amid the cries of a Morfay dispossessed, haggard, hands open? What if Mauda were to follow the crowd, wedding the world's revolution in a second marriage?

Oh! Madness then, the ultimate recourse, the Bomb! The assassination of masses, the Earth depopulated in three seconds, through the fault of a lost girl, through the rage of an old boy, through the misery of a love! Oh! The certainty of dying at the same instant, even if you're on the other side of the planet, even if you beg, even if you remarry, even if you repudiate me aloud in your dazzling cathedral!

But nothing can happen to this bitch. Only this.
Morfay, one night, makes her wash his feet. (98–100)

The first part of the book ends with several pages of sadomasochistic degradation and Morfay's discovery of Mauda's corpse in the kitchen the next morning. The second part of the book relates Morfay's despondency, the efforts of his daughter Marceline to both help him and escape his clutches, her eventual failure (and the clearest allusion to an act of incest), her attempt to flee into the arms of a farm boy Morfay murders in a fit of jealous rage, and the death of both father and daughter, along with the total destruction of the Morfay property in a cataclysmic fire, described in terms befitting thermonuclear annihilation. Thus concludes a novel "improvised in ten days, like a piece of jazz, fed by immense anger."

While the sexual content of the novel might have been the pretext for banning Genka's work, it's far more likely the picture it painted of French family life and *la France profonde* could not be tolerated by the authorities. "This novel tells us that where there is family, there is a structure carrying crime, incest, rape, madness, and death. It is this usually repressed truth that led to the ban by the Ministry of the Interior," writes Jacques Henric in his preface to the first reissue citing Aristotle: "The family is the tragic milieu par excellence."[9] Françoise d'Eaubonne suggests an additional, symbolic dimension that might have played a subliminal role in the government's reaction. According to her, *L'Épi monstre* constructs "the symbol of the relationship between power, Morfay, and the two pillars of society: Mauda, the peasantry, and Marcelline, the intelligentsia."[10]

While *L'Épi monstre* remains attached to or grounded in conventional narrative, despite its recurrent flights of dark lyricism and use of temporal

9. *L'Épi monster*, 20.
10. In *La plume*, 96.

shifts, Genka's second novel, *Jeanne la pudeur*, hardly ever sets foot on the ground. It is akin to a dream, and yet, once again, derives directly from Genka's experience. His sister Jeanne, the closest of his siblings growing up, a tomboy who introduced him to the work of André Gide, had simply disappeared. Rumor had it that she went to America. Years went by without news. Then, suddenly, when Genka was in Paris, after the publication and banning of *L'Épi monstre*, he received a call from the hospital in Brittany where his mother had died: "Your sister is hospitalized here in a terrible state. She has lost her mind."[11] Jeanne had been found wandering around her empty, ransacked former home "like a lost pet," toothless and wearing rags. She recognized her brother, but was unable to speak or communicate to anyone where she had been or how she had been living. *Jeanne la pudeur* imagines Jeanne as a prostitute returned to her native village from Pigalle in a state of utter destitution, raped by the locals under the leadership of the local priest. Soon her ex-lovers arrive to avenge her and to put her out of her misery: a mysterious man named Jean who moves in with and dominates the priest before raping and murdering a local boy; Michel, aka "Go Home," a black American GI, who murders Jeanne in what resembles a ritual sacrifice; and the memory of Yoshi, who died in Hiroshima, and with whom she is reunited in death. Or so it all seems, for this is a work of surreal and delirious imagination, as perhaps befit the real Jeanne, whose sufferings could only be imagined.

Nicolas Genka was a tragic figure, a gay man in a time of sanctioned homophobia and a likely sexual-abuse victim whose obvious love for the women in his family (when he spoke the word "sister," he would trace an upper case *S* in the air with his index finger) had been ravaged by forces beyond his control. Each of his sisters, as well as his mother, had been a victim he had been unable to rescue, and each of his attempts to use writing as a means of coming to terms with the rage he felt as a consequence of these experiences was foiled by the state. And his rage itself only made matters worse. According to Françoise d'Eaubonne, "[Genka] lived in a state of permanent provocation. His verbal aggressions, of a scatological nature, ridiculed people with such mastery that he

11. *La Plume*, 84.

terrified his entourage."[12] In 1964, when his sister Renée was involved in a divorce, her husband exploited the autobiographical elements in *L'Épi monstre* to win custody of their daughter by claiming that she was the product of an incestuous relationship between brother and sister. (In which, somehow, Genka's homosexuality was thought to be a contributing factor!) While his sister cried on the witness stand, and her husband's attorney exclaimed, "She shared the same little room in Paris with her brother!" Genka stood up in court and bellowed sarcastically "A love nest!" His antics helped Renée lose custody of her daughter, although all those close to Genka knew the accusation was an absurdity. In a 1999 interview on the occasion of the reissue of *L'Épi monstre*, Nicolas Genka said, "I was twenty-four. I was completely ignorant of legal procedures. Renée ended up swallowing a tube of Nembutal. They pumped her stomach so they could bring her back to court where they judged her in my name."[13] He survived by editing, rewriting screenplays, etc. But he died an alcoholic in 2009. He only published one other book in 1968, which went unnoticed.

JEAN SÉNAC

"Jean Sénac is little known today in either the United States or in France, yet his is one of the most powerful and original voices to have emerged from the bloody war of independence and the turbulent postcolonial period in his native Algeria. His name does not appear even within the most authoritative studies of gay literary history or in surveys of Francophone literature. And yet, this openly-gay Algerian of European descent, who is widely believed to have been the victim of a government assassination in 1973, was one of the most remarkable French-language authors of his generation and represents the struggle of intellectuals trying to bring a reconciliation between European and Islamic cultures in order to create a truly multi-ethnic, multi-religious, sexually liberated society."[14] So writes Katia Sainson, one of very few scholars

12. *Libération*, May 24, 1999.
13. *Libération*, May 24 1999.
14. From an unpublished translation proposal by Sainson.

working to preserve the legacy of this major poet. With David Bergman she translated and edited *The Selected Poems of Jean Sénac* (Rhinebeck, NY: Sheep Meadow Press, 2010), a bilingual edition that is in fact the only volume of his poetry currently in print.

Sénac was born in Algeria in 1926. His mother, Jeanne Comma, was Spanish. He never knew who his father was. He took the name of his French stepfather. Although he wrote in French and never learned Arabic, he early on devoted himself to the cause of Algerian independence and was associated with the FLN. This earned him the enmity of Albert Camus, another *Pied-Noir* who, along with René Char, had been a friend and an early champion of his poetry. When Camus called him "the cut-throat," alluding to the FLN's killing method of choice,[15] and referred to his poem "Salute to Black Writers and Artists" as "unacceptable, indecent and shameful,"[16] their long friendship came to an end. Sénac spent the war years in France, returning to Algeria as soon as independence was declared. There he joined the Ministry of Culture in the Ben Bella government, hosting two popular and influential radio shows (with a listenership that rivaled those for soccer matches and soap operas) that introduced a young North African audience to poetry from around the world. When Ben Bella was overthrown by the more Islamist Boumedienne regime, Sénac was forced out of his post and became increasingly isolated. Although he was threatened and denied citizenship (despite the fact that his patriotic and revolutionary poems had become standard schoolroom fare), Sénac refused to leave Algeria. By the early '70s he was living in a hovel in Algiers. It was there that he died of multiple stab wounds in 1973.

Sénac's poetry is abundant and wide-ranging. After Char's early influence, Sénac developed a style that evolved through many different periods, from militant revolutionary to intensely personal and erotic poems of the

15. As related in Sainson's introduction to *The Selected Poems of Jean Sénac*, with regard to Sénac's poem posthumously published poem entitled, appropriately, "To Albert Camus Who Called Me a Cut-Throat."

16. The slight was reported by Sénac in a letter to Jean Daniel, published in *Poésie au Sud: Jean Sénac et la nouvelle poésie algérienne d'expression française* (Marseille: Archives de la ville de Marseille, 1983), 65.

body (which Sénac called *corpoèmes*). His poetry reflects both the '60s countercultural desire to combine love, sex, and revolution, and what might be called the legacy of nineteenth-century French poetry: Baudelaire's conflation of aesthetics and existential necessity (poetry as a way of life) along with the twin ambitions of Rimbaud and Lautréamont, to "change life" and "change the world." Surrealism turned this legacy into a veritable program and neither the counterculture nor Sénac escaped this influence. Sénac however eschews what might be called the abstract and impersonal utopian tendencies of surrealism. Where Rimbaud, Mallarmé, and the Surrealists sought something like the dissolution of the self in the poem (Mallarmé's "elocutionary disappearance of the poet") Sénac is busy struggling to construct a gay French Algerian revolutionary bastard self. And he is inclusive, engaging in a dialogue with other poets—Whitman and Lorca, not surprisingly, as well as many others.

If, as the critic Arnaud Génon has said,[17] the essence of autofiction consists of the subject "laying claim to [its] fracture" then Sénac's "novel" *Ébauche du père: pour en finir avec l'enfance* (Sketch of the Father: To Be Done with Childhood) is a classic representative of the genre. Written between 1959 and 1962, it was meant to be the first volume of an autobiographical project that would cover Sénac's life. When Sénac returned to Algeria, his "life book" never advanced beyond this first installment. Dedicated to his mother, to his adopted son Jacques Miel, and to Patrick MacAvoy (who would dedicate his first novel to Sénac), *Ébauche du père* was published posthumously in 1989 by Gallimard. Besides reminiscences of childhood, it features most prominently the author's attempt to come to terms, by way of a suitable fractured structure, with the unknown father who is thought to have raped his mother:

> And now, what does it matter if he really forced her or if she consented! [. . .] What was his name? I don't know. I don't want to know. (Maybe Ruis Y Gongora.) I don't want to know [. . .] I am

17. In "Note sur l'autofiction . . ."

talking about it in this novel because my hand is pushing me. Is it a novel to tell one's life with a lot of imagination that reshapes things according to their true core? It is a novel, because I invent a bunch of truths whereas I only experienced approaches, passages, flashes. I crystallize, I petrify what were just glimpses, questions, whims. (23)

Sénac raises questions of culture and identity that speak directly to our historical moment, with his concerns having moved from the periphery toward the center of Western societies. (The same can be said of all the writers I am addressing: d'Eaubonne's promotion of ecology, gay rights, and women's rights; Genka's indictment of sexual abuse and patriarchy; MacAvoy's adolescent rage or disappointment with the conditions of modern existence.) He is the ultimate outsider: an openly gay European in an Islamic country that rejected him even as he embraced it; a man rejected by the country of his nationality because he fought against it; a traitor to a cause (colonialism) now almost universally despised; a man lacking even the basic knowledge of his own paternity. And yet a deep vein of optimism runs through Sénac's poetry, and the approach he took to his memoir-novel seems to have been motivated in part by a desire to maintain the integrity of his poetry: "For me it is the only way to not soil my poem. To shield it from my vacillating attachments and my duplicity. And it is why I go forth, sinuous and talkative, in order to reach the only thing that matters. The Father, the Country, the Flesh I have been given." Sénac the poet seems to have understood that his very singularity was the mark of his humanity, and that by embracing it he was on the right side of history.

PATRICK MACAVOY

Patrick MacAvoy won the second Prix des Enfants Terribles Jean Cocteau for *Les hauts fourneaux* (The Blast Furnaces) published in Paris in 1963 by

Julliard and dedicated to Jean Sénac. François Ruy-Vidal,[18] in the chapter of an unpublished memoir covering the years 1964–1965, has this to say about Patrick MacAvoy:

> Les hauts fourneaux was published by René Julliard when [MacAvoy] was only eighteen. And yet it has nothing in common with Bonjour tristesse [which Julliard had likewise published when its author, Françoise Sagan, was eighteen]. Neither did the two authors have anything in common. Save that it was possible to think, as Julliard would often have it, that the pages of these hauts fourneaux, written so quickly under the black suns of cruelty and madness, were only the baby steps of a unique and irreplaceable writer and the first contribution to a body of work that would turn out to be exceptional.

Julliard published MacAvoy's second book, La ballade, in 1966. In 1983, a collection of MacAvoy's poems written between 1960 and 1970, Les Fenêtres Rouges, was published by Éditions Saint-Germain-Des-Près. The first and apparently only edition was limited to eighty copies, decorated with an original lithograph by Edouard MacAvoy, the writer's father—an important portrait painter, the president of the Salon d'Automne, and friend to many other writers and artists. The nature of the relationship between father and son during this period is perhaps best expressed by a passage from Edouard's memoir, Le plus clair de mon temps 1926–1987 (Paris: Éditions Ramsay, 1988): "Thus do I witness the experiment my son Patrick is attempting, refusing any support, any love, any contact, living according to a rhythm of which I cannot approve and norms I find inexplicable. I hope that he is in the right, and not

18. François Ruy-Vidal, along with Harlan Quist, published a number of modernist children's books with such authors as Eugène Ionesco and Marguerite Duras. His blog (and, in greater detail, his memoir in progress) contains much discussion of his friends at the Café Flore in the early '60s, and the four writers featured in this article in particular. It is Ruy-Vidal who places them at the same table and also talks about them in the context of his work as an editor at Grasset. His blog and my own acquaintance with Patrick MacAvoy in 1968–1969 were the starting points of this article.

myself . . ." These lines were written in 1969 in the context of a discussion of the events of May 1968; today, Patrick MacAvoy himself doesn't approve of the young man he was at the time.[19]

The relative obscurity surrounding Nicolas Genka, despite an aura of *succés de scandale* and obvious literary merit (and ambition?) is a relatively straightforward matter, given his work's truly taboo subject matter and its innovative, outsider quality. Patrick MacAvoy, however, seems to have courted obscurity more actively, in part no doubt in reaction to his father's celebrity. His precociousness prompted both the Cocteau award and an article by his editor Jacques Brenner, entitled "Adolescent Genius,"[20] which compares MacAvoy to both Rimbaud and Lautréamont. Indeed, on the basis of literary virtuosity alone, it is nearly impossible to conceive of how a sixteen-year-old[21] could have produced such a text. Only the extremely dark themes and fervid emotional tenor of the prose provide clues to the writer's age. As Brenner put it in his essay:

> Adolescent genius is often a genius for revolt, especially when it manifests itself before [one's] twentieth year. It is a total revolt: one directed against the human condition in general. [. . .] Young poets tend to celebrate the dark aspects of life: boredom, pain, sadness, and death. 'It is to want at all costs to consider only the puerile dark side of things,' Lautréamont said, as he retrospectively passed judgment on his *Chants de Maldoror*.

The comparison to Rimbaud is even more striking, however. Both MacAvoy and the poet wrote with striking urgency and precociousness,

19. Related to me during telephone interviews, and during a visit to Patrick MacAvoy in the Aveyron.

20. In *Journal de la Vie Littéraire 1962–1964* (Paris: Julliard, 1965), 136–137. Elsewhere in this same volume is an article entitled "La Nouvelle Fable," in which Brenner situates Patrick MacAvoy in a "movement lacking only a theoretician," that is "a reaction against every form of realism, in particular the existentialist school and *l'ecole du regard*" (a term for the Nouveau Roman).

21. Jean Sénac submitted the manuscript of *Les hauts fourneaux* to René Julliard when Patrick MacAvoy was sixteen.

then abandoned writing at about the same age. Both left France: Rimbaud for Africa, MacAvoy for India. In addition, MacAvoy's work bears clear signs of influence by the Rimbaud of *Une saison en enfer*. Most of all, MacAvoy seems to have followed to the letter the prescription set forth by Rimbaud in his "Lettre du Voyant":

> You have to make the soul monstrous: in imitation of the Comprachicos, right! Imagine a man implanting and cultivating warts on his face. [. . . the poet himself] seeks out every form of love, of suffering, of madness. He exhausts every poison, to keep only their quintessence . . ."[22]

As might be expected, Antonin Artaud, Samuel Beckett, and Jean Genet also stand out as influences. These antecedents, and the surreal dimension of MacAvoy's writing, point to a rejection of realism, setting him apart from many of the other experimental French prose writers of his time, whose works often feature a kind of minimalist objectivism.

Les hauts fourneaux, which nonetheless describes itself as a novel, is made up of three tales. The first, "Blockhaus Définitif" (Terminal Blockhouse), is itself split into two parts. The first is forty-eight pages long, and is an extended interior monologue by a middle aged man named "Patrick MacAvoy," who is writing, or attempting to write, in order to remember, to be able to tell, eventually, the story of "what happened." Part two, at twenty-two pages, is (probably) the story the narrator of part one was attempting to remember: in the post-nuclear-holocaust French provinces, the narrator and his wife, Denyse Rolland (the name of the woman MacAvoy would indeed go on to marry) are the only ones who have not fled. The narrator experiences the deterioration and disintegration of his wife. As insects eventually devour her and her limbs fall off, he shows his love by embracing her putrefaction in any number of memorable ways. Prose style aside, part one is reminiscent of some of Beckett's novels and bears an uncanny resemblance to Paul Auster's relatively recent *Travels in the Scriptorium*. Part two has echoes of Edgar Allan Poe.

22. Rimbaud, *Œuvres completes*. Paris: Gallimard, 1972, 251.

The second tale of *Les hauts fourneaux* is titled "Le Fil de Nerf Barbelé" (The Barbed Wire Nerve) and is forty-three pages long: a mostly third-person narrative, with dialogue, relating from different points of view the short and violent life of an Algerian immigrant day laborer in Paris. The tale cuts back and forth between the story of Ahmed in Paris and its eventual conclusion: Ahmed, dead in the street (after committing random murders), surrounded by a knot of Parisians waiting for someone to pick up the body.

The third tale, "L'Epine" (The Thorn), at sixty pages, is a gothic horror story in the form of a journal kept by a fifty-year-old man, chronicling his descent into madness after welcoming into his home a once prominent attorney who killed his own daughter and gouged out her eyes, but has since been deemed cured after a stay in a mental institution: it's like nothing so much as Maupassant on LSD. Again and always, literary pyrotechnics propel these stories into uncharted territory. The writing is layered, dense, and dazzling, but without recourse to much in the way of allusion or symbolism. Instead, rather than a representation of everyday reality enriched by the symbolic or seen from a new perspective— or both—precedence is given to the creation of a more purely textual reality:

> The other day the luminous globe that lights the room began to swell. It was full of water in which not entirely coagulated clots of an unknown, other liquid were swimming, their yellowish color tending toward ochre. But no, they were yellow. I no longer have any doubt. Yesterday, just as I finished writing this first page, I came across, or at least my eyes came across, a photograph that, as it aged, had taken on exactly this same shade of yellow. Since it had yellowed under my own light, it's quite possible that it is the lamp itself that contains this fluid and imprints its color on every object within its reach. And what if I myself were discolored in this way, I wondered? That is probably just what's happening, for I am now yellow, the same shade as that somewhat ochre, dirty yellow. In spots my skin is lighter, and my most private parts reach lemon yellow, a violent and laughable yellow . . . I am in the depths of a malady as foolish and cruel as impotence. (12–13)

Published when MacAvoy was twenty-one years old, his second book, *La ballade,* is the sixty-page, first-person narrative—a monologue, mostly—of a hospitalized prostitute. It was written while MacAvoy was convalescing in a veteran's hospital outside Paris, and then in the south of France, after an operation to remove one of his lungs. The title is best translated as "The Stroll" or "The Ramble." In her imagination, MacAvoy's narrator embarks on a lyrical search for her lover (pimp? Death itself?). Both the lover and the search are of monumental proportions, and *La ballade* features writing in which the author's command of the language seems total, with the text taking on the appearance of an irrefutable stylistic proof of concept:

> In this village that he frightened by putting on the airs of a fakir, old women and children pointed him out. In this other one he sowed the rye, irrigated the scrub, picked the vegetables, and harvested the grapes. Farther on, I hear him talked about as an untouchable, impenetrable mikado, who is supposed to have reserved a room in a luxury hotel for one night. He had the moon as a monocle and no luggage. Farther still, distrustful peasants tried to kill him with pitchforks; in a stream he laid traps, bathed, dried off on the bank, and seeing him so beautiful, the washerwomen stopped rinsing their laundry and, chirping, stood up, leaning again as though they did not want to see, caryatids suddenly surrounded by a farandole of crazed fauns, bent over by the weight of the erect poem.
>
> I know every location he chose to rest, every pond where he dipped his face. He avoided such and such a group of farms access to which was barred by mastiffs, he snuck in at night like a fox into hen houses to break the necks of badly guarded chickens, but my suffering pursues an uncatchable trade wind, a Tamerlane, the only visible aspect of which are the roofs torn away, the damage after his passage.
>
> I let myself fall on a bale of hay that has kept the shape of his body, a shape that for a moment I thought was on top of me. And it burned me. I hit the road again! "Anne, Anne, he is in the little wood," said the oak, "he is in that farm shed, in front of you . . ."

I fight wild hogs for potato peels, I too thread my way through henhouses, my stomach clenched from hunger, and I call you from the hilltops, from the steeples. The road is long. It leads to my grail under fiery skies, vehement dreams of nettles or hyacinths, to the rhythm of my step, which is a loving, regular, almost joyful rhythm. My love, the shepherd returning home for the winter Angelus, the kid in clogs playing in a puddle, the suspicious patrolman, the women chatting in front of the church, the horse thief, all have watched you leap over walls or run through the brush; the flowers too remember you and try to imitate your odor. (52–53)

A documentary from 1970 tells us that Patrick MacAvoy was a serious candidate that year for the Prix Goncourt, France's most important literary prize.[23] The film contains a short interview in which MacAvoy dismisses the prize as "commercial" and "petit bourgeois," and says that if he won it would mean he had written "a very bad book" In any case, he would refuse it, since he would refuse "rewards and punishments alike." His intransigent, militant stance was certainly a factor in why the literary world seems to have forgotten him despite the magnitude of his achievement in *La ballade*— and, in turn, perhaps the degree to which *La ballade* has been marginalized contributed to MacAvoy's decision to give up writing. More likely, this slim volume simply exhausted or fulfilled his literary project. That he has devoted himself in the intervening years to Indian classical music is no fluke: there, MacAvoy says he finds "the ideal balance between structure and improvisation." It is clear that his writing already sought that balance, and to a great extent found it.[24]

23. *Le Prix Goncourt* pourquoi pour qui? available online at http://www.ina.fr/art-et-culture/litterature/video/CPF10005685/le-prix-goncourt-pourquoi-pour-qui.fr.html
24. Speaking personally, I reconnected with Patrick MacAvoy after a forty-two year hiatus. We had been friends in Paris in 1968–69, and he had dropped completely out of sight after that. I eventually found him in 2012 thanks to the Internet and blind luck, combined with my need to inquire about the translation rights to *La ballade* and some of his poems. During our phone conversations and a later visit, it seemed as though

According to an October 2011 article in the newspaper *Sud Ouest*, about the sale of several Edouard MacAvoy paintings, his son, now known as Nala, had this to say: "My father's work languishes in purgatory." The same could be said of his own work, and to a lesser extent of the works of Nicolas Genka, Jean Sénac, and Françoise d'Eaubonne, all of whom deserve a wider audience, both in French and in translation.

---

no time had passed since we last met. Patrick remains perhaps the most compelling person I have ever known, a man who combines joie de vivre with the honesty of those who live without illusions. His physical ailments now interfere with the demands of the sarod. Thus he is considering a return to writing because he says he cannot live without creative activity.

CONTRIBUTORS

Luis Chitarroni was born in Buenos Aires in 1958. He is a writer, critic, and editor, and has to date published two novels, including *The No Variations*, and two collections of nonfiction and critical writing.

S. D. Chrostowska is the author of the novel *Permission*, and the critical volume *Literature on Trial: The Emergence of Critical Discourse in Germany, Poland & Russia, 1700–1800*. She is Assistant Professor of European Studies in the Department of Humanities at York University.

Thalia Field is a third generation Hyde Parker, attended lycėģe in France, and worked in theaters in France, Berlin and New York. Switching to fiction, she won the first John Hawkes Prize from Brown. Her collections include: *Point and Line, Incarnate: Story Material,* and *Bird Lovers, Backyard* (all New Directions) as well as a collaboration with french author/translator Abigail Lang, *A Prank of Georges* (Essay Press). A second collaboration, *Leave to Remain,* is underway. Thalia has written one full-length experiment in the novel, *Ululu (Clown Shrapnel)* (Coffee House) and is wrestling with the blissful irrationality of completing another.

John Griswold is an assistant professor in the MFA program at McNeese State University and the editor of the *McNeese Review*. He is the author of the novel *A Democracy of Ghosts* and of the nonfiction narrative *Herrin: The Brief History of an Infamous American City*. He lives in Lake Charles, Louisiana.

Lily Hoang is the author of *The Evolutionary Revolution, Changing, Parabola,* and *Unfinished: Stories Finished by Lily Hoang*. She serves as Prose Editor for Puerto del Sol. She teaches in the MFA program at New Mexico State University.

JACQUES HOUIS is a French Teacher at the Brearley School in New York City, as well as a literary translator, editor, and writer. *The Comic Romance*, his translation of Paul Scarron's 1651 seminal classic novel *Le Roman Comique*, was published by Alma Classics in 2012.

ANTONI JACH is a novelist, painter and playwright. He is the author of the novels *Napoleon's Double*, *The Weekly Card Game*, and *The Layers of the City*, a meditation on contemporary Paris, civilization, and barbarism. In addition, he is the author of a book of poetry, *An Erratic History* and two limited-edition artist's books: *Still River in the Numinous World* and the recently published, *Faded World: Fragments from the Description de l'Égypte*.

JACQUES JOUET was elected to the Oulipo in 1983. He is the author of more than sixty texts in a variety of genres—novels, poetry, plays, literary criticism, and short fiction—including the novels *Mountain R* (part of his *La République roman* cycle), *Savage*, *Upstaged*, and *My Beautiful Bus*, all published in English by Dalkey Archive Press.

BHANU KAPIL has written five books: *The Vertical Interrogation of Strangers* (Kelsey Street Press, 2001), *Incubation: a space for monsters* (Leon Works, 2006), *humanimal [a project for future children]* (Kelsey Street Press, 2009), *Schizophrene* (Nightboat Books, 2011) and *notes for a novel never written [a novel of the race riot]: Ban* (forthcoming: Nightboat Books, 2014). Her recent work and teaching has unfolded at the intersection of performance art and the novel. She teaches classes on anti-memoir, architecture and the animal at Naropa University. At Goddard College, she makes videos in a wintertime forest with Douglas Martin, on his phone.

WARREN MOTTE is Professor of French and Comparative Literature at the University of Colorado, Boulder. He has written several studies of contemporary French Literature, including *Fables of the Novel: French Fiction Since 1990*, *Small Worlds*, and *Fiction Now: The French Novel in the*

Twenty-First Century. Translator and editor of *Oulipo: A Primer of Potential Literature*, he also edited an issue of the journal *SubStance* dedicated to the work of Jacques Jouet, and is a contributing editor to *CONTEXT* magazine. His next book, *Mirror Gazing*, focusing on his collection of "mirror scenes" in fiction, will be published by Dalkey Archive Press in the spring of 2014.

GERALD MURNANE was born in Melbourne, Australia in 1939. He is the author of nine books of fiction, including *Barley Patch, Inland, The Plains,* and *Tamarisk Row,* as well as a collection of essays, *Invisible Yet Enduring Lilacs.* Murnane has been a recipient of the Patrick White Award and the Melbourne Prize. His most recent book is entitled *A History of Books.*

ADRIAN WEST's short fiction has been published in *McSweeney's, 3:AM,* and *Evergreen Review.* His numerous translations from German, Spanish, and Catalan can be found in *Fwriction, Intranslation, Words Without Borders,* and *Asymptote,* where he is also a contributing editor. His translations of Josef Winkler's novels *Natura Motra* and *When the Time Comes* were recently published by Contra Mundum. He lives in Philadelphia with the cinema critic Beatriz Leal Riesco.

TRANSLATORS

Sarah Denaci is from Doylestown, Pennsylvania. She is currently a student in the Masters in Creative Writing program at the Universidad Nacional de Tres de Febrero in Buenos Aires.

E. C. Gogolak is a journalist and translator living in New York City whose writing appears in publications including the *New York Times*, the *Village Voice*, and the *New York Observer*. She graduated from Brown University in 2012 with a BA in Comparative Literature and currently works for *The New Yorker*.

ACKNOWLEDGMENTS

Luis Chitarroni's "Five Silhouettes" consists of five sections from his "biographical" story collection *Siluetas*. © 1992, 2010 by Luis Chitarroni.

John Griswold's "Looking for Writers Beyond Their Work" is excerpted from *Pirates You Don't Know, and Other Adventures in the Examined Life: Collected Essays*, by John Griswold. Copyright © 2014 by John Griswold. Reprinted by permission of the University of Georgia Press.

Jacques Jouet's "Nine Suppositions Concerning *Bouvard and Pécuchet*" is excerpted from his *A supposer . . .* © 2007 by Jacques Jouet. Appears by permission of Éditions Nous.

BOOK REVIEWS

Thomas Pynchon. *Bleeding Edge*. Penguin Press, 2013. 477 pp. Cloth: $28.95.

Thomas Pynchon has continuously returned to those geographic spaces—the Zone in *Gravity's Rainbow*, the West in *Mason & Dixon*, Shambhala in *Against the Day*—that represent openness, innocence, and an infinity of possibilities faced with the inevitable process of rationalization, corruption, and control. In *Bleeding Edge* he offers two such spaces: twenty-first century Manhattan (of all places), where everything unique, quirky, and eccentric is being bludgeoned into conformity by an ideology of real-estate development; and the Deep Web, specifically a Second Life-type platform called DeepArcher, where hackers can escape our commodity-driven culture—for the moment. One wonders if this is Pynchon's most pessimistic take on our world, where the last refuges of innocence and possibility are a claustrophobic island and a virtual amusement park. Pynchon fans will find much that's familiar here: accounting detective Maxine Tarnow stumbling into a multi-tendrilled financial conspiracy, the outcome of which may be 9/11; Gabriel Ice, entrepreneurially evil dot-com mogul; Nicholas Windust, globetrotting Reagan administration and IMF thug; an enormous cast of computer geeks, Italian mobsters, rogue Russian secret police, old leftists, Jewish mothers, and others; a host of high- and pop-culture references; hilariously bad jokes the narrative goes many paragraphs out of its way for. Fans might be surprised not to find multiple narrative focalizations, complex leaps backward and forward in time, or excursions to exotic locales. In fact, this may be Pynchon's most straightforward novel, the narrative tied to Maxine's consciousness and to a chronological arc with 9/11 its apex, just as the setting is tied to Manhattan. However, straightforward doesn't mean simple. One point of the novel is to complicate the official narrative of 9/11, multiplying motives, participants, outcomes, and especially stories about the event, but unlike other Pynchon novels, this complication doesn't seem subversive or liberatory as much as it seems bitter and sad, a mourning for the loss of innocence. *Bleeding Edge* is poignant and funny, despairing and hopeful, bearing brilliant witness to the wound of the twenty-first century. [Robert L. McLaughlin]

László Krasznahorkai. *Satantango*. Trans. George Szirtes. New Directions, 2012/2013. 320 pp. Paper: $15.95.

Krasznahorkai's first novel (ca. 1985) draws us into a dismal, perpetually raining countryside reeking of human effluvia of a peculiarly disheartening sort. Its action, rising and falling back upon itself, underscores the dispatch of hope, the victory of fear haunting the depiction of each character's pathetic nature. As the precarious existence of an isolated, faded community in rural Hungary unfolds, its residents' anxieties, delusions, and desires collide in an infernal stasis. These wretched remnants of what was once a thriving cottage industry set on a country estate, now fallen into ruin, have no idea how to improve their lot, so they drink, whore, and grumble, invariably getting in each other's way in their sodden inanition, until word of a fabled leader's return from the dead inspires in some apprehension, in others hope. While awaiting this event, the villagers revel in a drunken dance, the tango of the title, which symbolizes their frustrations and speaks to their sense of perpetual betrayal. At length, when a sudden minor tragedy coincides with the arrival of the feared leader, it serves as an ideal opportunity for him to persuade his downtrodden followers that, with faith in him, in his oracular voice and steadfast vision, their eventual restoration, even return to prosperity lies within reach. Yes, comrades, there will be risks, but what is life without them? Years of petty jealousies, rivalries, even such semblance of security as remained in the quagmire of the villagers' dashed expectations—the dogged quotidian of their lives—fall of their own weight as the newly enlightened devotees gather their belongings to trek to the estate, awaiting deliverance in another dance of a decidedly different sort. Krasznahorkai's mordant voice sends up the squalor of these lives, imprisoned in the passage of time, in an unsettling fable of sardonic regret. [Michael Pinker]

Eric Lundgren. *The Facades*. Overlook Press, 2013. 224 pp. Cloth: $25.95.

Set in Trude, a thinly disguised substitute for St. Louis, *The Facades* is a very literary novel about a very literary place—a city where librarians take up actual arms against mayoral budget cuts, and a nursing home designed by an émigré Austrian architect includes a Robert Walser room. (Its inhabitants are required to write memoirs justifying their institutionalization.) In this sinister fading metropolis we meet one Sven Norberg, a man of little consequence; he narrates his inept search for his wife, Molly, the town's prize opera star, who never returned home from a rehearsal one evening, and yet is rumored (in acrostics in newspaper columns) to still be singing, somewhere. At the same time, the middle-aged man is dealing with his son's conversion to fundamentalism, and the fleshy attentions of a teenage baker, even while he lusts after—what else?—a bookshop owner. Nestled amid nods to Wittgenstein and Calvino are literal red herrings and games of Scrabble and the sense that the whole thing is based on some underlying Oulipo-style constraint (although I never found that suspicion distracting). It's also a Pynchonian tangle of conspiracies and arcane clues that at times recalls Auster's *City of Glass*: the town mall is an unsolved labyrinth, and—fittingly, given the book's title—nothing is as it seems. But lest this description make the whole thing sound too highfalutin or allusively "postmodern," rest assured that Lundgren's tricky Trude is his own creation, and that Norberg's dispirited search proves consistently moving and compelling. While the book is highly digressive, and arguably more scenario-driven than densely plotted (the chapter order sometimes feels arbitrary), it still qualifies as a page-turner for its overall sense of suspense, and the enviable confidence with which it's written. Every sentence interesting, it all adds up to a novel deeply in love with language and with literature. With *The Facades*, Lundgren takes his place alongside very fine company. [A D Jameson]

Amina Cain. *Creature*. Dorothy: A Publishing Project, 2013. 144 pp. Paper: $16.00.

Amina Cain's second book, *Creature*, is a collection of fourteen delicate stories about women on the precipice, women whose lives have been altered by past events—events not necessarily seen but felt, in the present, in this moment. Cain's prose captures the quiet present: its loneliness, the want for relief and release, the realness of consequences and desolation. "Like a day in the mouth, and me in it," Cain writes. But they are also stories about hope, small moments of respite that indicate potential enlightenment, Cain's creatures are learning and questioning: "So there is a web, but that web doesn't actually exist, and sometimes it is multiple. / Do you think you are walking around in a web?" The protagonists in *Creature* spin multiplicity. Often bearing a striking resemblance to Cain herself, her heroines are flawed creators, struck by the wonder of the now, survivors by intuition alone. "Together the rocks formed a micro-climate for plants that grew in the shade they made, and for animals who could also survive there, because of shade." So Amina Cain's characters survive in shadow, observing geography saunter discreetly by, in love and suffering the now. [Lily Hoang]

Laird Hunt. *Kind One*. Coffee House Press, 2012. 213 pp. Paper: $14.95.

This novel begins with an "Overture" that cuts the legs right out from under you, and it is as devastating a piece of writing as anything one is likely to find in contemporary literature. Laird Hunt conjures up a world where movement is most often vertical, either up or down, and where people dig graves for others who haven't yet died. We are in our very own heartland here, in Kentucky and Indiana, from the middle of the nineteenth century to the beginning of the twentieth, and it is a very tenebrous place indeed. Its currencies are crudely wielded force, oppression, cruelty, prejudice, and the joyless revenge that necessarily attends them. Suffering is endless and irremediable. Those who are called upon to bear that suffering will eventually inflict it on others in their turn. The protagonist is Ginny Lancaster, married at fourteen to a man who preferred her mother, widowed at twenty by a stroke that many will approve. Thereafter she is known as "Scary Sue," first because of her scars both visible and invisible, then because of the lesson she embodies in the minds of god-fearing folk. It is she who speaks for the most part, and her language is hieratic and incantational, as if her story were to be intoned, rather than merely spoken. For a world such as this one tests the power of mere speech. Individuals come back from the dead as if naturally here. Their bodies sprout supplemental mouths, the better to wail, and additional eyes, to gaze and accuse. Amputated limbs come back as well—but not necessarily to the people from whom they were severed in the first instance. Other specters wander through these pages. One thinks of Faulkner for the unblinking critique of American myth. Yet Gombrowicz also comes to mind, because of the absolute strangeness of things. *Kind One* can certainly be read as an account of where we've been, but one can also see in it a parable of where we are, right now, as we try to rid ourselves of some of the ghosts that haunt us. [Warren Motte]

John Kinsella. *Morpheus: A Bildungsroman: A Partially Back-Engineered and Reconstructed Novel*. BlazeVOX, 2013. 414 pp. Paper: $22.00.

Morpheus, its tertiary title informs us, is "partially back-engineered and reconstructed," meaning that the now well-known, fifty-year-old John Kinsella has here reassembled what was salvageable and otherwise completed a novel begun in high school, worked on at university, then abandoned, its pages dispersed, mislaid, or destroyed (appropriately, my copy came apart as I read). An amalgamation of narrative fragments, poems, quotations, scribbles, diagrams, playlets, dreams, Q & A, and more, *Morpheus* is, the author tells us in his preface, an attempt to "undo" literature. This undoing requires several hundred pages of bricolaged anamnesis—in the dual sense of psychiatric case history and reminiscence, the latter doubled insofar as the recalling necessitates remembering recollections decades ago. If Kinsella is his novel's great rememberer, his narrative consciousness is the often incoherent and self-indulgent Thomas Icarus Napoleon, an underappreciated young poet and polymath riddled with self-doubt and self-inflicted woes. Having dropped out of school and been kicked out by his parents, Thomas eventually finds himself institutionalized, his breakaway precipitating a sometimes acerb, sometimes giddy breakdown. Under such circumstances, what is delusion, what braggadocio, and what (fictional) fact is not always clear. Does Thomas drop acid? Is he a closet racist? Does he have sex with old men in the park, rob a bank, knock up the local druggist's wife? Does his friend Henry actually exist? "I fear I am trapped inside my reading and my note-taking," Thomas confides midway through his story, forgetting momentarily the tight snare of his delusional imagination. "I am culpable . . . I am accountable" (412), he cries two hundred pages later, this mea culpa an epiphany of sorts that perhaps adjudges his obsessive reading and writing—along with the self-inflating fantasies, the insane self-destructiveness, and the self-medicating— to have been unsuccessful attempts to erase or replace a so far disappointing life. Alas for Thomas, that life continues to prove unrewritable, for the past "always catches up" and finally trips him up. [Brooke Horvath]

Craig Foltz. *We Used To Be Everywhere*. Ugly Duckling Presse, 2013. 107 pp. Paper: $16.00.

The new collection by Craig Foltz, *We Used to Be Everywhere*, traces the boundary between fiction and prose poetry, using a somewhat Language-centered writing that is self-referential in places, identifying a slippery, indeterminate discourse. Foltz's prose takes its novel and sometimes startling juxtapositions at face value, so that the pleasures of these texts are to be found in the surfaces, in the author's facility with arresting details and imaginative incongruities, and in the strong musicality of the prose. In terms of tone, this collection is contemporary in its disconnected affect, with its strong sense of having been blitzed by the intensities of our milieu. However, because these "post" narratives are wryly humorous, the overall mode is initially more bemused than tragic. This is in the service of a thematics of absence/presence that registers with the reader as a displaced sensuousness, a longing for things here and then gone, manifested in a surfeit of the immediate. The writing also has the quality of being utterly unselfconscious, with these texts generating a strong sense of an author/narrator as *persona*. It's a curious effect, the way identity is both foregrounded and problematized throughout the text by the focus on surface detail, and it does much to strengthen the tone overall. And the tone becomes increasingly dark as the collection continues, as the refusal of interiority, and the displacement of the subject into every scenario, every image, creates an ever-greater sense of unease. If there is a narrative momentum to the collection, it involves the gradual erosion of ironic detachment, the loss of a carefully constructed sense of self. [Gary Lain]

Yuri Rytkheu. *The Chukchi Bible*. Trans. Ilona Yazhbin Chavasse. Archipelago Books, 2011. 362 pp. Paper: $16.00.

In this account of the history of his people and their way of life from their remote origins to the mid-twentieth century, Rytkheu mingles myth, history, and imaginative recreation of individual lives to achieve a fascinating synthesis. The Chukchi, or as they call themselves, the Luoravetlan, live in far northeastern Siberia near the Bering Strait. For centuries almost totally isolated from the rest of the world, they hunted whales, walruses, and seals, and herded reindeer after those creatures were introduced from the west. Mastering their harsh environment, they created a rich tradition that conveyed their respect for and dependence on what nature afforded. Rytkheu, a descendant of shamans, follows his ancestral line as gradually they meet and are caught up by incursions from the outside world—first Russian, then American—as commercial whaling and fur trading overwhelm the subtle arts and seasonal rituals sustaining the cultures of the northern latitudes. As he relates the careers of several of his ancestors, major figures in their small community, by telling their stories through their own eyes, Rytkheu is no longer a historian and anthropologist, but a remarkable storyteller. His forbears display how the Luoravetlan maintained their cherished customs until the Tangitans, white people, began to arrive. In the case of Mletkin, the last shaman, Rytkheu's grandfather, whose life from cradle to grave comprises the latter two-thirds of the book and whose adventurous spirit and love of learning ultimately transported him to America, the conflict between tradition and its inexorable uprooting palpably lives. For despite Mletkin's efforts to preserve the old ways upon his return to Uelen, the empire builders of the nascent Soviet Union prove too determined, too powerful to withstand. Rytkheu's portrayal of his people's ancient and new legends, a work of art in the guise of a chronicle, is mesmerizing. [Michael Pinker]

Paula Bomer. *Inside Madeleine*. Soho Press, 2014. 240 pp. Paper: $16.00.

Dynamite and obscene, Paula Bomer's third book *Inside Madeleine* is a collection unapologetic stories. They are stories of feminine defiance without shame. In an increasingly politically correct word, Bomer refuses, screams *no*, ignores all the warning shots. But where the author rejects, her characters succumb, boldly, like the hideous can also be fragile grace. The collection is bookended with two stories, "Eye Socket Girls" and the eponymous "Inside Madeleine"—the latter arguably a novella. Inside these stories: a landscape of the hospital made romantic: girls with anorexia, bodies made effulgent from lack, a world where the skeleton is a beauty mark, like Marilyn's mole. The corporeal is a site for ugliness, "Her armpits and inner thighs began smelling musty like a dirty drain in a bathtub. They stunk like brown hay, like a sink full of dirty pots. Her crotch smelled of lukewarm shrimp, salty and damp." The protagonists in Bomer's stories are girls coming into sexuality, and although they are only still learning, they allow the process of discovery to swan them into unabashed sluts, begging boys and men alike to devour their cunts, the erudition of pleasure. These girls engender their own objectivization as a mode of understanding: "Her right nipple burst, popped out like a tight wad of bubble gum, a pink swelling that felt itchy. She scratched it relentlessly." But even more resonant and true than their transformation into tramps is the cruelty of girlhood—the way girls badger and despise each other under the artifice of a smile. Friendship is only potent in the moment, and it is just as quickly abandoned—asunder—as it is formed. *Inside Madeleine* is an honest and urgent collection, one that examines girlhood, a yearning to move beyond Midwestern trashiness, domesticity all grown up and in the very real of the contemporary. [Lily Hoang]

Jeff Jackson. *Mira Corpora*. Two Dollar Radio, 2013. Paper: $16.00.

Mira Corpora, the visceral debut novel of playwright Jeff Jackson, is a work of startling intensity and punk anguish. More a hallucinatory collage or mix tape than traditional coming-of-age tale, the book is based on journals Jackson kept in his youth, according to an author's note. While we should assume, at the very least, that the novel represents a free and revisionist honing, Jackson's use of aporia and contradiction allows him to harness the emotional power of the diary. On one level we have the story of an abused child struggling to find a way out—but Jackson finds an oneiric intensity in this familiar narrative, which he portrays not a progressive series of self-realizations but a series of advances and retreats, dislocations, erasures. "I was on a need-to-know basis with myself," says the narrator, Jeff, and later: "The body is mine, technically speaking." In one memorable scene, a teenage oracle tells Jeff's fortune, producing only a blank sheet, leaving "a coastline of torn paper that clings to the margins of her notebook." Other images of blankness and annulment recur: graffiti images of a crossed-out king's crown, rumors of a reclusive rocker with a bitten-off tongue. Deconstructing a baby doll, Jeff thinks, "it's as if the poor creature was made to be dismembered." Numbed by his own dreadful experience, Jeff can barely understand his own situation, let alone control it, and he often observes his life as if it were a bewildering art film. However, the dangers of his situation are all too real, as proven by the menacing Gert-Jan, a pimp and dealer who poses as Jeff's "guardian" and stalks him toward the novel's conclusion. Childhood is a wilderness in *Mira Corpora*, which begins and ends in the woods, where Jeff must ultimately confront his mother's estate (in every sense of the word). Jackson handles his difficult material with verbal prowess and the eye of a video artist, quoting Eluard, Blanchot, and the Mekons along the way. He averts melodrama by acknowledging the weird and hard truths about growing up that other bildungsromans avoid. [Eric Lundgren]

Cyprian Norwid. *Poems*. Trans. Danuta Borchardt with Agata Brajerska-Mazur. Archipelago Books, 2011. 140 pp. Paper: $16.00.

The Polish poet Cyprian Norwid (1921–1883) looked like a character out of Dostoyevsky. Ridiculed when not ignored, he died, lovelorn and tubercular, weeping in a Paris charity hospital. His major collection, *Vade-Mecum*, was not published until 1953, but since then he has slowly been taking his place as one of the major poets of the nineteenth century. He has a reputation (often overstated) for difficulty—"every poem has to be read syllable by syllable ten times over," observed the nineteenth-century critic Józef Tokarzewicz—and critics are still trying to decide if he was a tardy Neo-Classicist, a post-Romantic, a Parnassian pre-Symbolist, or a precocious modernist. He described himself as "the last one in the world of poetry, the one who came late." What is clear is that Norwid was an original. His use of punctuation, for example, is not intent on making the relation of sentence parts clear but on scoring the poems, indicating silences and hesitations, as in this line from "Fatum": "Will, man, swerve?" He was a Christian, a nationalist, an autodidact, an eccentric, a political exile, and a bohemian. The poems in this new collection are ably translated, which is to say they read like poetry in their English rendering, the nuances and ambiguities firmly in place. The lyrics by which the poet is best remembered—"Chopin's

Grand Piano," "To Bem's Memory," "Marionettes"—are included. (It should be noted that of the forty-three poems in what is now the third collection of Norwid in translation, twenty-five also appear in Adam Czerniawski's 2004 *Selected Poems of Cyprian Norwid*.) Whether mocking the phoniness of polite society or brooding on exile, Norwid's poems are perhaps less visionary than the means of conjuring elusive visions in the reader. However difficult these poems may sometimes be, they are worth the effort. [Brooke Horvath]

Xu Bing. *Book from the Ground*. MIT Press, 2014. 112 pp. Cloth: $24.95

Xu Bing is a prominent Chinese painter who, in the late 1980s, published *Book from the Sky*, an illegible text written with thousands of characters of made-up, pseudo-Mandarin. Almost twenty-five years later, Xu has reverse tacked semantically with a graphic novel composed of emoticons, numerals, corporate logos, standardized signs, mathematical operators, and cartoon stick figures. It has no words, yet tells the story of twenty-four hours in the life of a white-collar, urbanite bachelor who is, visually, a twin of the guy you see on the door of men's rooms everywhere—dot for a head, shoulders square, circular nubs for his hands and feet. Mr. Black (as the protagonist is referred to in the book's meta-book, *The Book about Xu Bing's Book from the Ground*), is part Dilbert, part Little Tramp, part "Buddy Boy" Baxter. He's romantic but obedient. Skeptical but loyal. He gets excited to see he's got e-mail. He plays video games when he can't fall asleep. He fantasizes about sex with the strangers that pass him in the hallway And he has issues with constipation. He's the twenty-first-century grandchild of all those brow-furrowed proletarians at the center of such worldess, woodcut, proto-graphic-novels as *Passionate Journey* by Frans Masereel or *Gods' Man* by Lynd Ward. That Mr. Black can be so thoroughly portrayed via a universal pictographic rebus is proof, perhaps, that Xu is onto something, or that the average white-collar bureaucrat just isn't that deep inside, or that a Bible-grade rending-apart of civilization is at hand. Though if at times the story feels simple and silly (as when Mr. Black extinguishes his burning eggs and bacon with a cupful of hot coffee), you can't help but think that an infant's first words are also simple and silly. Reading this book makes you feel as though you're looking through a window to the future, and while that future may be sad and techno-alienated and irrevocably urban, it is, alas, the place to where each of us is headed. [Tim Peters]

BOOKS RECEIVED

Appel, Jacob M. *The Biology of Luck.* Elephant Rock Books, 2013. Paper: $16.00. (F)

Arias-Misson, Alain. *Tintin Meet the Dragon Queen in The Return of the Maya to Manhattan.* Black Scat Books, 2013. Paper: $16.95. (F)

Bell, Eleanor, and Linda Gunn, eds. *The Scottish Sixties. Reading, Rebellion, Revolution?* Rodopi, 2013. Paper: €67.00. (F)

Blanqui, Louis-Auguste. *Eternity by the Stars. An Astronomical Hypothesis.* Trans. Frank Chouraqui. Contra Mundum Press, 2013. Paper: $20.00. (F)

Branscum, John, and Wayne Thomas, eds. *Red Holler. Contemporary Appalachian Literature.* Sarabande Books, 2013, Paper: $16.95. (F)

Bronk, Jerry. *Belinda's Law.* Trafford Publishing, 2013. Paper: $13.96. (F)

Brown, Ian. *Scottish Theatre: Diversity, Language, Continuity.* Rodopi, 2013. Paper: $74.25. (F)

Buckeye, Robert. *Waiting in the Rain for the Last Streetcar.* Amandla Publishing, 2013. Paper: $15.00. (F)

Cage, Patricia. *Justice for #997543.* Tigress Publishing, 2012. Paper: $14.95. (F)

Cărtărescu, Mircea. *Blinding.* Trans. Sean Cotter. Archipelago Books, 2013. Paper: $22.00. (F)

Césaire, Aimé. *Return to My Native Land.* Trans. John Berger and Anna Bostock. Archipelago, 2014. Paper: $16.00. (P)

Chapman, Jennie. *Plotting Apocalypse: Reading, Agency, and Identity in the* Left Behind *Series.* University Press of Mississippi, 2013. Cloth: $55.00. (F)

Corral, Will H., and Juan E. De Castro, Nicholas Birns, eds. *The Contemporary Spanish-American Novel.* Bloomsbury, 2013. Paper: $39.95. (F)

Crace, Jim. *Harvest: A Novel.* Vintage Books, 2013. Paper: $15.00. (F)

Crosthwaithe, Luis Humberto. *Out of Their Minds.* Trans. John William Byrd. Cinco Puntos Press, 2013. Paper: $14.95. (F)

Eaglestone, Robert, and Martin McQuillan, eds. *Salman Rushdie.* Bloomsbury, 2013. Cloth: $90.00. (F)

Edwards-Stout, Kergan. *Gifts Not Yet Given (and Other Tales of the Holidays)*. Circumspect Press, 2013. Paper: $15.99. (F)

Fagunwa, D. O. *Forest of a Thousand Daemons. A Hunter's Saga*. Trans. Wole Soyinka. City Lights Books, 2013. Paper: $14.95. (F)

Ferry, Jean. *The Conductor and Other Tales*. Trans. Edward Gauvin. Wakefield Press, 2013. Paper: $13.95. (F)

Freeman, Brian. *The Cold Nowhere*. Quercus Publishing, 2014. Cloth: $24.95. (F)

Friedman, Jason K. *Fire Year: Stories*. Sarabande, 2013. Paper: $15.95. (F)

Fuller, Thomas. *Monsieur Ambivalence: A Post-Literate Fable*. IF SF Publishing, 2013. Paper: $15.00. (F)

Germanà, Monica, and Emily Horton, eds. *Ali Smith*. Bloomsbury, 2013. Cloth: $90.00. (F)

Godbersen, Anna. *The Blonde: A Novel*. Weinstein Books, 2014. Cloth: $29.00. (F)

Graves, Robert. *The White Goddess*. Farrar, Straus & Giroux, 2013. Paper: $18.00. (F)

Groes, Sebastian, ed. *Ian McEwan*. Bloomsbury, 2013. Paper: $27.95. (F)

Harryman, Carla. *W—/M—*. SplitLevel Texts, 2013. Paper: $12.00. (P)

Hrabal, Bohumil. *Harlequin's Millions*. Trans. Stacey Knecht. Archipelago Books, 2013. Paper: $18.00. (F)

Jeppesen, Travis. *The Suiciders*. Semiotext(e), 2013. Paper: $16.95. (F)

Katz, Steven. *The Compleat Memoirrhoids*. Starcherone Books, 2013. Cloth: $23.00. (NF)

Lewitscharoff, Sibylle. *Apostoloff*. Trans. Katy Derbyshire. University of Chicago Press, 2013. Cloth: $21.00. (F)

Luiselli, Valeria. *Faces in the Crowd*. Trans. Christina MacSweeney. Coffee House Press, 2014. Paper: $15.95. (F)

Luiselli, Valeria. *Sidewalks*. Trans. Christina MacSweeney. Coffee House Press, 2014. Paper: $15.95. (F)

Mansfield, Melody. *A Bug Collection*. Red Hen Press, 2013. Paper: $15.95. (F)

Merkner, Christopher. *The Rise & Fall of the Scandamerican Domestic*. Coffee House Press, 2014. Paper: $15.95. (F)

Mikesch, Elizabeth. *Niceties: Aural Ardor, Pardon Me*. Calamari Press, 2014. Paper: $12.00. (F)

Mitchell, Kaye, ed. *Sarah Waters*. Bloomsbury, 2013. Cloth: $100.00. (F)

Orlan, Pierre Mac. *A Handbook for the Perfect Adventurer*. Trans. Napoleon Jeffries. Wakefield Press, 2013. Paper: $12.95. (F)

Pava, Sergio De La. *Personae*. University of Chicago Press, 2013. Paper: $17.00. (F)

Perec, Georges, et al. *Georges Perec and the Oulipo: Winter Journeys*. Atlas Press, 2013. Cloth: $34.00. (F)

Petrocelli, William. *The Circle of Thirteen: A Novel*. Turner Publishing Company, 2013. Cloth: $26.95. (F)

Pizer, Donald. *Toward a Modernist Style: John Dos Passos*. Bloomsbury, 2013. Cloth: $120.00. (F)

Pritchard, Melissa. *Palmerino*. Bellevue Literary Press, 2014. Paper: $14.95. (F)

Schwartz, Howard. *The Library of Dreams: New & Selected Poems 1965-2013*. BkMk Press, 2013. Paper: $15.95. (P)

Schwartz, Jason. *John the Posthumous*. OR Books, 2013. Paper: $17.00. (F)

Segura, Mauricio. *Eucalyptus*. Trans. Donald Winkler. Biblioasis, 2013. Paper: $15.95. (F)

Spahr, Juliana, and David Buuck. *An Army of Lovers*. City Lights Publishers, 2013. Paper: $13.95. (F)

Steinmetz, Andrew. *This Great Escape. The Case of Michael Paryla*. Biblioasis, 2013. Paper: $16.95. (F)

Stevenson, Wade. *The Electric Affinities*. BlazeVOX [books], 2014. Paper: $18.00. (F)

Stockenström, Wilma. *The Expedition to the Baobab Tree*. Archipelago Books, 2013. Paper: $18.00. (F)

Szentkuthy, Miklós. *Towards the One and Only Metaphor*. Contra Mundum Press, 2013. Paper: $22.00. (F)

Washburn, Frances. *The Red Bird Al-Indian Traveling Band*. University of Arizona Press, 2014. Paper: $16.95. (F)

Winkler, Josef. *When the Time Comes*. Trans. Adrian West. Contra Mundum Press, 2013. Paper: $16.00. (F)

Yamashita, Karen Tei. *Anime Wong: Fictions of Performance*. Coffee House Press, 2014. Paper: $19.95. (F)

ANNUAL INDEX FOR VOLUME XXXIII

Contributors

Améry, Jean. "From *Charles Bovary, Country Doctor*," 2: 11–19.

Bock, Raymond. "From *Atavisms*," 1: 11–21.

Brooke, D. E. "Translator's Introduction to *A Sentimental Novel*," 1: 131–135.

Chevillard, Eric. "From *The Author and Me*," 2: 20–31.

Chitarroni, Luis. "Five Silhouettes," 3: 51–65.

Chrostowska, S. D. "Five Stories," 1: 22–35.

————. "Seven and a Half Studies," 3: 66–86.

Cox, Jack. "From *Dodge Rose*," 1: 36–45.

Dvoryanova, Emiliya. "From *Concerto for a Sentence*," 1: 46–51.

Field, Thalia. "Irrationality, Situations, and Novels of Inquiry," 3: 94–106.

Gál, Róbert. "From *On Wing*," 1: 52–55.

Gavarry, Gérard. "From *Allada* and *Experience of Edward Lee, Versailles*," 2: 32–48.

Goytisolo, Luis. "From *Antagony*," 2: 49–75.

Grill, Evelyn. "From *The Antwerp Testament*," 2: 76–86.

Griswold, John. "Looking for Writers Beyond Their Work," 3: 41–50.

Hoang, Lily. "The Colon," 3: 121–123.

von Hofmannsthal, Hugo. "From 'A Letter,'" 2: 87–96.

Houis, Jacques. "Transgressive Autofictions," 3: 135–156.

Jach, Antoni. "An Interview with Gerald Murnane," 3: 11–40.

Jouet, Jacuqes. "Nine Suppositions Concerning *Bouvard and Pécuchet*," 3: 87–93.

Kapil, Bhanu. "The Colon," 3: 121–123.

Kleeberg, Michael. "From *A Garden in the North*," 2: 97–103.

Koeppen, Wolfgang. "From *Youth*," 1: 56–63.

Kofler, Werner. "From *At the Writing Desk*," 1: 64–71.

Laederach, Jürg. "From *The Whole Of Life*," 1: 72–79.

Levé, Edouard. "From *Works*," 1: 80–87.

Malouf, Melissa. "From *More Than You Know*," 1: 88–94.

Machado De Assis, Joaquim Maria. "From *Selected Stories*," 1: 95–104.

Medina, Susana. "From *Philosophical Toys*," 1: 105–115.

Mirbeau, Octave. "From 'The Death of Balzac,'" 2: 104–118.

Motte, Warren. "Margins and Mirrors," 3: 107–120.

Pittler, Andreas. "From *Inspector Bronstein and the Coup d'état: Tacheles 1934*," 2: 119–141.

Radvilavičiūtė, Giedra. "The Problems of the Near East," 1: 116–124.

Renouard, Madeleine. "From *Barbara Wright: Translation as Art*," 1: 125–130.

Robbe-Grillet, Alain. "From *A Sentimental Novel*," 1: 136–144.

Saiko, George. "From *On the Raft*," 2: 142–152.

Schrott, Raoul. "From *The Sex of the Angel—The Heaven of the Saints: A Breviary*," 2: 153–167.

Snijders, A. L. "Banana," 2: 168–171.

Sperl, Dieter. "From *Unintentional*," 2: 172–182.

Tsepeneag, Dumitru. "From *Waiting: Stories*," 1: 145–153.

West, Adrian. "The Fragile Shelter of the Declarative: on Edouard Levé," 3: 124–134.

Books Reviewed

Ashley, Robert. *Atalanta (Acts of God)*, 2: 194. (A D Jameson)

Blackwell, Gabriel. *Critique of Pure Reason*, 2: 195–196. (Greg Gerke)

Breckenridge, Donald, ed. *The Brooklyn Rail Fiction Anthology 2*, 1: 176–177. (Jill Magi)

Bomer, Paula. *Inside Madeleine*, 3: 169–170. (Lily Hoang)

Cain, Amina. *Creature*, 3: 165. (Lily Hoang)

Callahan, Jonathan. *The Consummation of Dirk*, 2: 195. (Levi Teal)

Chevillard, Éric. *Prehistoric Times*, 1: 172. (James Crossley)

Clabough, Casey. *George Garrett: A Critical Biography*, 2: 199. (Nicholas Birns)

Corin, Lucy. *One Hundred Apocalypses (and other apocalypses)*, 1: 171. (Brendan Riley)

Couto, Mia. *The Tuner of Silences*, 1: 167. (Brendan Riley)

Edwards, Ken. *Down with Beauty*, 1: 173. (Joseph Dewey)

Foltz, Craig. *We Used To Be Everywhere*, 3: 167–168. (Gary Lain)

Forrest, Tara, ed. Alexander Kluge: *Raw Materials for the Imagination*, 2: 200–201. (Karen Mauk)

Gorodischer, Angélica. *Trafalgar*, 1: 166. (Pedro Ponce)

Hemon, Aleksandar. *The Book of My Lives*, 1: 160–161. (James Crossley)

Hilst, Hilda. *The Obscene Madame D.*, 1: 168. (Rhett McNeil)

Hogan, Desmond. *The Ikon Maker*, 1: 175–176. (Thomas McGonigle)

Howe, Susan. *Sorting Facts: or, Nineteen Ways of Looking at Marker*, 2: 197–198. (David Seed)

Hunt, Laird. *Kind One*, 3: 165–166 (Warren Motte)

Ibrahim, Sonallah. *That Smell and Notes from Prison*, 1: 174–175. (Stephen Fisk)

Jackson, Jeff. *Mira Corpora*, 3: 170–171. (Eric Lundgren)

Jergović, Miljenko. *Mama Leone*, 2: 196–197. (Trevor Laurence Jockims)

Kadare, Ismail. *The Fall of the Stone City*, 2: 191–192. (Brooke Horvath)

Kasischke, Laura. *If a Stranger Approaches You*, 1: 174. (Levi Teal)

Kinsella, John. *Morpheus*, 3: 166–167. (Brooke Horvath)

Kluge, Alexander, and Gerhard Richter. *December: 39 Stories, 39 Pictures*, 2: 200–201. (Karen Mauk)

Knausgaard, Karl Ove. *My Struggle Book Two: A Man in Love*, 1: 163. (Jeff Bursey)

Krasznahorkai, László. *Satantango*, 3: 163. (Michael Pinker)

Koeppen, Wolfgang. *Journey through America*, 1: 177–178. (Nicholas Birns)

Lundgren, Eric. *The Facades*, 3: 164. (A D Jameson)

Marinkovic, Ranko. *Cyclops*, 1: 165. (Michael Pinker)

Norwid, Cyprian. *Poems*, 3: 171–172. (Brooke Horvath)

Perec, Georges. *La Boutique Obscure: 124 Dreams*, 1: 159–160. (Warren Motte)

Pynchon, Thomas. *Bleeding Edge*, 3: 162 [Robert L. McLaughlin]

Rytkheu, Yuri. *The Chukchi Bible*, 3: 168–169. (Michael Pinker)

Sarduy, Severo. *Firefly*, 2: 190–191. (Rhett McNeil)

Schwob, Marcel. *The Book of Monelle*, 1: 162–163. (David Cozy)

Simon, Christoph. *Zbinden's Progress*, 2: 192–193. (D. Quentin Miller)

Szentkuthy, Miklós. *Marginalia on Casanova: St. Orpheus Breviary, Vol. I*, 1: 169.

Tavares, Gonçalo M. *The Neighborhood*, 1: 161–162. (Rhett McNeil)

Tawada, Yoko. *The Bridegroom Was a Dog*, 1: 164. (Peter Grandbois)

Tsypkin, Leonid. *The Bridge Over the Neroch and Other Works*, 1: 170. (Michael Pinker)

Whalen, Tom. *The President in Her Towers*, 2: 193. (Gary Lain)

Xu Bing. *Book from the Ground*, 3: 172–173. (Tim Peters)

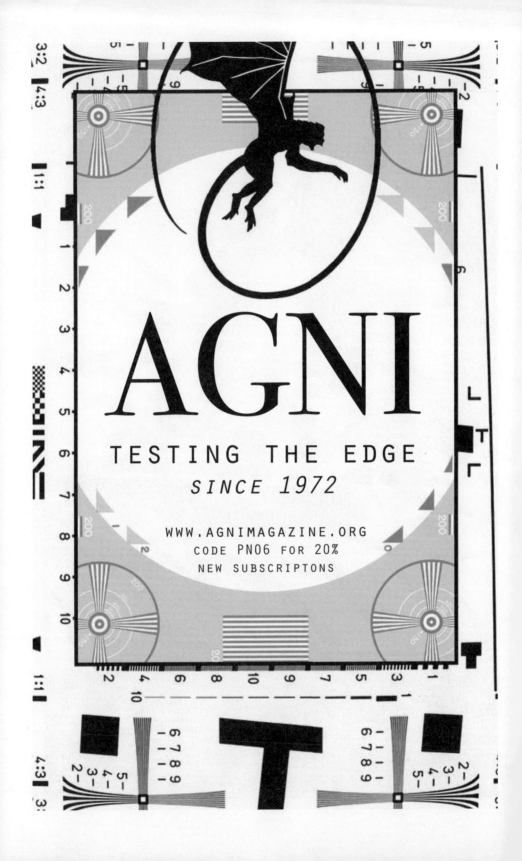

AGNI

TESTING THE EDGE
SINCE 1972

WWW.AGNIMAGAZINE.ORG
CODE PN06 FOR 20%
NEW SUBSCRIPTONS

NOON

A LITERARY ANNUAL

1324 LEXINGTON AVENUE   PMB 298   NEW YORK NY 10128

EDITION PRICE $12 DOMESTIC $17 FOREIGN

DELILLO FIEDLER GASS PYNCHON
University of Delaware Press
Collections on Contemporary Masters

UNDERWORDS
Perspectives on Don DeLillo's *Underworld*

Edited by Joseph Dewey, Steven G. Kellman, and Irving Malin

Essays by Jackson R. Bryer, David Cowart, Kathleen Fitzpatrick, Joanne Gass, Paul Gleason, Donald J. Greiner, Robert McMinn, Thomas Myers, Ira Nadel, Carl Ostrowski, Timothy L. Parrish, Marc Singer, and David Yetter

$39.50

LESLIE FIEDLER AND AMERICAN CULTURE

Edited by Steven G. Kellman and Irving Malin

Essays by John Barth, Robert Boyers, James M. Cox, Joseph Dewey, R.H.W. Dillard, Geoffrey Green, Irving Feldman, Leslie Fiedler, Susan Gubar, Jay L. Halio, Brooke Horvath, David Ketterer, R.W.B. Lewis, Sanford Pinsker, Harold Schechter, Daniel Schwarz, David R. Slavitt, Daniel Walden, and Mark Royden Winchell

$36.50

INTO *THE TUNNEL*
Readings of Gass's Novel

Edited by Steven G. Kellman and Irving Malin

Essays by Rebecca Goldstein, Donald J. Greiner, Brooke Horvath, Marcus Klein, Jerome Klinkowitz, Paul Maliszewski, James McCourt, Arthur Saltzman, Susan Stewart, and Heide Ziegler

$35.00

PYNCHON AND *MASON & DIXON*

Edited by Brooke Horvath and Irving Malin

Essays by Jeff Baker, Joseph Dewey, Bernard Duyfhuizen, David Foreman, Donald J. Greiner, Brian McHale, Clifford S. Mead, Arthur Saltzman, Thomas H. Schaub, David Seed, and Victor Strandberg

$39.50

ORDER FROM ASSOCIATED UNIVERSITY PRESSES
2010 Eastpark Blvd., Cranbury, New Jersey 08512
PH 609-655-4770   FAX 609-655-8366   E-mail AUP440@ aol.com

Dalkey Archive
Scholarly Series

Available Now

Surface Tension
JULIE CARR

Approaching Disappearance
ANNE MCCONNELL

Robert Coover & the Generosity of the Page
STÉPHANE VANDERHAEGHE

Critical Dictionary of Mexican Literature
(1955–2010)
CHRISTOPHER DOMÍNGUEZ MICHAEL

Iranian Writers Uncensored:
Freedom, Democracy, and the Word in Contemporary Iran
SHIVA RAHBARAN

Pop Poetics
Reframing Joe Brainard
ANDY FITCH

Dumitru Tsepeneag and the Canon of
Alternative Literature
LAURA PAVEL

This Is Not a Tragedy:
The Works of David Markson
FRANÇOISE PALLEAU-PAPIN

The Birth of Death and Other Comedies:
The Novels of Russell H. Greenan
TOM WHALEN

When Blackness Rhymes with Blackness
ROWAN RICARDO PHILLIPS

A Community Writing Itself:
Conversations with Vanguard Writers of the Bay Area
SARAH ROSENTHAL, ED.

The Subversive Scribe:
Translating Latin American Fiction
SUZANNE JILL LEVINE

Taking Dante Gabriel Rossetti, William Morris, and Gerard Manley Hopkins as its primary subjects, *Surface Tension* reveals how these later Victorian poets repeatedly imagine the aesthetics of their historical moment—charged, variegated, intensely focused—as capable of birthing a new, and newly redemptive, culture. Turning to contemporary experimental poets and theorists of poetry, such as Andrew Joron, Lisa Robertson, Christopher Nealon, and Joan Retallack, it goes on to reveal how our own poetry's fascination with complex surfaces and imagined social transformation has deep and under-recognized ties to Victorian concepts. *Surface Tension* offers new insights into the debt we owe to the most radical of the Victorians while yielding new understandings of how late Victorian poetry, even when least explicitly political, engages and often re-envisions the period's pressing anxieties about progress, decadence, and revolution.

Surface Tension

JULIE CARR

Dalkey Archive Scholarly Series
Literary Criticism
$35.00 / paper
ISBN: 978-1-56478-809-2

Julie Carr is the author of four books of poetry, *Mead: An Epithalamion*, *Equivocal*, *100 Notes Violence* (winner of the Sawtooth Award), and *Sarah—Of Fragments and Lines* (a National Poetry Series selection). She is an associate professor of poetry and poetics at the University of Colorado in Boulder and is the co-publisher, with Tim Roberts, of Counterpath Press.

Maurice Blanchot (1907–2003), one of the most influential figures of twentieth-century French literature, produced a wide variety of essays and fictions that reflect on the complexities of literary work. His description of writing continually returns to a number of themes, such as solitude, passivity, indifference, anonymity, and absence—forces confronting the writer, but also the reader, the text itself, and the relations between the three. For Blanchot, literature involves a movement toward disappearance, where one risks the loss of self; but such a sacrifice, says Blanchot, is inherent in the act of writing. *Approaching Disappearance* explores the question of disappearance in Blanchot's critical work and then turns to five narratives that offer a unique reflection on the threat of disappearance and the demands of literature—work by Franz Kafka, Jorge Luis Borges, Louis-René des Forêts, and Nathalie Sarraute.

Approaching Disappearance

ANNE MCCONNELL

ANNE MCCONNELL

APPROACHING
DISAPPEARANCE

"*Approaching Disappearance* is an invigorating and intellectually mobile piece of work, one that focuses boldly on the anxieties of contemporary literature, without compromise or appeal to easy orthodoxy." —Warren Motte

Dalkey Archive Scholarly Series
Literary Criticism
$34.95 / paper
ISBN: 978-1-56478-808-5

Anne McConnell is an Assistant Professor in the English Department at West Virginia State University. She completed her graduate work in Comparative Literature at the University of Colorado at Boulder in 2006, specializing in twentieth-century European and Hispanic literature and literary theory. She currently teaches world literature, literary criticism, and writing at West Virginia State University.

Robert Coover and the Generosity of the Page is an unconventional study of Robert Coover's work from his early masterpiece *The Origin of the Brunists* (1966) to the recent *Noir* (2010). Written in the second person, it offers a self-reflexive investigation into the ways in which Coover's stories often challenge the reader to resist the conventions of sense-making and even literary criticism. By portraying characters lost in surroundings they often fail to grasp, Coover's work playfully enacts a "(melo)drama of cognition" that mirrors the reader's own desire to interpret and make sense of texts in unequivocal ways. This tendency in Coover's writing is indicative of a larger refusal of the ready-made, of the once-and-for-all or the authoritative, celebrating instead, in its generosity, the widening of possibilities—thus inevitably forcing the reader-critic to acknowledge the arbitrariness and artificiality of her responses.

STÉPHANE VANDERHAEGHE

ROBERT COOVER

&

THE GENEROSITY OF THE PAGE

Robert Coover & the Generosity of the Page

STÉPHANE VANDERHAEGHE

Dalkey Archive Scholarly Series
Cultural Studies
$34.95 / paper
ISBN: 978-1-56478-807-8

Stéphane Vanderhaeghe is Associate Professor at the University of Cergy-Pontoise, France, where he teaches American literature. His research focuses on contemporary, avant-garde writers and he has published essays on Robert Coover, Ben Marcus, and Shelley Jackson.

The *Critical Dictionary of Mexican Literature (1955-2010)* is both a personal anthology and a highly subjective and unscientific reference work, marrying the often acerbic, always poetic reviews and essays written on Mexican literature by renowned critic Christopher Domínguez Michael over the past thirty years to the quixotic ideal of a comprehensive dictionary of Mexico's recent literary history. With well over 150 entries, the *Dictionary* both introduces and interrogates the work of novelists, poets, essayists, and journalists working in Mexico between 1955 (date of the publication of Juan Rulfo's watershed Mexican Revolution novel *Pedro Páramo*) and the present day.

Critical Dictionary of Mexican Literature

(1955–2010)

CHRISTOPHER DOMÍNGUEZ MICHAEL
TRANSLATION BY
LISA DILLMAN

Dalkey Archive Scholarly Series
Literary Criticism
$29.00 / paper
ISBN: 978-1-56478-606-7

Christopher Domínguez Michael was born in Mexico City in 1962. He is a literary critic, historian of ideas, and novelist. He's a contributor to such prestigious periodicals as *Vuelta*, *Letras Libres*, and the literary supplement of the newspaper *Reforma*. His biography *Vida de Fray Servando* was awarded the Xavier Villaurrutia Prize in 2004, and one of his books on literary criticism (*La sabiduría sin promesa*) was awarded the international prize of the Art Circle of Santiago de Chile in 2009.

As poet Mohammad Hoghooghi says, "[Writing] constitutes resistance. Because, in any age, the poet has been a protestor of a kind; resisting the thought-molds of the day. However, this protest might be political, it might be social, or it might even be philosophical. At any rate, the artist is at odds with the prevalent conduct and thinking of his age; this has always been the case." The 1979 Revolution in Iran was meant to bring freedom, hope, and prosperity to an oppressed people, but the reality is well known—the poets and writers interviewed by Shiva Rahbaran in *Iranian Writers Uncensored* speak instead of humiliation, despotism, war, and poverty. These interviews with poets and writers still living and working in Iran demonstrate their belief that literature's value is in opening spaces of awareness in the minds of the reader—and pockets of freedom in society.

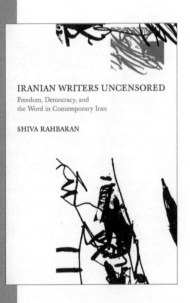

IRANIAN WRITERS UNCENSORED
Freedom, Democracy, and
the Word in Contemporary Iran

SHIVA RAHBARAN

Iranian Writers Uncensored:
Freedom, Democracy, and the
Word in Contemporary Iran

SHIVA RAHBARAN
TRANSLATION BY
NILOU MOBASSER

Dalkey Archive Scholarly Series
Cultural Studies
$17.95 / paper
ISBN: 978-1-56478-688-3

Shiva Rahbaran was born in 1970 in Tehran. She left Iran for Germany in 1984, where she studied literature and political science at the Heinrich-Heine-Universtät Düsselorf. She continued her studies at Oxford University, where she was granted a Ph.D. in English literature. She is also the author of *Nicholas Mosley's Life and Art: A Biography in Six Interviews* and *The Paradox of Freedom*, both published by Dalkey Archive Press.

Pop artists (painters and poets) often get praised or criticized for their use of low-brow commercial iconography. Yet either appraisal obscures the rigors of Pop serial design.

Adopting artist-poet Joe Brainard as its principal focus, this project presents Pop poetics not as a minor, coterie impulse meriting a sympathetic footnote in accounts of the postwar era's literary history, but as a missing link that potentially confounds any number of familiar critical distinctions (authentic record versus autonomous language, the "personal" versus the procedural). Pop poetics matter, argues Andy Fitch, not just to the occasional aficionado of Brainard's *I Remember*, but to anybody concerned with reconstructing the dynamic aesthetic exchange between postwar New York art and poetry.

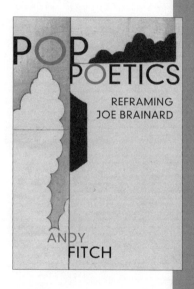

Pop Poetics
REFRAMING JOE BRAINARD

ANDY FITCH

Dalkey Archive Scholarly Series
Literary Criticism
$34.95 / paper
ISBN: 978-1-56478-728-6

Andy Fitch, along with Jon Cotner, is the author of *Ten Walks/ Two Talks*, which was chosen as a Best Book of 2010 by *Time Out Chicago*, The Millions, The Week, and Bookslut. He teaches in the MFA program at University of Wyoming.

It wasn't until after Dumitru Tsepeneag fled Romania for France in 1971 that he was able to speak frankly about the literary movement that he had helped create. "Oneiricism" wasn't just a new, homegrown form of surrealism, but implicitly a rebuke to the officially mandated socialist and nationalist realism imposed by Ceaușescu on all Romanian authors: here was writing devoted to the logic of dreams, not the grim reality policed by the communist regime. As such, *Dumitru Tsepeneag and the Canon of Alternative Literature* is not just the study of one man's work, but of an entire nation's literary history over the latter half of the twentieth century. The first monograph to appear in English on perhaps the most idiosyncratic and influential Romanian writer working today, *Dumitru Tsepeneag and the Canon of Alternative Literature* places Tsepeneag among the ranks of the great literary innovators—and pranksters—of the twentieth century.

DUMITRU TSEPENEAG AND THE CANON OF
ALTERNATIVE LITERATURE BY LAURA PAVEL

Dumitru Tsepeneag and the Canon of Alternative Literature

LAURA PAVEL
TRANSLATION BY
ALISTAIR IAN BLYTH

Dalkey Archive Scholarly Series
Literary Criticism
$23.95 / paper
ISBN: 978-1-56478-639-5

Laura Pavel is a Romanian essayist and literary critic. She is Associate Professor at the Faculty of Theater and Television of the Bábeș-Bolyai University, and Head of the Department of Theater Studies and Media.

The very first book-length study to focus on this seminal American author, *This Is Not a Tragedy* examines David Markson's entire body of work, ranging from his early tongue-in-cheek Western and crime novels to contemporary classics such as *Wittgenstein's Mistress* and *Reader's Block*. Having begun in parody, Markson's writing soon began to fragment, its pieces adding up to a peculiar sort of self-portrait—doubtful and unsteady—and in the process achieving nothing less than a redefinition of the novel form. Written on the verge of silence, David Markson's fiction represents an intimate, unsettling, and unique voice in the cacophony of modern letters, and *This Is Not a Tragedy* charts Markson's attempts to find, in art and language, the solace denied us by life.

This Is Not a Tragedy:
The Works of David Markson

FRANÇOISE PALLEAU-PAPIN

Dalkey Archive Scholarly Series
Literary Criticism
$49.95 / paper
ISBN: 978-1-56478-607-4

THIS IS NOT A TRAGEDY **THE WORKS OF DAVID MARKSON**
FRANÇOISE PALLEAU-PAPIN

Françoise Palleau-Papin teaches American Literature at the Sorbonne Nouvelle University-Paris 3. She has edited a critical study of Patricia Eakins, and published articles on Willa Cather, Carole Maso, John Edgar Wideman, William T. Vollmann, and others.

Russell H. Greenan's *It Happened in Boston?* is one of the most radical narratives to appear in the late 1960s ("this is a book that encompasses everything," as David L. Ulin noted in *Bookforum*). Yet due in large part to the difficulty of classifying Greenan's fiction, many readers are unaware of his other novels. In *The Birth of Death and Other Comedies: The Novels of Russell H. Greenan*, Tom Whalen, drawing widely from the American literary tradition, locates Greenan's lineage in the work of Hawthorne and Poe, "where allegory and dream mingle with and illuminate realism," as well as in the fiction of Twain, West, Hammett, Cain, and Thompson. Examining Greenan's characteristic themes and strategies, Whalen provides perceptive readings of the dark comedies of this criminally neglected American master, and in a coda reflects on Greenan's career and the reception of his work.

The Birth of Death and Other Comedies:
The Novels of Russell H. Greenan

TOM WHALEN

Dalkey Archive Scholarly Series
Literary Criticism
$23.95 / paper
ISBN: 978-1-56478-640-1

Tom Whalen is a novelist, poet, translator, and author of numerous stories and critical essays. He has written for *Agni, Bookforum, Film Quarterly, The Hopkins Review, The Iowa Review, The Literary Review, Studies in Short Fiction, The Wallace Stevens Journal*, the *Washington Post*, and other publications, and he co-edited the *Review of Contemporary Fiction*'s "Robert Walser Number."

In *When Blackness Rhymes with Blackness*, Rowan Ricardo Phillips
pushes African-American poetry to its limits by unraveling "our
desire to think of African-American poetry as African-American
poetry." Phillips reads African-American poetry as inherently alle-
gorical and thus a successful shorthand for the survival of a poetry
but unsuccessful shorthand for the sustenance of its poems. Argu-
ing in favor of the counterintuitive imagination, Phillips demon-
strates how these poems tend to refuse their logical insertion into
a larger vision and instead dwell indefinitely at the crux between
poetry and race, where, when blackness rhymes with blackness, it
is left for us to determine whether this juxtaposition contains a
vital difference or is just mere repetition.

When Blackness Rhymes with Blackness

ROWAN RICARDO PHILLIPS

Dalkey Archive Scholarly Series
Literary Criticism
$25.95 / paper
ISBN: 978-1-56478-583-1

when
blackness
rhymes
with blackness

ROWAN RICARDO PHILLIPS

Rowan Ricardo Phillips's essays, poems, and translations have appeared in numerous publications. He is also the author of *The
Ground* (2010). He has taught at Harvard, Columbia, and is currently Associate Professor of English and Director of the Poetry
Center at Stony Brook University.

A Community Writing Itself features internationally respected writers Michael Palmer, Nathaniel Mackey, Leslie Scalapino, Brenda Hillman, Kathleen Fraser, Stephen Ratcliffe, Robert Glück, and Barbara Guest, as well as important younger writers Truong Tran, Camille Roy, Juliana Spahr, and Elizabeth Robinson. The book fills a major gap in contemporary poetics, focusing on one of the most vibrant experimental writing communities in the nation. The writers discuss vision and craft, war and peace, race and gender, individuality and collectivity, and the impact of the Bay Area on their work.

A Community Writing Itself:

Conversations with Vanguard
Writers of the Bay Area

SARAH ROSENTHAL, ED.

Dalkey Archive Scholarly Series
Literature
$29.95 / paper
ISBN: 978-1-56478-584-8

A Community Writing Itself Conversations with Vanguard Writers of the Bay Area

Sarah Rosenthal in conversation with:
Michael Palmer **Nathaniel Mackey** Leslie Scalapino
Brenda Hillman Kathleen Fraser **Stephen Ratcliffe**
Robert Glück **Barbara Guest** Truong Tran
Camille Roy Juliana Spahr Elizabeth Robinson

"Sarah Rosenthal's interviews with some of the most engaging and important American poets of the time, all working in the Bay Area, provide vivid commentary on the state of the art and some of the most useful commentary available on the work of each individual writer."

——Charles Bernstein

Drawing together a wide range of focused critical commentary and observation by internationally renowned scholars and writers, this collection of essays offers a major reassessment of Aidan Higgins's body of work almost fifty years after the appearance of his first book, *Felo de Se*. Authors like Annie Proulx, John Banville, Derek Mahon, Dermot Healy, and Higgins himself, represented by a previously uncollected essay, offer a variety of critical and creative commentaries, while scholars such as Keith Hopper, Peter van de Kamp, George O'Brien, and Gerry Dukes contribute exciting new perspectives on all aspects of Higgins's writing. This collection confirms the enduring significance of Aidan Higgins as one of the major writers of our time, and also offers testament that Higgins's work is being rediscovered by a new generation of critics and writers.

Aidan Higgins:
The Fragility of Form

NEIL MURPHY, ED.

Dalkey Archive Scholarly Series
Literary Criticism
$29.95 / paper
ISBN: 978-1-56478-562-6

AIDAN HIGGINS:
THE FRAGILITY
OF FORM

edited by Neil Murphy
with essays from

ANNIE PROULX
JOHN BANVILLE
DERMOT HEALY
DEREK MAHON
GERRY DUKES
KEITH HOPPER
GEORGE O'BRIEN
PETER VAN DE KAMP
& AIDAN HIGGINS

Neil Murphy has previously taught at the University of Ulster and the American University of Beirut, and is currently Associate Professor of Contemporary Literature at NTU, Singapore. He is the author of several books on Irish fiction and contemporary literature and has published numerous articles on contemporary Irish fiction, on postmodernism, and on Aidan Higgins. He is currently writing a book on contemporary fiction and aesthetics.

To most of us, "subversion" means political subversion, but *The Subversive Scribe* is about collaboration not with an enemy, but with texts and between writers. Though Suzanne Jill Levine is the translator of some of the most inventive and revolutionary Latin American authors of the twentieth century—including Julio Cortázar, G. Cabrera Infante, Manuel Puig, and Severo Sarduy—here she considers the act of translation itself to be a form of subversion. Rather than regret translation's shortcomings, Levine stresses how translation is itself a creative act, unearthing a version lying dormant beneath an original work, and animating it, like some mad scientist, in order to create a text illuminated and motivated by the original. In *The Subversive Scribe*, one of our most versatile and creative translators gives us an intimate and entertaining overview of the tricky relationships lying behind the art of literary translation.

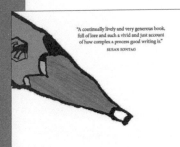

"A continually lively and very generous book, full of lore and such a vivid and just account of how complex a process good writing is."
SUSAN SONTAG

The Subversive Scribe:
Translating Latin American Fiction

SUZANNE JILL LEVINE

Dalkey Archive Scholarly Series
Literary Criticism
$13.95 / paper
ISBN: 978-1-56478-563-3

THE SUBVERSIVE SCRIBE
Translating Latin American Fiction
Suzanne Jill Levine

"A fascinating glimpse into the mental gyrations of a first-class literary translator at work."
—Clifford Landers, *Latin American Research Review*

ORDER FORM

Individuals may use this form to subscribe to the *Review of Contemporary Fiction* or to order back issues of the *Review* and Dalkey Archive titles at a discount (see below for details).

Title	ISBN	Quantity	Price

Subtotal _____

Less Discount _____
(10% for one book, 20% for two or more books, and
25% for Scholarly titles advertised in this issue)
Subtotal _____

Plus Postage _____
(U.S. $3 + $1 per book; foreign $7 + $5 per book)

1 Year Individual Subscription to the **Review** _____
($17 U.S.; $22.60 Canada; $32.60 all other countries)

Total _____

Mailing Address _____

_____

_____

_____

---

xxxii/1

Credit card payment ☐ Visa ☐ Mastercard

Acct. # _____ Exp. date _____

Name on card _____ Phone # _____

Billing zip code _____

Please make checks (in U.S. dollars only) payable to *Dalkey Archive Press.*

mail or fax this form to: Dalkey Archive Press, University of Illinois,
1805 S. Wright Street, MC-011, Champaign, IL 61820
fax: 217.244.9142 tel: 217.244.5700